"We can talk here.
Do you have any other children?"

Turning back to face Peter, Marie steeled herself with a gulp of air. "The only other child I have is in your house."

An agonized roar tore from his chest as he bolted to his feet.

"Mr. Hallock, I have to see my baby."

"We don't know for sure that Luke is your son." Even as he spoke, his face flushed. Was it from anger, or guilt?

Marie felt sick at how she'd torn this man's world apart, but she couldn't leave without learning the truth. "What does he—your son, Luke—look like?"

"You're not getting my son." His eyes bored through her. His volume dropped ominously, but the rumble carried conviction. "The Hallocks are never losing another child."

CATHY MARIE HAKE

walked five miles uphill in the Southern California snow (both ways) every week to check out books from the library. Then she grew up. Discovering the real mystery and adventure in life was men, Cathy fell head over heels for romance. She married the high school sweetheart she met at church, and now has two kids, two dogs and a fulfilling job as a nurse and Lamaze teacher. She enjoys writing stories that combine love and faith in a romance you can believe in.

MIXED BLESSINGS

CATHY MARIE HAKE

Published by Steeple Hill Books™

STEEPLE HILL BOOKS

Steeple Hill®

ISBN 0-373-87272-0

MIXED BLESSINGS

Copyright © 2004 by Cathy Marie Hake

This edition published by arrangement with Steeple Hill Books.

® and TM are trademarks of Steeple Hill Books, used under license. Trademarks indicated with ® are registered in the United States Patent and Trademark Office, the Canadian Trade Marks Office and in other countries.

www.SteepleHill.com

Printed in U.S.A.

But God commends His own love toward us,
in that while we were yet sinners, Christ died for us.

—*Romans* 5:8

To Andrea, who had faith with me and in me.
To Krista, who held my hand through cyberspace.
To my family, who believed and waited with me.
To Deb, who blessed me with her insights.
And most of all, to the Lord,
for His mercy and grace.

Chapter One

"Mr. Hallock, the Cadant woman is out here. She pulled right up to the gate and is blocking the driveway. I've already notified the police."

Peter Hallock gripped the receiver. "I'll be right there to handle her. Don't let her in." He slammed down the phone and headed for the front walkway. This woman had pursued them zealously, and he was going to put an end to it—here and now. No one threatened his son.

Four days ago, she'd tilted his world when she called and introduced herself, then rasped, "We have to talk. I—I have your son." Peter could see Luke with his nanny just outside the window, so he'd hung up and immediately called them inside. He refused to accept three other subsequent calls from Ms. Cadant.

When Ms. Cadant persisted by sending a letter marked "Urgent!" via next-day mail, he consulted a security specialist and returned it unopened, as recommended. He also hired a security guard. Worried, he'd taken off from his job as the CEO of the local hospital. Luke was the joy of his life, and as long as there was even a hint of danger,

Peter would do everything in his power to safeguard his son. At the moment, that meant confronting the woman. He'd make it clear she'd tangled with the wrong man.

He couldn't believe she had the gall to show up—but that just reinforced how dangerous and mentally unstable she must be. Each long, purposeful stride he took down the cobblestone walkway took him away from his son's giggles that spilled from the backyard and closer to the opportunity to tell Marie Cadant she'd gone too far.

When she came into view, Peter felt a jolt of surprise. Marie Cadant wasn't anything like what he'd expected. Instead of a vampy siren or an unkempt bag lady, she looked like an ordinary, albeit pretty, housewife. She stood beside the open door of a road-weary blue sedan. A snarled skein of shoulder-length, buttery yellow hair glowed in the midday sunlight. It framed big blue eyes and dimples. Her rumpled apricot-colored dress looked like she'd sneaked a nap in it, and the run in her nylons called his attention to ankles that were just as trim as the rest of her.

As he passed through the heavy wrought-iron gates, she stepped forward and gave him a tentative smile. "Thank you for coming!"

He scowled back. "Miss Cadant, I thought I'd already made myself abundantly clear. I don't deal with seedy little opportunists or con artists. Now leave."

Her smile faded. "Please! This is terribly important—"

"The police are on the way."

She folded her arms across her chest and leaned against the car. "Please, listen! You've got to listen to me."

"Not a chance, lady." Peter spun away and took a step back toward the house. Just then, he realized the giggles he thought had been Luke's were coming from the neighbor's grandchildren.

"I have your son!" Ms. Cadant cried.

He wheeled around quickly, but she'd already dipped her head into the car. He saw chubby toddler arms around her neck. A wild surge of adrenaline flooded him. "Nooooo!" he roared as he shot toward her car before she could take his precious boy. "Luke!"

Everything clicked into eerie slow motion. The woman straightened and turned. Her arms encircled a little boy. A red plastic toy firefighter's hat tumbled off the child, revealing wide, frightened eyes as he screamed in terror. Peter came to an abrupt halt, but his hands still closed around the boy's ribs.

"Police!" someone boomed. "Freeze!"

Instinctively protecting the boy, the woman held him tighter. Her hand came up and cupped his head to her shoulder. Every speck of color drained from her face. The officer continued, "No one's going to get hurt if you let the boy go."

Peter shouted, "It's not Luke!"

In spite of his assertion, four officers all converged on the car, their weapons still drawn. "Is there anyone in the back seat?" one officer called to another.

So close he could see the woman's whole body shuddering, Peter felt some of his furor fade. Hopefully, she'd learned her lesson and would leave him alone now. For a brief second, her tongue loosened. "Let us go. I'll never come back. Please—"

"Mr. Hallock." An officer drew him off to the side to talk as his partner interviewed Ms. Cadant. Clearly, Marie wanted nothing to do with the officer. After stammering something, she desperately started to stuff her child into the car. The cop firmly drew her to the back end of her sedan and tried to calm her. Peter couldn't hear much of what she said over the boy's frightened wails.

The officer with him gained his attention. "Sir, she's made threats and trespassed."

"No. Wait." He'd just heard her mention Melway General. Peter's heart kicked into overdrive. Luke was born at Melway.

The tyke's pitiful sobs tore at Peter. Ms. Cadant didn't indulge in tears, but she looked ready to collapse. Whatever she said made the cop shoot a quick glance from the boy, over to Peter, then back again.

Her little boy. Hers? *I have your son...* The child she held sported red hair and black-brown eyes. He was the only person Peter had ever seen with that unique combination—other than when he glanced in the mirror. This boy looked like a twin to the pictures in Peter's own baby book—and he seemed to be about the right age, too....

It can't be. It can't.

Peter agonized over what to do. Something was wrong, dreadfully wrong. Her impulsive appearance was bad enough, but his rash actions had undoubtedly made things far worse. Prompted by painful memories, he'd responded in such a way that he'd jeopardized this woman and her little boy. "We'll...talk. Give me a minute with her."

"No," his security guard protested. "You can't do that. Never give in to these tactics. It's a big mistake."

The police officer cast a disparaging look at the guard and muttered something under his breath about wanna-be cops and rent-a-thugs. "No one," he grated, "is doing anything until she calms down."

"I'll talk to her," Peter reiterated in a louder tone.

"No." Marie cringed and stammered, "It w-was all a m-m-mistake. I'll go—"

"Ma'am," the officer interrupted, "you're in no condition to drive."

The little boy clung to her for dear life. His arms and

legs twined tightly about her neck and waist. Something about the way she cradled him spoke eloquently of love and protection. A woman who cherished her child wouldn't ever intentionally endanger him. She'd obviously anticipated no possible jeopardy since she'd brought along the boy.

The little guy was big for her to hold. He had to be heavy, but her arms stayed wound about him. She kissed his unruly curls, then rested her cheek on them.

"She needs to sit down." Peter pointed past the gates toward a small garden. "There's a bench over there."

The two cops got together and exchanged information. The one who had been talking to Peter looked at the child, then back at him. A less astute person would have missed the subtle grimace, but Peter read body language as a matter of course. In dealing with staff, families and attorneys, he'd learned to pick up faint cues, and it stood him in good stead. Clearly, the cops felt something vital was going on between him and the Cadant woman.

Whatever the issue, Peter didn't want an audience. He took control. "Ms. Cadant is rattled, but it's apparent she doesn't mean any harm. I appreciate your response, but I'm confident we can handle this matter, ourselves." As he spoke, Peter closed the distance between them. He cupped Marie's elbow and marveled she'd stayed upright. Uncertain her legs would hold much longer, he knew he'd better hustle her to the bench. "Here." He tugged her lightly.

Instead of taking his cue, she tilted her face up to his. Peter inhaled sharply when he saw her expression. He'd expected to see fear, but the total devastation painting her features stunned him. Shock and tears glazed her huge eyes. "Come with me, Marie. There's a little bench in the garden."

"Let us go!"

"You wanted to talk to me."

"Not anymore!"

"You cannot hold her against her will," said the officer who had been interviewing her.

She'd pursued him almost fanatically, yet now when he granted her his attention, Marie Cadant looked as if she'd give all she owned to be anywhere else. Peter knew he couldn't allow her to go until they resolved the matter. "I can't let you leave. You heard the cop—you can't drive right now. It's too dangerous." His fingers tightened until he managed to make her focus on him again.

Marie gulped in several deep breaths. In spite of the terror of the moment, Peter's assertive tone sliced through some of her fear. She felt his body ease away a bit, felt his sigh gust across her face, and barely heard his soft praise. "Good. There you go. You're going to be all right. Come sit down."

When he shifted to the side, his hand rotated so he kept hold of her, but his arm slipped beneath hers to brace her. He executed the move easily, capably, as if he were accustomed to dealing with balking, emotional women. Her fright caused a strange split to take place. Marie felt oddly removed—almost as if she were a spectator who could see silly details. The numbness wore off the second his other hand came across and pressed against Ricky's little back.

Her hold on Ricky tightened so intensely, she accidentally squeezed Mr. Hallock's arm between her arm and ribs. He studied her for a long moment, then gently stroked up and down Ricky's back. "I'd offer to carry him, but he needs you too much right now."

She bobbed her head in jerky affirmation. When Peter Hallock tried leading her off to the right, she couldn't

seem to comply. Her feet stayed rooted to the ground.
Every shred of maternal instinct screamed at her to shove
Ricky back into the car and flee, yet she couldn't.

Peter gave her arm a tiny squeeze. Tall and broad-
shouldered as he was, he overshadowed Marie and inten-
sified her sense of vulnerability. It took a moment for her
to realize his eyes no longer snapped with temper—they
were dark brown pools of concern. "Ms. Cadant," he said
quietly, "that was a bad scare, but it's over. You and the
boy are safe."

She shook her head. Safe? Oh, no. Peter Hallock simply
didn't know the truth—and her truth jeopardized all they
both held dear. With a stilted gait, Marie accompanied
him down a herringbone brick path to a bench that
couldn't be seen from the road. It rested in the shelter of
a long, tall hedge and faced a small, circular patch of
bright, multicolored spring flowers.

"See? Nice and quiet." Peter's voice took on a coaxing
tone. "We can talk here."

A verdant lawn dotted with croquet wickets stretched
almost fifty yards between that area and the house. Marie
looked back over her shoulder and felt a small flash of
relief that the cops hadn't left. Peter Hallock led her over
to a wrought-iron bench. She sank onto it and automatically turned to the side, away from Peter, in a vain effort
to keep little Ricky as her very own for even a few more
precious seconds.

Peter sat down right beside her and stayed silent—as if
he expected her to explain everything. Though she tried
to gather her wits, Marie knew no matter how much she'd
prayed, she wasn't ready for this moment. Firmly, yet
gently, Peter managed to wrap an arm about her shoulders
and turn her around. He tenderly ran his long fingers
through Ricky's hair. "Hey, tiger."

"Mommy!"

"He's a mama's boy?"

Marie nodded. She gratefully accepted the snowy handkerchief Peter produced from the inside chest pocket of his stylish, charcoal suit coat and still kept hold of Ricky. She mopped her boy's sweet little cheeks, then nestled the child's face in the crook of her neck and rested her cheek on his crown. Giving Peter a stricken look, she took several choppy breaths. *I can't do this. I can't tell him.* She'd come this far, but her courage failed her. "We won't ever bother you again."

The way he stared at her for many long seconds and carefully scanned each of her features heightened her anxiety. She felt a small flash of relief that she'd tucked Ricky in so closely. Mr. Hallock wouldn't be able to see his features well at all. Maybe she could still slip away from him.

Seconds ticked by. Each heartbeat hurt more than the last. The man beside her had razor-cut mahogany hair that glinted in the sun, just like Ricky's did. His eyes were the color of dark chocolate—just like Ricky's. His look of intense concentration, the shape of his nose…*just like Ricky's.* Though everything within her railed against it, Marie couldn't deny the truth. *This is Ricky's fath—*

He shattered the fragile stillness. "How old is he, Marie?"

She nervously licked her lips. In a thin voice, she offered, "Three." She patted her son's back and murmured his name over and over again in a mournful chant as his tears tapered off into the hiccups.

"So you named him Ricky. What's his birth date?"

She didn't want to tell him. Now that the time arrived, it was too hard, too miserable. Marie gnawed on her trembling lower lip. *God, he's not going to let me slip away.*

I'm going to have to go through with it. Please give me strength....

He jostled her a little and persisted, "Marie, when's Ricky's birthday? Tell me."

"April Fool's Day."

Peter closed his eyes for a second, then opened them again. In a slowly exhaled breath, he asked for confirmation, "Did I hear you tell the cop he was born at Melway General?"

Marie nodded. She held her little boy and began rocking to and fro, as much to comfort herself as to soothe him. She desperately needed comforting. Steeling herself with a deep breath, Marie forged into the dark waves of doubt. "I started to have seizures during the labor, so they did an emergency cesarean. I didn't get to hold him for the first three days. My grandmother had red hair, so I didn't think anything was wrong." She studied Peter's mahogany hair and fell silent.

"What happened?"

Still remembering the hazy days surrounding the birth, she murmured a rambling, "I had severe toxemia...sedated me...said I had a seizure, but I don't recall it...woke up in the intensive care unit..."

He nodded sagely as he absorbed her explanation, then asked, "How did you decide Ricky isn't yours?"

Her arms spasmed around her son. "He is mine! Ricky is mine! I've loved him and—"

Peter gently pressed two fingers to her lips to quiet her and interrupted, "I meant biologically unrelated, Marie." He gave her an apologetic smile, then broke contact.

She tried to settle down. "The last week has been horrible. I'm sorry I'm so snappish."

"It's understandable. Tell me what happened last week."

"The day-care center where I work had medical students come do physicals on the children. They did lab work and head-to-toe checkups. When I got Ricky's results, I thought they'd made a mistake. A kid can't have AB-negative blood when both parents have O positive."

"I'm AB negative," he whispered hoarsely.

She closed her eyes, as if it would make the problem disappear. Trying to ignore Peter's revelation, she whispered, "I made them test Ricky again. I had them test me, too. When it came back conclusively that he couldn't…"

He seemed to know she wouldn't finish the sentence. Those words were too painful to say aloud. Swirling his big hand on Ricky's back, he asked, "How did you find me?"

"I know I've been a pest, but I couldn't help it. The hospital—I didn't go to them because I don't trust them. It seemed wrong, letting them control this when they'd already messed it up so badly."

"So you did all of the legwork, yourself? You didn't hire anyone to help you?"

"I went to the county registrar's office and checked in the Hall of Records. It's a small community hospital, so there weren't all that many birth records to wade through. Only four boys were born during that time. One was a stillbirth, so that left three, and I knew the boy who weighed in at over ten pounds couldn't have been switched with a seven-pounder, so that left me with you."

"You don't have any real proof yet." He sounded like she had a few short days ago—anxious to deny the truth. Desperate.

"I wouldn't have come if I wasn't sure, Mr. Hallock. The doctor guaranteed me Ricky isn't—that biologically, he can't be…" She sucked in a deep breath. "The only time I've been separated from him was during the hospital stay. There's no other possibility."

"What does your husband say about all of this?"

She averted her face as a wave of grief washed over her. Her heart contracted as she watched the flowers in the patch flutter in the breeze, just as she'd watched the ones in the bouquets flutter at Jack's graveside. Their scent suddenly grew just as cloying, too.

"You're wearing a wedding ring," he prompted tentatively.

"Jack was a police officer. He got shot and killed in the line of duty almost two years ago." She heard the sharply indrawn breath Peter took and didn't dare look at him for fear she'd start weeping all over again.

"I'm so sorry, Marie. I'm sorry they pulled guns just now, too. That must've brought up painful memories." He paused, and she slowly nodded confirmation. Birdsong filled the silence—so out of place in the midst of a catastrophe. "Do you have any other children?"

Turning back to face him, Marie steeled herself with a gulp of air. "The only other child I have is in your house."

An agonized roar tore from his chest as he bolted to his feet and paced away a few steps. He turned back again. His mouth opened and closed several times, as if he were going to say something and then decided not to.

"Mr. Hallock, I have to see my baby."

"We don't know for sure that Luke is your son." Even as he spoke, his face flushed. Was it from anger, or guilt?

Marie felt sick at how she'd torn this man's world apart, but now that she'd calmed down a bit, she couldn't leave without learning the truth. "What does he—your son, Luke—look like?"

"You're not getting my son." His eyes bored through her. His volume dropped ominously, but the rumble carried conviction. *"The Hallocks are never losing another child."*

Chapter Two

His words and tone stunned her. Had one of his other children died? Had he lost one in a custody battle? It wasn't her place to ask, but Marie could tell from those agonized words Peter Hallock fiercely loved and protected his own. A host of primitive emotions crackled between them. Ricky squirmed and broke the tense silence. "I gotta go potty!"

When Peter failed to react, Marie prompted, "Could we please go inside?"

"Yeah. Sure." He got up and helped her to her feet. "Give me a few days to get over the shock. No, give me a lifetime. This is a hideous nightmare!"

"I know." His look of mixed anguish and bewildered hurt struck a common chord. Marie struggled to keep her voice steady, "I keep praying I'll wake up and it'll be behind me."

Peter eased Ricky from her arms and glanced at her, then down at Ricky and back at her. His face appeared even more haunted. "I don't know if we'll wake up, Marie."

The officers still hovered close by. "Ma'am? Sir—"

Peter took charge. "We appreciate your assistance. No one is at risk—unless it's Ricky and me in danger of getting drenched. You can leave." The cops chuckled as Peter increased his pace.

She hastened alongside him, up a cobblestone walk bordered by perfectly manicured hedges and lawn. His home looked like a Georgian mansion. It stood as evidence of power, class, and wealth. Marie hadn't researched him— all she'd gotten were a name, address and phone number. She'd tried to get more information, but she didn't know the ins and outs of investigating someone, and the few leads she had were useless. The gates hadn't been mere façade—the home behind them and the man who lived in it were steeped in money. That fact increased her wariness.

When they reached the bathroom and Ricky fumbled to pull down his elastic-waisted jeans, Peter braced himself against the marble pullman. "I don't want to believe it." In a sickened hush he added, "But I think I do."

His words only confirmed her worst fears. The days of praying and nights of sleeplessness all came down to this. Marie wanted to turn back the clock and return to the days when she innocently mothered the child she'd always thought was hers. As she soaped Ricky's hands over the sink, she felt his slippery hand slide away from hers and knew it was symbolic. It took every last shred of her self-control to keep from weeping.

Peter stared at Ricky. His eyes held a dazed cast. "I hoped you were mistaken. We'd do tests—you know— and realize you'd just been...wrong. This nightmare is real. You have my s—"

"Daddy?" a high voice piped out in the hallway. "Lookie! I gots a—" As soon as the toddler discovered strangers, he halted midsentence and clutched his father's slacks for security.

Transfixed, Marie stood still and stared at the boy. His corn-silk hair matched hers, as did his dimples. He had her small, straight nose and gently rounded chin, but he also carried some of Jack's traits. She folded her wet hands to her chest to still the thundering in her heart. His name whispered between her lips.

Peter immediately grabbed the boy by the shoulder and turned him to divert his attention. "Hey, sport! I found someone to be your friend. Let's go to the playroom." He scooped up the child before Marie could even reach out for him. Peter threw a towel at Marie, grabbed Ricky, and headed down the hall.

"Wait!" She hurriedly dried her hands and chased after him. The man had an impossibly long stride. She kept her eyes on them—the boy who matched his red hair, and the boy who matched her blond. A jumble of emotions muddled her brain.

She hurriedly caught up with him at the doorway to a playroom. Sunlight streamed through gleaming windows, illuminating the bold primary colors of the simple furniture and toy shelves. Every imaginable thing a child might dream to possess filled the place. A very young woman in overalls carefully stacked blocks back into a red plastic bin and gave the boys a warm smile. *Mrs. Hallock?*

"Anne, we have guests," Peter said in a friendly tone that still carried authority. "Please ask Mrs. Lithmas to bring lunch here for the four of us. You may have the rest of the day off. Have her call Paulette to cancel my twelve o'clock, too."

"Yes, sir." The nanny nodded and left.

Marie glanced around, then asked, "Is your wife home?"

"I'm widowed, too."

"Oh, I'm so sorry!" Her heart twisted. How long had little Luke lacked a mommy's love?

Peter put both of the boys down, then held Marie back. "Please let them have time together. Don't rush Luke. He's shy, and you don't want to scare him. He's been taught not to go near strangers."

Marie shot him a pained look.

Peter gently squeezed her arm and urged, "Give him time. It'll be worth it—I promise." He frowned a few minutes later. He and she still stood side by side in tense silence while the boys played with toys and ignored one another. "Why won't they play together?"

Kneeling on the floor, Marie stated softly, "I work in a day care, so I see this all of the time. Kids this age do what's called parallel play. They play alongside of one another and sense companionship, but they don't necessarily interact. In a while, they will." She turned back to Ricky and laughed as he worked the jack-in-the-box.

Luke let out an unholy screech and grabbed for the toy. "Mine!"

"Share!" Ricky yelled back.

"Let's take turns," Marie intervened. "Ricky, it's Luke's turn next." She slowly reached out to the son she'd never held. Her heart almost beat out of her chest as he stared at her with wide blue eyes. He turned his gaze toward his father and received a nod of approval. Very tentatively, he drew closer.

Lord, he's all I have left of Jack. You already instilled a mother's love for him in my heart. Please, Father, stir the love of a son in his heart for me.

Marie wanted to grab him and hold him close, but she knew she'd spoil everything if she did. Summoning control she didn't know she possessed, she gently hitched the children by their waists and held one on each knee. In her softest voice she prompted, "Okay, Luke, show me how to do it."

She wanted to squeeze him silly. She wanted to cover his dear little face with kisses and vent the laughter and tears that warred within her breast. She couldn't do any of that—not here, not now. She felt Peter watching how she handled both boys. Glancing at him, she cocked a brow as if to ask what he thought.

"He doesn't usually take kindly to strangers. He kicks up a royal fuss."

"Really?"

Marie remained motionless as Luke curiously raised a finger to trace her dimple, then she took his finger and guided him to touch one of his own. Afterward, she took that finger and drew it toward her face. Suddenly, she turned her head and gobbled up his arm and neck. He dissolved into gales of laughter.

"Me, too!" Ricky demanded, and she pulled him right into the fun.

To Marie's amazement, Peter Hallock forced out a lion's roar. He disregarded his beautifully tailored, visibly expensive suit and pounced from the sofa. Both boys shrieked, and Peter grabbed Luke. He tossed him in the air, caught him amidst squeals of joy, and then did the same to Ricky. He lay on the floor and wrestled gently with the boys. They piled all over him, wiggled and kicked and screeched. Marie giggled, but her mirth came to a quick halt as Luke pressed a sloppy peck on his father's cheek.

Marie went stark still. She felt the blood drain from her cheeks, and her stomach plunged to the hardwood floor.

Peter stopped chortling, sat up and leaned closer. "Marie?"

Fearing she was going to be sick, she dipped her head and rasped, "Give me a minute."

"Marie, I know this is hard. Take a few deep breaths." He knelt directly in front of her and cupped both of her shoulders, as if to brace her. "That's right. Take your time."

A few minutes passed, and Marie earned an approving nod from him. "There. Much better," he said softly. She struggled to contain her feelings. Countless emotions flickered across his features. He cradled her cheek in one hand, and the other slid off to feather her hair back from her temple. "Marie, I know this is hard, but I don't understand what happened. You were okay one minute, and then…what's wrong?"

"What's wrong? That's my baby! He's mine and he doesn't even know me. He calls you Daddy. He's never even kissed me." Her trembling whisper finally cracked and she said, "He should have played with Jack."

"You're right." The agreement whispered between them.

"He looks like Jack, too. Through the eyes. And the shape of his lips. The right arch of his lip is just a shade higher." She drew in an aching breath. "Jack would have been so proud."

Peter's eyes glowed with love. For all the horror of the moment one thing came across very clearly—he cherished his son. "Luke is a very special child, Marie. Of course Jack would have been proud. I'm sure he was proud of Ricky, too."

"Oh, he adored him! He had father-son portraits taken just the week before…the week before…"

"I understand," he said, saving her from saying the words she found so difficult. "I'd like copies of those pictures, Marie. I'll duplicate my favorite pictures of Luke for you, too. You'd like that, wouldn't you?'' Peter gave her a bolstering smile when she nodded.

''Mommy, I'm hungreeee!'' Ricky stood next to Peter and gave her an accusing look.

''Yeah, tiger,'' Peter chuckled, ''I'll bet you're always hungry. A lady is going to bring us lunch in a minute.''

Gathering her wits, Marie tugged her rumpled dress down a few inches to her knees. ''That's not necessary.''

''But it would be nice.'' Peter slipped his arm around Ricky's hips and gave him a possessive squeeze. ''I want you to stay. We ought to all get to know one another.''

''After lunch, we'll need to leave. Ricky can nap in the car, but I have a fair drive home.''

''Where do you live?''

''Orange County.''

His jaw dropped, then his brows knit in vexation. ''That's over two hundred fifty miles away!''

Marie rubbed her forehead back and forth in line with the furrows. ''I know. I said the same thing when I found out where you live. I'd hoped you lived much closer to the hospital. It's halfway between us.''

''Why were you so far from home for delivery?''

''We lived in Melway at the time. Jack got a position down in Orange County, so we moved soon after I had Ricky.''

''I see,'' he said tightly. ''Where were you staying?''

''Staying?''

''Last night. Where did you spend last night?''

Marie gave him a puzzled look. ''We were at home.''

Raking his hand through his hair, he scowled. ''You drove all of the way up here this morning and plan to turn back around and go home again? That's a ten-hour round-trip!''

''I have commitments.''

"What could possibly be more important than getting to know our sons?"

Marie took a deep breath, let it out slowly, and remembered how shocked and angry she'd been when she discovered the awful truth. Peter Hallock probably felt just as appalled.

"At least stay for the weekend."

The lump in her throat worsened. The anguish in his eyes nearly took her breath away. She empathized. From the moment she'd discovered her son was elsewhere, she'd hungered to hold him. Peter Hallock clearly felt that same longing to be with his son. *Her son.* She said very quietly, "I can't stay."

"You can't mean to dash off!"

Marie pulled a slip of paper from her pocket and extended her hand. "I've written my address and phone number down for you. Here. You can reach me anytime. My business number is there, too."

Peter took the paper and barely glanced at it before slipping it into the pocket of his slacks. "Stay for lunch. We'll come up with plans. We have to do something. I don't want you to leave."

"Ricky and I will have lunch with you and Luke." She looked at her son—her biological son—and whispered, "I didn't know it was going to be this hard."

The housekeeper's arrival cut short Peter's response. The aproned woman pushed in an elegant, inlaid wood tea cart laden with four china plates and beverages. She proceeded to set the small trestle table over by the window with linen napkins. Marie thought she must be hallucinating. It looked like someone had clipped this scene straight from a soap opera. She glanced at Peter and Luke. Neither of them paid any attention to the housekeeper.

Marie gulped. A very ordinary woman who lived an

average middle-class life, she knew she was in way over her head.

Peter nudged Luke toward the table, then plucked Ricky out of Marie's arms. "We'll have to get you a booster seat just like Luke's. Today, you'll sit on my lap."

Marie hesitantly took the seat Peter pulled out for her, then looked at Ricky. He'd curled his fingers around Peter's collar and grinned up at him, so she couldn't very well protest, even though her heart twisted at the sight of them together. *You knew you'd have to learn to share him.* She daintily settled her napkin in her lap, then reached over to take Ricky's outstretched hand. She cast a wary look at Peter.

He took Luke's hand. "Do you normally say grace, too?"

She nodded. *Too.* That one word relaxed her a bit. At least they held some common ground. Building bridges between their families would be easier if they shared a foundation of faith.

Luke and Ricky singsonged, "God is great, God is good..." in a sweet duet, and Peter's voice quickly blended with them. Marie finally caught up and added, "Amen!"

Peter's intense stare made Marie shift in her seat. "What?"

"If you're upset about missing church, you can attend ours."

She broke eye contact and picked up her sandwich. "I'm so confused." She put down the sandwich without taking a bite. "I'm torn between needing to stay and needing to go."

"Staying is only right. There's no question. You can't tease me with one short hour of being with my—" he paused and shot a quick look at Luke, then back at Ricky.

His voice vibrated with restrained emotion "—With my flesh and blood, then snatch him away!"

Despair flooded her. "I care for my sister. She was injured in an accident."

He frowned. Marie wasn't sure whether it was from vexation that she didn't accede to his wishes at once or concern for Sandy. "How is she managing without you today?"

"She's at the rehab facility. One of our church family is picking her up. He'll keep her company at home until I get there."

"Surely he can watch her overnight."

Marie winced. "The gentleman involved isn't exactly versed in giving her the particular type of care she'll require."

"That's not a problem. We'll call and arrange for a private nurse to stay with her tonight. You can't leave."

"Mr. Hallock," she paused and watched as Peter playfully stuck an olive on Ricky's thumb. Both of their faces lit with glee. Cuddling Ricky closer, Peter grabbed another olive and did the same to Luke. All three of them laughed. *If it's so cute, why do I want to cry?*

Peter looked at her and raised his brows. "What were you going to say?"

"I know I said it before," she whispered, "but this is even harder than I thought it was going to be."

His smile faded. "We have to work together, Marie…for their sakes."

"I know."

He shook his head. "It's so hard to believe. We've got a lot to do." He accepted a carrot from Ricky. "First off, I—"

"I think," she interrupted, "we'd be wise to not make

any immediate decisions. It's going to be complicated. Can't we please have today to just share our sons?''

''That would be easier if you'd change your plan to flit out of here.''

She tried to calm down with a sip of iced tea, but it didn't help. Her hand shook as she set the crystal goblet back down on the table. ''Mr. Hallock—''

''Peter. It seems crazy to be formal when we're going to be sharing kids.''

Marie dipped her head in acknowledgment. ''Peter, I learned about this a week ago. The first day, I was in shock. You're that way now. I'm falling apart, and you're acting like nothing is wrong. In a day or two, the reality will hit you full force.''

''So you're dropping a bomb, listening to it tick for a few minutes, then running before it detonates?''

She granted him a wobbly smile. His words were clever, but the reality hurt too much. Her eyes burned and her nose tingled with suppressed tears.

''Hey,'' he said softly, ''I'm sorry. That joke was in poor taste. I think you were incredibly brave to come here. I don't know what I would have done.''

''I admit, I'm frazzled. I prayed all of the way here, but my focus was on the boys.'' She shrugged. ''I'm not ready to think about all of the consequences or plot a future course.''

''Okay. We'll just concentrate on the guys today.''

Marie didn't eat much. Her nerves were strung too tight. Nothing seemed to fit past the big ball in her throat. By the end of lunch, Luke started rubbing his eyes. Marie looked at Peter. ''Would you mind if I tucked him in for his nap?''

He rubbed his chin on Ricky's crown. ''How 'bout if we let Ricky nap a while, too?''

"He naps well in his car seat. It might be easier if we slip out while they're sleepy. If you're free next weekend, why don't you and Luke come for a visit?"

"Nothing is more important than this, Marie. We have to make a pact that the boys come first. I'll clear my calendar and jump through whatever hoops I have to."

Peter sat on the couch and held Ricky while Marie tucked in Luke by herself. Those few moments she spent alone with Jack's little son were bittersweet. Even after he'd fallen asleep, she held him close to her heart. Finally, she whispered a prayer over him, slipped him onto his bed and covered him with a satin-edged baby blanket. One kiss wasn't enough. The second and third were just as precious.

She knew she had to leave. It felt like a giant was reaching in and tearing her heart from her breast. Each step she took from his room and down the hall took monumental effort.

Peter rose from the couch as she reentered the playroom. Ricky lay in his arms like a boneless cat. He'd fallen asleep, just like Luke. "I'll carry him out for you."

She blinked back tears and reached out. "My arms feel too empty. Please—" To her relief, Peter relinquished Ricky.

Peter's face was pale and taut. Marie suspected his composure was starting to crack. Part of her wanted to stay so he wouldn't have to bear the anguish alone, but she had no emotional reserves and couldn't do anything to lessen the impact of this disaster. Left alone, he'd at least keep his dignity.

She made it to the front door, but Peter pressed a hand to the oak panel, blocking her exit. "Marie—"

"Peter, you have to let us go."

His troubled gaze held her captive. "For now—but things are far from resolved."

Marie nodded. Ricky stirred and lifted his head. Marie shrank as Peter completely closed the few inches between them. Back pressed against the wall, she gulped and her eyes widened. Then his head dipped.

"Bye-bye, tiger. You're a wonderful boy. I was so happy to meet you. I'll see you again, soon." He spoke the words very softly, very tenderly, before he kissed Ricky's cheek and rumpled his hair. Genuine affection glowed in his eyes.

His sweetness to her son meant the world—until he whispered to her, "You take good care of him until I can."

Chapter Three

The phone rang as Marie crossed the threshold. Too tired to care, Marie let go of Ricky's hand and smiled wearily at her sister. "I don't know how people commute long distances to work."

Sandy gave her a sympathetic look, then glanced at the still-jangling phone and made a wry face. "You'd better answer that. Some guy named Peter has been calling every fifteen minutes for the last two hours. He's frantic."

"Great." Marie rubbed her aching back as she headed for the phone. "Hello?"

"Marie! It's eight forty-seven! You've been driving long past dark. What took you so long? Was there a problem?"

Her purse strap slid down from her shoulder, and Marie let her bag drop onto the battered, white kitchen counter with a muffled thump. Shoving her hair back from her forehead, she sighed, "We're fine."

"What took you so long?"

Peter's voice sounded ragged with concern, but Marie didn't want to think about him or his feelings at the moment. His parting words kept echoing in her head. *You take good care of him until I can.* All the way home, she'd worried that Peter meant to try to take Ricky away. She'd been so absorbed, she'd failed to look at the gauges and run out of gas.

"I said, we're fine."

"Thank heavens! Marie, your car is leaking oil. I saw a pool of fresh oil right where you were parked. I worried you broke down or something."

"We made it home in one piece."

"Good!" His sigh of relief flowed over the line.

Marie cleared her throat. "When I stopped to get gas, my license and cards were in the wrong places in my wallet."

The line went silent.

"Mr. Hallock? I believe an answer is in order." She could hear his steps as he paced back and forth on a hard surface someplace. The silence told her he was considering several possible explanations. That fact irked her. She wanted the truth.

"While you were in my house," he said in a well-modulated tone, "the security officer did a search of the car and your purse. He copied your identification and put it back."

I wanted him to be honest—but I also hoped he'd be honorable. Fatigue gave way to anger. "I'm so mad, I could spit nails! How dare you do such a thing!"

He made an impatient sound. "I didn't have a choice! You have my son!"

"How am I supposed to respond to that?" She glanced behind herself to be sure Ricky wasn't in the room. Taking care to lower her voice, she hissed, "Am I expected to scream that Ricky is mine, or do you want me to lay claim to Luke?"

Another silence ensued. Peter finally admitted, "That didn't come out right. You were wise to leave. I'm starting to go nuts already, and I really don't want anyone seeing me when I feel this out of control. I'm glad you got home safely. Good night, Marie."

"Good night, Peter." Marie hung up the phone.

"Oh, sis! It sounds bad." Sandy's eyes held consolation as she maneuvered her wheelchair closer. When her chair came to a halt, she pushed her headband back to restrain a fall of sun-bleached blond hair.

"I've opened Pandora's box."

"I told you to get a lawyer or a private investigator. You could have at least let one of the guys on the force run a sheet on Peter Hallock."

Marie compressed her lips and tried to ignore the storm of emotions raging inside her. She hadn't wanted to get anyone else involved. She didn't have money to hire professional help, and it felt creepy to ask one of Jack's old buddies to pull strings. Any number of them would have done so in a heartbeat. Now she wished she would have.

"What's he—your real, biological son—like?"

Marie flopped down on her brown tweed couch. She gave Ricky a vague smile as he came out of the bathroom. "Go get your jammies, Rick. It's bedtime."

"So?" Sandy prompted as Ricky disappeared into his room.

"He's beautiful, Sandy. Beautiful. His eyes are blue, but they're shaped just like Jack's. His mouth is, too. He looks like a cherub. He's a few inches shorter than Ricky, but maybe a bit stockier."

"What did they name him?"

"Luke." She closed her eyes. "My day was a disaster. How was yours?"

"Rehab went well. They're pushing me to join an independent living group. Do you think I'm ready?"

"I think you will be soon." Marie accepted the race-car-printed flannel pajamas she'd made and helped Ricky into them. Ordinarily, he'd try to change all on his own, but after a long, trying day, he'd come out to seek her help and reassurance. She gave him an extra hug after she buttoned his shirt.

While Ricky stayed in the living room with them, she and Sandy took care to discuss Sandy's future instead of the catastrophic events of the past week. Marie wanted to shield her son from as much of the ordeal as she could until the adults all managed to iron out the issues. She'd never imagined her sweet little tyke would be in the line of fire as he'd been today. The memory left her shaken— and more than willing to distract herself with the exciting prospects opening up for Sandy.

"My physical therapist said I've stabilized," Sandy said as she whizzed in and out of the kitchen. She brought a pair of Red Delicious apples.

"You've worked hard," Marie praised. "I'm really impressed by how much you can do."

They discussed the merits of such a plan as they shared the apples with Ricky for a bedtime snack. Marie tucked him into his bed. He mumbled a nighttime prayer and fell asleep at once.

The minute Marie came back into the living room, Sandy demanded, "Okay. Now that he's in bed, give me the scoop."

"I'm in big trouble." Marie sank onto the couch, stared straight ahead at the brick fireplace and sighed. "Peter Hallock is rattled. From what I gather, he's an administrator at a hospital—powerful. Rich, too." She took a deep breath and slowly let it out. "To top it off, he's possessive. When I left, he told me to take good care of Ricky until he can.''

Sandy's jaw dropped. ''You have to be kidding me!''

''Nope.'' Marie wearily propped her feet up on the coffee table.

''He's nuts! What did you do?''

''I got out of there as fast as I could.''

''So he's going to be ugly?''

''I can't say. It wouldn't be fair to judge that yet. Sandy, I'm just sick about it all. I know he is, too.''

''What's his wife like?''

''He's widowed.'' Other than that fact, he hadn't alluded even once to his wife. Marie tried to rub away her headache and wanted to pretend nothing had happened. ''Let's get you ready for bed. You know, I didn't see Brent when I came in. I wanted to thank him for helping you.''

''*I* thanked him.''

Marie stopped and gave her sister a searching look. ''Oh? That sounds interesting.''

Sandy grinned. ''We thought so.''

''What are you telling me?''

''He asked me out to lunch after church. We're going on a picnic. He said he's tired of pretending to be my buddy. His kiss backed up that claim, too.''

''Wonderful!'' Marie gave her a hug. ''What will you wear?''

They chattered about that issue as Marie helped Sandy transfer from her wheelchair to bed. She'd learned all of the necessary skills to take care of Sandy since she'd hurt her back in a freak surfing accident. With the passage of time and rehabilitation, Sandy had regained most of the use of her arms. She needed to build up more muscle strength so she could move herself independently, but she was nearly to the point of being able to care for herself with a minimum of help.

Marie changed and crawled into the other bed in the same room. As she curled up under the blankets, she tried to block the image of a large, mahogany-haired man reaching for Ricky.

You take care of him until I can. Until I can... His words kept echoing in her mind. Marie shuddered and dragged the covers up higher.

She sensed Peter Hallock dearly loved children. The protective urge he'd shown at the outset with Luke now extended toward Ricky, too. What had he meant, *the Hallocks are never losing another child?* Had there been a kidnapping? A murder? Was Luke safe? Tired and worried as she felt, Marie didn't sleep well.

Peter's nerves stretched taut. Darlene took their baby when she left him; yesterday, as Marie left with Ricky, the landslide of feelings and memories nearly buried Peter. Peter tried to book a flight to Orange County last night, but the galling fact that John Wayne airport closed at ten each night foiled his plan. This morning's whole flight down seemed to go in slow motion, and Peter got unaccountably impatient with the rental agency when his car wasn't ready as promised.

He swerved and focused his attention on the road again. Marie had better be an easygoing hostess, because he was dropping in without warning. If he called again, he'd only put his foot in his mouth. He even missed the freeway turnoff to her place and needed to backtrack.

Marie lived in an older tract neighborhood where it looked like an unimaginative architect had taken a pair of cookie cutters to design only two floor plans. Places of this vintage invariably needed upkeep, but most carried the air of being well-tended.

Peter pulled up to the curb and gave the pink, purple and white flowers edging her yard an assessing look. The mailbox out in front of her house bore a shiny gold icthus. Instead of steps, a wooden ramp led to the front door. Painted along the widest side beam was a verse he recognized. ''As for me and my house, we will serve the Lord.'' Clearly, yesterday's lunchtime prayer wasn't a mere ritual. Marie lived her faith. *Good thing she does. Only God will be able to solve this for us.*

He swept Luke out of the car seat, strode up the ramp and rang the doorbell.

Tired of being confined by the flight and his car seat, Luke wiggled. ''Want down.''

''Okay.'' Peter set him on the porch, and he immediately scampered off and grabbed for a marble-blue plastic ball that rested against the garage.

A young woman in a wheelchair opened the door. Her beaming smile and ''Hi!'' took Peter off guard. So did the sight of Marie, barefoot, in a pair of walking shorts and a cherry-red T-shirt. Oblivious to his arrival, she and Ricky screeched and giggled as she chased him into the corner with the hose attachment of a noisy vacuum cleaner. Peter's uneasiness evaporated.

''Can I help you?''

He refocused on the woman in the wheelchair. She had to be Marie's sister. Her wheelchair was one of the slick customized jobs, cueing him in to the fact that the injury to which Marie had alluded was significant and permanent. He cleared his throat. ''I'm Peter Hallock. You must be Sandy.''

She'd already cocked her head and gazed at him suspiciously. The moment he confirmed his identity, her face grew wary. "I don't think you should have come here, Mr. Hallock. Ricky is ours."

He gave no reply. Marie switched off the vacuum. Though Ricky continued to shriek with glee, Peter noted Marie's laughter died the moment she spied him. Her eyes narrowed and she studied him for a second before she quickly pivoted, as if to block his access to the little boy. Clearly, this mother was protecting her young. Peter wanted to protest—but in that moment, he realized he'd managed to scare her. He'd instilled in her the selfsame sickening fear he lived with—that someone was going to harm or take away a very precious child. The thought appalled him.

Marie patted her son on the backside. "Go to your room. Put away Noah and the animals. Mommy will come check on you in a minute." She waited until Ricky obeyed and was safely out of sight before she walked to the door. "I'll take care of this, Sandy."

Her sister didn't budge. She kept her chair in place as a barrier and looked like a bulldog. "You don't have to talk to him."

"I know I don't." Marie glanced over her shoulder, as if to reassure herself Ricky was safely out of reach, then turned back toward him. "Mr. Hallock, I'll be hiring an attorney on Monday. You'll be contacted thereafter. Do you have a lawyer yet?"

"I was hoping we could share an attorney."

She gave him an incredulous look.

Sandy scoffed, "There's a great idea. I can already see who would end up the victor."

Marie put her hand on her sister's shoulder. Was it a move to silence her, or to protect and side with her? "If you wait at the foot of the ramp, Mr. Hallock, I'll get you a few pictures of Ricky."

Peter noticed she still didn't look him in the eye, and that bothered him. Sandy's bitter words took him off guard, too. Still, he had no right to complain. He refocused his attention. "Luke, come back here!"

"Luke!" Marie's face transformed at once. She scrambled past her sister and plowed down the ramp. She swung Luke in a big circle, then cuddled him close. Head tilted so she could rub her cheek in Luke's soft hair and relish every last inch of contact, she turned her gaze to Peter. "You brought him!"

Peter felt a jumble of emotions. A stab of jealousy pierced him. Then, too, anger hit. How dare she think he'd leave Luke behind? Ah, but the wariness on her face had been replaced by sheer joy.

Something tugged on his shirt. Sandy laughed. "Hey, would you mind moving? That's my nephew down there."

Peter stepped aside. As Sandy rolled over the threshold, Marie brought Luke up the ramp. "Lookie, Luke! It's Auntie Sandy!"

Luke grabbed fistfuls of Marie's shirt and buried his face in her shoulder. Peter watched how Marie held him a bit more possessively. "It's okay, punkin." She smiled at Sandy. "He's shy."

"Compared to Ricky," Sandy said, "anyone is shy."

Peter felt relieved that they accepted Luke just as he was.

"Can I come out?" Ricky's shout from the bedroom made them all laugh again.

The second Marie called her permission, Ricky rocketed out of his room and onto the porch. Peter caught him and held him tight. In that moment, every bit of doubt he'd held about coming south disappeared. He'd done the right thing.

"It's getting kinda crowded," Sandy said. "This porch isn't made for family reunions."

They went into the house and the joy suddenly dissipated, only to be replaced with awkwardness. For a brief pause, no one said a thing. Then, they all started to speak. "We didn't—"

"I know—"

Marie and Peter both went silent as Sandy finished her statement. "Those kids look—" she hesitated as she looked from Peter to Marie, then finished "—like very good boys."

Ricky poked himself on the chest a few times directly over a badge-shaped patch. "I'm a fireman!"

"You don't got a hat," Luke countered.

"I gots two." Ricky wiggled, so Peter set him down. Luke followed suit, and they scrambled out of the room. Peter looked back at Marie and cleared his throat. "After you left, I got mad. Not at you—at Melway General. I called my lawyer. I'd like to discuss what he said."

Sandy piped up, "How 'bout if I take the boys for a walk?"

Marie's shoulders melted with obvious relief. "That would be great! Thanks."

Ricky, wearing a plastic fire helmet, came back into the room. Luke trailed along behind him. Instead of a hat, he sported a toy tool belt. Peter wasn't sure if Sandy could handle one kid, let alone two, but how could he diplomatically ask? He watched as Luke tentatively ran his hand over a wheel of her chair. Sandy didn't reach for him. Instead, she leaned a bit closer and asked in a quiet, sweet voice, "I'm going to take Ricky to the park. He rides in my special chair with me. We'll take a bag with juice and cookies. Do you want to come?"

Luke shook his head. Peter was secretly glad he did.

Ricky grabbed a lumpy canvas bag from a nearby shelf. As he dragged it over, one of the straps caught Sandy's foot and pulled it off her wheelchair's footrest. "Hey, buster! No fishing in these waters."

Ricky untangled the webbed strap, then hooked the bag over the handles of Sandy's chair. His intense concentration struck Peter as both adorable and a sign of his intelligence.

Sandy tried to use her hands to tug her pant leg so she could lift her foot, but her shoe got stuck between the footrests. Peter knelt and slipped Sandy's foot back in place. "Are you always this fun to be with?"

"Not by a long shot. Four months ago, I strongly contemplated suicide. Marie managed to keep me patched together and dragged me to church until I got my head screwed on straight. I decided landing in a wheelchair was a disaster, but it wasn't the worst thing that ever happened. If anything, it made me take stock of my life and change things for the better. Marie made me face things and helped me get through. She's got a knack for doing that."

"You sisters are quite a twosome."

"She's the loyal one. I'm the deserter. After all, I'm leaving her with you right now." Sandy straightened her clothes and looked at him intently. "Marie would eat ground glass before she ever left me with a guy who wanted my kid."

Peter looked up at her somberly. "I'd never intentionally hurt either of them."

"I know. Before I ever let Marie go, I called and had one of Jack's friends on the force run a sheet on you. You came out totally clean."

"Sandy!" Marie gasped.

"Hey, you can't blame me! This guy could've been

dangerous. I wasn't willing to risk you or Ricky.'' The little boy scrambled up onto Sandy's lap. She dipped her head and rubbed her nose to his in an Eskimo kiss. ''We'll be back soon. Behave yourselves.'' She set her wheelchair into motion.

As it rolled down the ramp, Ricky started making fire-engine siren sounds.

Peter turned to Marie and cocked a brow. ''So she ran a check on me.''

''You had your security guard search my car and purse!''

''True.'' He couldn't quell a grin at her outrage. ''Are we even?''

Marie shook her head adamantly. ''Nothing, but nothing, is as bad as a purse search! Half of my life is in that bag!''

''I see…'' he mused. He chuckled and couldn't resist. ''I think you lied about your height on the driver's license. You're at least two inches—''

She wheeled around. ''I didn't, but you looked!''

''Nope. Honest, I didn't. I was tempted, but I didn't. It was a stupid way of me trying to break the tension.'' He forked his fingers through his hair. ''This is all so unbelievable.''

The fire in her eyes went out and compassion replaced it. Quietly, she asked, ''Would you and Luke care for some juice? Water?''

''Juice for him, please. Do you have any coffee?''

''I'm out of it right now. Sorry.''

''Okay. Juice will do.'' He hefted Luke and ventured, ''I'll bet this little guy would rest if we laid him down. I gave him a decongestant so his ears would clear on the plane. It makes him sleepy, but he's getting over another ear infection, so I didn't have much of a choice.''

"Poor guy. Let's tuck him into Ricky's bed." They coaxed Luke out of the tool belt and laid him down. As they left the bedroom, Marie said, "I've heard ear infections are brutal."

"He's had them constantly since birth. Hasn't Ricky?"

She shook her head. "No, breastfed babies rarely get them."

It took every shred of discipline to keep from zeroing in on her T-shirt. "You nursed my son?"

"My son. Or at least I thought he was." She folded her arms across her chest and her cheeks turned the same cherry-red as her shirt. "Didn't your wife want to?"

"My wife died as a result of a car accident. The doctors at Melway General delivered our child as a last-ditch effort."

Marie gave him a startled look. "That's why you were so adamant about not letting me go! I was pretty surprised."

He nodded. "Probably. Some wounds don't heal very easily." His gaze slid over her face. "Your reaction to the guns yesterday was probably magnified because of how your husband died."

"We've both stumbled onto each other's vulnerabilities, haven't we?"

"Let's make allowances for that and try to start over."

She nodded hesitantly.

"So tell me why Ricky is crazy about firefighters when your husband was a cop."

"Sandy mail-ordered a costume and the truck for Christmas. It's grown into a full-blown fascination. I bought a bunch of patches that look like badges and added them to his shirts just to save my sanity."

They walked into the kitchen. Peter passed the round oak table and noted a dinky acrylic holder full of tiny, colorful paper strips. A pale blue one lay on the table. *Lo, I am with you always, even unto the end of the earth.* That Bible promise seemed particularly apropos. Ever since Marie's revelation, he felt like he stood teetering on the edge of the safe, happy world he'd built for himself and his son. He needed to be reminded the Lord was with him—with them—in the midst of this earth-shattering mess.

''You mentioned consulting an attorney.'' Marie took two green striped glasses from the cupboard. ''So what happens next?''

''So far, we're basing everything on simple blood type and deductive reasoning. We'll undoubtedly have to have DNA testing done to confirm the boys were swapped. We could go the rapid route and have an answer back in a couple of days, but since things will get sticky, I'd rather spare the boys a second blood draw and have all of the specimens go through the full battery.''

''It sounds to me like you still aren't convinced there was a switch.''

Peter frowned. ''On the contrary. As far as I'm concerned, doing the lab work is a mere formality. I always thought Luke looked like my wife until you came along, Marie. Now I know he has to be yours. The similarity is stunning—just like the match between Ricky and me. Even a fool could plainly see whose child is whose.''

''But everyone else will demand proof.''

He nodded. ''This week we'll all have to get to a lab, but for the sake of streamlining things, I'm going to assume our suspicions are a confirmed fact.''

''Okay.'' Her hand shook as she poured the orange juice. ''I'll have the doctor call in an order to the lab. Ricky and I can go after work on Monday.''

Peter had thought about having them all go in and getting the blood drawn at a clinic today, but he could see that wouldn't be wise. He'd rattled her badly enough yesterday, and he still had something on the agenda that meant more to him at the present. He cleared his throat.

"Did you need something?"

"As a matter of fact, yes. I want to spend the weekend. I went crazy without Ricky last night."

Marie gave him a stricken look. "You can't get possessive like that, Peter."

"He's my son, Marie."

"And Luke is my son." Marie could see the strain in his eyes. She drew in a deep breath to steady her nerves and whispered a quick prayer for wisdom. She wanted her voice to stay strong, even though everything inside quivered like pudding. Quickly, before her words would quaver, she shoved his glass at him. "It's practically tearing me apart, but I'm trying hard not to make any demands and to be scrupulously fair."

"I think you ought to come live with me."

Chapter Four

Her own glass slipped from her fingers and shattered on the floor. Marie ignored it as she gaped at him.

"Did you cut yourself?" Peter carefully walked on the clean spots between the glass and juice. He wrapped his hands around her waist and lifted her onto the counter.

She practically shrieked, *"Live with you?"*

"Yes. You're a mess. Swing around here and put your feet in the sink so you can rinse the juice off of your legs and feet."

Stunned, Marie sat there and looked at him as if he'd suddenly sprouted cloven hooves. "I can't live with you!"

"Marie, take care of your legs, then we'll see to the other issues. Where's your trash?"

She mutely pointed at a cabinet. Turning around, Marie followed his suggestion and put her feet in the sink. Rinsing off took no time at all, but she sat on the counter and stared at the water as it cascaded over her feet. Clearly, Peter Hallock wasn't going to be a take-things-slowly kind of man. He blazed his own path; she carefully con-

sidered and weighed her options. That personality difference wasn't going to make coping with the situation any
easier. *Lord, this would be a great time for a miracle. If*
You're not dispensing those, then that wisdom I just re-
quested? Please double it and add on a side order of
patience!

"Are you okay?"

His concern jarred Marie out of her prayer. She turned
off the water. "I'm fine. Please hand me a towel."

He tossed a dishcloth to her. "There you go." Gingerly, he picked up large shards of glass and put them in
the trash, then sopped up most of the remainder of the
mess with a few paper towels. "Your floor is going to be
sticky."

"I planned to mop it today, anyway."

"I'll mop it."

"No, thank you." His offer surprised her. "I'll sponge
it for now and take care of it after Ricky goes down for
his nap. He'll slip on a wet floor."

"I hoped we could use that quiet time to talk through
some plans."

Marie gave him a stern look. "Peter, I don't know exactly what you have in mind, but I'm not ready to pull
up stakes and move. I have a steady job and, though it
may not compare in any way to your mansion, this is my
home. I have ties to the community, and stability is important to me. It's vital in a small child's life, and I'd be
a fool to give all of that up because you snap your fingers."

"I'm not asking for myself. I'm asking because I firmly
believe it's in the boys' best interests."

Marie took a deep breath in a vain attempt to settle her
nerves. The man was as calming as a stick of lit dynamite.

"If your concern is for Sandy, let me assure you, she'd

be welcome. My home is big enough, and since it's a single story, she'd have full access to the whole place. Think of it. You could stop working and spend all day with the boys. You'd have more time to work with Sandy, too.''

Marie twisted sideways. She concentrated on rubbing her feet dry and tried to block out the temptation of his offer. She shook her head and whispered, ''We can't do that.''

''Why not?''

''Can't we come up with another option? Maybe have a weekend together, then swap kids for the next weekend or something?''

''That's too disruptive and awkward.'' Several glass shards clinked as he dropped them into the trash. He turned and gave her a level gaze. ''You're the one who just pointed out how important stability is.''

''It's morally wrong, Peter.''

''Your sister will be there! Isn't that enough?''

''We're total strangers!''

''It wouldn't take long for that problem to be resolved.''

''Stop it. Just stop!'' She wanted to turn back the hands of time and make it so she'd have never discovered the baby swap. *But then I'd never have seen Luke....*

''We can't just sit around and do nothing, Marie.''

''There isn't any big hurry,'' she countered.

''If you really like working outside the house, Anne can handle the boys. All of my sisters work, Marie. If you enjoy having a job, we'll find something up there that you like.''

''You're trying to tempt me, and you've tossed in everything a woman might hope for, but, Peter, it's still wrong. I can't go against my moral code. It's a terrible message for the boys, and we still don't know how well they—or we—will get along. I'd be a fool to accept this cockamamie plan."

Peter had finished up cleaning the floor. He planted his hands on the counter on either side of her. His eyes searched hers for a long count. "You're going to have to work with me. What is it you want, Marie?"

Nervously crushing the dishcloth into a ball, she blurted out, "I want the nightmares to stop!"

Peter took the dishcloth from her and set it off to the side. He slid his hand over hers. "Tired of it all?"

She bit her lip and nodded. Blinking madly, she pleaded, "Don't get me started crying. I can't do that."

"But, Marie, in less than two years you've suffered not one, but three staggering blows. Think about it. You've lost your husband, your sister got injured and became totally dependent on you and you've discovered your son isn't yours. How are you supposed to cope? I think you're more than entitled to sob your guts out."

She averted her face. "It upsets Ricky and Sandy too much," she whispered thickly. "I need to be strong for them."

Peter gently tilted her face and forced her to look back at him. In a low, insistent tone, he asked, "But, Marie, who's strong for you?"

Chapter Five

The obnoxiously loud buzzer on the dryer sounded. Startled, Marie jumped. "I have to get that."

His hands immediately went to her waist. He gently squeezed, then pulled her to the edge of the counter and lifted her down. She shivered from the contact—or was it from the emotions shimmering just below the surface that he'd almost bared? He didn't know. Clearly, Marie was a woman of great depth, but she guarded her heart just as closely as she guarded her child.

"You do too much," Peter decided aloud a few minutes later as he watched her sit on the couch and fold clothes. The vacuum cleaner still rested in the corner, and a grocery list lay beneath a toy car on the coffee table.

"I do what every other mother does. I'm not complaining."

His hands itched to pull away the laundry basket and make her stop taming the jumbled clothes into neatly folded squares. The intense concentration she aimed at the simple task seemed ridiculous—but then he realized she was trying to get lost in the rhythm of a familiar task so her life wouldn't feel so chaotic.

"How can I get you to reconsider, Marie? I really want you to move in with Luke and me."

The distinctive fragrance of fabric softener drifted in the room as Marie folded a pair of Ricky's pants with jerky motions. *They look just the same as the pairs in Luke's drawers—same pint size, same style, same fold.* That odd fact strengthened his resolve.

"I'll do whatever it takes to make this work, Marie."

"There's nothing you can do. I'm not about to change my mind." The next few garments were disciplined into perfection under her moves.

"I'm not trying to put you on the defensive, Marie. It's the best option available, especially since we live several hours apart with the wrong biological kids."

"Give me other possibilities, Peter."

He sat opposite her and let out a heavy sigh. "We can trade. We each keep the child we've been rearing during the week, then switch them on the weekend."

"That's pretty disruptive. As soon as they start school and ball teams that won't work."

Peter reached up and rubbed the awful knot of tension at his nape. "Let's try to limit our plans to the present."

She nodded and smoothed a collar on a tiny, golden yellow rugby shirt.

"I could have them both one weekend, then you could have them the next."

"I don't think that's workable—at least not now." She tilted her head to the side a bit and shot him a rueful look. "Luke is too shy, and Ricky hasn't ever been away from me."

"All of that is probably valid, but I like the idea of them being together. Right now, you and I are feeling the impact of this whole mess, but in later years, they will. I want them to have each other. No one else could possibly understand how this upheaval will affect them.''

Marie's fingers curled into the little shirt, and she unconsciously brought it up and crushed it to her heart. She looked at him, her eyes pleading. ''I could keep both boys down here during the week, then bring them up for the weekends—''

''No!'' Peter scowled. ''I'm not one of those cardboard fathers. I take my place in my son's life—in my *sons' lives*—seriously. That plan makes it impossible for me to see my sons each day!''

Marie bit her lip. Blinking furiously, she set the shirt aside. Her hands shook terribly and tears shimmered in her eyes. Finally she whispered unsteadily, ''No matter what we do, we're not going to be able to see both of them on a daily basis.''

''If it upsets you so much, Marie, why don't you accept my offer?''

Raw pain ravaged her features, twisted her mouth and leeched the color from her cheeks. In a low, pained rasp, she asked, ''How can I? I don't know you at all. We're total strangers.''

''We're both motivated. We could make it work.''

She shook her head. ''You've been masterful at this, Peter. I can see why you're so successful. You've enticed me with everything I could want. The temptation is incredible—to have both boys all of the time, to be able to help Sandy more. You offered me everything my heart longs for—but it goes against my soul.''

Peter winced. She certainly knew how to hit the bull's-eye. He tried to hide his feelings by momentarily cranking his head to the side. He drew in a steadying breath, then turned back. "You're mobile. I'm not. I'm locked into a five-year contract with the hospital."

"Sandy's doctors and rehab experts are down here. She's made such good progress."

"I guarantee you the rehab department at my place is top-notch. If you came up there, Sandy would get excellent attention, and I'll put in whatever equipment she needs or adapt her room so she'll be comfortable."

Marie shook her head. "It's not just a matter of physical care. Tomorrow she's supposed to go out on her first date since the accident. At some point in the fairly near future, she'll move into a living center, but until then, I can't abandon her, and I can't take her away from here." She pulled another of Ricky's little shirts from the basket and shook it out, almost as if the action were sketching an exclamation point to the end of her assertion.

Peter groaned, "Solomon had it easy. Those two women only brought one kid to him."

"He had God's blessing and wisdom, too," Marie tacked on.

"We're both believers. God can and will grant us wisdom if we ask."

The little shirt rumpled into a messy knot in Marie's hands. "I've been praying for His wisdom and will, but I still don't have any sense of direction. I don't want you to put pressure on me to act in haste."

"I'll try my best. Look—you're understandably distraught, but I want you to know it's not my intent to make things harder on you."

"You just want to make them easier on yourself—even though it costs me everything."

"But you'll gain seeing Luke every day."

"Don't you think I know that?" she cried. "But I refuse to be reliant on your whims and goodwill. I can't leave this house. Jack bought it for me. He was fixing it up on his days off. It's all I have left.''

"Why don't you look at me?" He didn't understand her aversion to him. It stung.

Swallowing hard, as if trying to dislodge the huge ball in her throat, Marie confessed, "You look too much like Ricky. I love his dear little face, and when I see you..." She shrugged.

"It's confusing," he finished softly. He gently set the shirt aside and folded her hand between both of his. "You look so much like Luke, it takes my breath away. Because of it, I feel as if I already know more about you than two short meetings would yield. My impulses to protect, keep and touch you probably come from that."

"But you can't be that way. You can't act like an authoritative parent and dictate what happens. I won't accept it. It's a struggle to wait for God's will, but that's far better than rushing to make decisions I'll regret later."

Peter's brows knit in consternation that she still wore her wedding ring. After his wife died, he'd jerked off his band and known beyond a shadow of a doubt he'd never replace it. He kept Marie's hand encased in his and slowly rubbed up and down the length of the back of her slender fingers. He'd barely kept his marriage patched together; Marie still hadn't even let go. *This woman honors her commitments at all costs. Such devotion!*

"I don't know what I want or expect," she admitted. "I prayed for wisdom and guidance, but that prayer hasn't been answered yet."

"It sounds to me like that prayer was more for the situation than it was for the feelings and dynamics between us." He curled his fingers so he engulfed her hand. "Until yesterday, Luke and I were just names to you. Now we're real people. These things take time, Marie."

She finally looked up at him. "If they take time, how can you want us to move in with you now?" She slowly pulled her hand from his grasp. "I don't know you at all, and I'm not sure how to interpret this situation...between us, you know...?"

"What don't you understand? This isn't a time to mince words, so I'm going to be forthright. I'm financially more than comfortable, Marie. You and Ricky can simply move in and—"

Color filled her cheeks. "I won't live with a man to whom I'm not married."

Peter decided to ease off a bit. He'd come here with that one plan and it seemed so direct and simple. A business deal. They'd be platonic roommates who shared their kids. No fuss, no nonsense, no emotional attachment between the two of them. No chance he'd ever let her close enough to hurt him. Clearly, he needed to spell it out. "I'm not trying to offend you, Marie. If you thought I was using the boys as a means to seduce you—"

The faint wash of color in her cheeks cued him in that he'd just jumped feetfirst into a sensitive topic and needed to be a shade less blatant.

"Marie, let me put your mind at ease. I'm not suggesting anything immoral at all. Sandy would come, too. You'll have your own bedroom—one with a lock on the door so you can have peace of mind—and I'll respect your privacy."

She signed deeply. "I still can't agree with your plan. I can't live with a man—even if it is platonic."

Peter sighed. Bitter memories of his wife surfaced. Darlene wasn't willing to get married at first. Neither of them had been Christians. Because he loved her, he agreed for her to move in with him for almost a year until he could convince her marriage held any importance. The wedding was more a formality and capitulation than a true commitment on her part. It wasn't until he'd lost her and started to rear Luke that Peter began going to church or paid much attention to old-fashioned morals. He wondered if Marie was as conservative as she seemed. He tried to delicately fish for information. "Your notions are pretty traditional. Have you always—"

"Let me save you from walking on eggshells. I'm very old-fashioned. I was twenty-two when Jack and I got married. We were very much in love, but we waited until our wedding night because it was the right thing to do. We conceived our child the second month of our marriage. He was a planned baby, and we were thrilled. After knowing the joy of a loving marriage, I'd never settle for anything less, so you can forget any plans for cohabitating—even if it is completely innocent."

Peter fell back against the couch cushions. He gave her a lopsided, self-conscious smile. "I needed to know where you stood."

"Now you know." She gave him a wry look. "If you're feeling that brazen, is there anything else you want to pry into?"

He spread his hands in a what-else-am-I-to-do? gesture. "This is a high-speed beginning. It isn't conventional, but for the boys' sakes, I think we have to hurdle over the usual constraints and forge a decent working relationship."

"I'm accustomed to doing that with preschoolers. They're a lot easier. They want to know if I have a pet and if I can hop on one foot. I'm not exactly the most coordinated person in the world, and you want me to jump hurdles!"

He chuckled. "Our cat ran away. I can hop on one foot, but I can't skip. What about you?"

"We had a solemn burial for our goldfish last month."
When he quirked a brow, she nodded, "Prayers and por-
celain. I can hop and I can skip. There? Does that satisfy
your curiosity?"

"Not really, but it's a start." He gave her a boyish grin.
"So far, I know you have a sister. What about your folks
or Jack's parents? Are there doting grandparents in
Ricky's world?"

"I have a stepfather, but he lives in Ohio. Jack's parents are missionaries in Thailand. They write, and we send
pictures."

"So you're doing it alone...unless you have a boy-
friend?"

Marie blanched. "I'm not interested in dating."

She looked like she needed a whole lot of space. He'd
pushed her too far and gotten a wealth of personal information, so Peter decided to bail her out by giving her
some basic information on himself. Reciprocating only
seemed fair.

"Darlene's parents aren't involved at all. A Christmas
picture is about all they want or expect. On the other hand,
my folks are wild about Luke. Until now, he's been their
only grandchild. I have three sisters—all single and madly
in love with him, too. I have one more sister out there
somewhere. We still have investigators working on trying
to find her. It's been eighteen years. She was kidnapped
when she was two. As for my personal status—I'm not
dating anyone, either."

He paused and noted how Marie stayed silent. Peter
looked around her living room and back at her. "Marie,
please forgive me," he pleaded softly. "I know we got
off to a ragged start, but I want us to get along."

"I understand." Compassion filled her voice. "It made
me sick, exploding your happy little world."

"You did the right thing. Why don't we start from scratch? We can trade stories about the kids and ease into things a bit. With time, we'll create ways to blend our families."

Marie stacked all of the neatly folded clothes back into the laundry basket. "I'm not good at diving into relationships."

He hunkered down and tried to take away the basket. "We have to make an effort to get along."

She gnawed on her lip and nodded slowly. Her fingers released the basket into his keeping, and at that moment, he wondered if it was somehow symbolic of so many little things she'd inevitably be placing in his care. The way the muscles in her arms tensed, he could see she fought to keep from snatching it back. *Was she thinking the same thing?*

"Marie—"

At the sound of his voice, she jerked away. Peter knew she had more than enough cause to be wary, but it still nettled him. She needed a lot of cosseting, loads of reassurance and a gentle approach. With so much at risk, he'd do that. "I tell you what—let's just keep the mix-up between ourselves for now. Luke doesn't understand anything's up. We can keep it a secret until the lab work gets back if Ricky doesn't know the score."

Her shoulders drooped with relief. "Other than yesterday, he's been in the dark, and he was too upset then to catch on."

Peter grinned. "Luke thinks *aunt* is part of my sisters' names, so 'Auntie Sandy' didn't hit his radar screen at all. So far, so good, right?"

She nodded.

"I saw your grocery list on the table. When Sandy

comes back with Ricky, why don't we all go do the marketing together?"

A tiny sparkle of humor glinted in her eyes. "Are you that desperate for coffee?"

Relieved that she'd recovered enough to tease him, he chuckled. "I will be by lunchtime."

"Hmm. Addicted to caffeine?"

He propped the basket against his thigh and held up the other hand in a gesture of mock surrender. "I plead guilty. I'm pathetic. I love coffee—any kind of coffee—as long as it isn't decaffeinated. In fact, while I'm confessing my darkest secrets, you may as well hear it straight from me—I'm just as bad when it comes to pie. I'll eat anything served in a pie tin."

"Anything?"

"Up 'til now. You name it, I've probably tried it."

She cocked her head to the side and assessed him slowly. "Baked beans from a campfire?"

He perked up. "Do you like to camp?"

"Love to. I already bought Ricky a little backpack. We strap it on him, and he wears it around so he can carry a tiny bit of gear when I take him to Yosemite."

"I love Yosemite."

"My goal is to take him on a trip when he turns five. By then, Sandy will be out on her own and independent, so we can slip off without too much concern. Ricky enjoys going on walks, and he'd love to see the flowers and squirrels." She paused, then added, "By that point, I have no doubt he'll be able to swim and climb trees. Besides, he's a trouper when it comes to walking. He doesn't often ask me to carry him anymore."

"Just as well. He's a pretty good-sized tyke." He smiled. "I used to do serious, backwoods survival hiking a couple of times a year. Since I lost Darlene, I stick to safer hobbies.''

Her hands fisted tightly. ''Everything changes, doesn't it?''

Peter set down the basket. Her hair looked as baby soft and fine as Luke's. Though the same color as Luke's, her eyes held the haunted cast of someone who suffered terrible heartache. He knew he'd only made her hurt more by being insensitive, and it bothered him. He wanted her to know he cared, and that he shared some of those same lonely feelings. Reaching over, he slowly took her fist into his hand and gently unknotted it as he spoke. ''With a little one underfoot, you have to keep going, even when you feel like you can't make it another minute more.''

''Did you feel that way?''

''Sometimes I still do,'' he confessed. ''I'm lucky to have a household staff. They ease things considerably. I can't figure out how you get everything done.''

''I don't. Just look around you!'' Marie pulled her hand free and flung her arm in an arc to encompass the room.

''You're too hard on yourself.''

A tense moment passed. Their lives and opinions differed so dramatically, bridging the gulf seemed almost insurmountable. She glanced at the front door. ''Ricky and Sandy ought to be home any minute.''

''Marie, I want us to get together each weekend and on holidays until we settle the details.'' Peter lowered himself into a battered leather chair and looked at her carefully. ''How about if we alternate weekends? I'd expect Sandy to join you when you come up to my place.''

The expression on her face made his stomach flip. ''What is it?''

She shook her head. ''It won't work.''

''Ricky's room is big enough for Luke to share.''

"You'd let him spend the night here with me?"

His mind whirled. "Why not? I'd be here, too." Something in her expression made him lock eyes with her. "You can't exclude me, Marie."

"There's nowhere for you to sleep. There are only two bedrooms."

"You already know I camp. I'd be happy out here on your floor or couch."

Nervously wetting her lips, she managed to avoid his eyes. "I'm going to have to watch out for you. You have a knack for making impossible things seem reasonable."

The front door swung open. Sandy and Ricky came in. "I've got a droopy kid here."

"Luke's sleeping on Ricky's bed," Peter realized aloud as he crossed the room to hoist his son off Sandy's lap.

"I gots two beds." Ricky tried to hold up a pair of fingers but didn't quite manage the necessary coordination. After they put him on his nap mat on the trundle, Marie led Peter out of the room and left the door open a mere crack.

She turned to Peter and shook her head. "You talked him out of that shirt." She referred to the juice-and-cookie-crumb covered Junior Fireman shirt Ricky had been wearing. "I was right—you make the impossible seem reasonable."

"No, I don't. Otherwise, you'd be packing right now."

Chapter Six

Marie groaned. "I can't believe I said that to you."

"We're both raw. I can't see any sense in wasting our energy putting on a big act with each other. I'm not myself right now, either. I'm blurting out stuff and look—I grabbed Luke and jumped on the plane without even calling ahead."

"So you're not usually this impulsive?"

"The most impulse thing I've done in the recent past is—" He had to pause and think. "Probably to whistle along with something on the radio. From the way I've acted in the last twenty-four hours, you'd never guess I'm the most boring man in the world."

"You? Boring? Based on your *boring* track record, I wouldn't let you read Ricky a bedtime story. He'd be up all night with nightmares!"

Peter turned the tables on her. "Bet you didn't sleep much last night."

She hitched her shoulder.

"Go ahead and take a nap."

"Can't."

She lowered her lids, and Peter knew full well she was trying to shield him from the emotional tumult in her eyes. "Even if you can't sleep, rest a little. Sandy is able to hold down the fort."

Peter shepherded Marie to the door of the master bedroom. The room looked off balance. A cherrywood dresser stood to the extreme side on one wall. Sandy's hospital bed was next to the door, but they'd left enough room for her to maneuver her wheelchair. That left barely enough room for Marie's double bed to be crammed into the remaining space. Even so, both beds had white eyelet dust ruffles and matching mint-and-white striped comforters.

She'd moved everything like puzzle pieces until they fit. It reminded Peter of how complex it would be for her to account for all of the factors in her life. He softened his voice into a rare mildness and said, "We'll work things out in time. If you're worn to a frazzle, it'll complicate matters."

"They can't get any more complex than this."

He winked. "Then imagine—they can only improve."

"Are you usually an optimist, Peter Hallock?"

"I'm a realist." He resisted the impulse to caress her cheek. "If you come out of here before three o'clock, I'm going to do something drastic."

"Three!"

"Three."

"I don't take kindly to threats."

"I don't make them lightly," he shot back. "If I shut the door, can Ricky open it?"

"He just learned that stunt."

"Luke can't—at least, not that I know of—but he's chunky enough that if he bumps into the door a few times, the latches give. I can see these two are going to teach each other any number of naughty tricks.''

Marie leaned against the doorsill and gave him a jaundiced look. ''I'm supposed to sleep after you said that?''

''I'll bet you could sleep through a six-point earthquake once you close your eyes.'' He nudged her inside, pulled the door shut and stood on the other side for a minute. He caught himself just before he used the adjective *pretty* when he mentioned her eyes. They were pretty. Beautiful, as a matter of fact. Marie Cadant was a very attractive woman. He rubbed his hand over his jaw and shook his head to clear away those errant thoughts.

Sandy's wheelchair whirred down the hall. She looked at the closed door, at him and then jerked her head toward the living room and spun back around. Once they both got out of Marie's earshot, Sandy warned, ''Don't even think of asking to sleep here tonight. When Marie has nightmares, she comes out here to read her Bible. Upset as she is, she's going to be up again tonight.''

''Has it occurred to you that maybe I could keep her company and calm her?''

''Not a chance. The only man who ever got past her guard was Jack.''

''Jack died two years ago,'' he said in an equally muted tone.

''In that very room,'' Sandy informed him. ''She brought him home to die. He was shot in the head.''

Peter sucked in a sharp breath.

''The doctor gave him maybe two weeks.'' Sandy shook her head. ''For three months, Marie tended him and did everything he needed. She was too proud to ask for help, and I was too selfish to think of offering.''

''Sandy—''

She shook her head to cut him off. ''I see how hard

she has to work to help me. It must've been ten times harder with Jack. She took care of him all by herself, and Ricky was younger and more dependent.'' Tears streamed down her cheeks. ''I swear, Peter Hallock, I'll do anything to protect her. If you hurt her…''

Peter half collapsed on the sofa. He shook his head dumbly. ''What it took for her to get through all of that…''

''Don't make it harder on Marie. She can't take anything more. She can't!'' Sandy wiped her face with her sleeve.

''How much does Ricky understand?''

Her eyes darkened with pain. ''He doesn't remember Jack at all. No matter how bad things are, Marie is always patient with Ricky. He trusts her to be the center of his world, and he depends on her to be stable.''

Staring at a picture on the mantel of Marie holding Ricky, Peter let out a noisy gust of air. ''And the earth just shifted in its axis.''

When Marie woke up, she felt completely disoriented. She couldn't remember the last time she'd taken a nap. Her head felt stuffy, and she had a weird kink in her neck. She listened for a minute as she sat on the edge of her bed. The silence unnerved her. She bolted to her feet and flew to the door.

Marie came to a skidding halt at the end of the hall. Sandy was chattering on the telephone. Ricky was nowhere in sight. ''Where is he?''

Sandy tilted her head and mouthed, ''In the backyard.''

Spinning back around, Marie almost lost traction on the freshly polished hardwood. She regained her balance, darted down the hallway and headed toward the porch. Her impulse was to open the door and shout Ricky's name, but the sound wouldn't come as she spied them through the window that comprised the upper half of the door.

Peter knelt in the dirt between Luke and Ricky. Their heads were together, glowing in the afternoon sunlight and they all made truck sounds as they played with an assortment of vehicles. Clearly, they were having a wonderful time. Marie carefully opened the door and eased it shut behind herself.

"Okay, speedy guys," Peter said. "We have a nice, smooth course. Grab your cars. We're going to race now."

"My fire truck is fast," Ricky boasted.

"Yeah, tiger, I'll bet you're the fastest thing around here." Peter must have sensed Marie's presence, because he turned toward her, winked and said, "I'll bet we're all the dirtiest things around here, too."

"Dirt washes off," Marie said softly.

"Daddy, I want to race!" Luke yanked on Peter's arm.

"Me, too!" Ricky zoomed his fire truck across a dirt path.

"Hang on, boys." He stood up and dusted his knees. "Did you have plans, Marie?"

She watched the uncertain look in Peter's eye and she felt a surge of generosity. If she and Peter were ever going to work out this mess and get along, she would have to allow him to get to know Ricky. "Go ahead and have fun. I've got a few things to do inside. You boys behave yourselves and have a good time."

Peter's face split into a beaming smile. "We'll do our best."

Marie went back inside and searched for the grocery list. "Sandy, have you seen—"

"Peter went to the grocery store while you and the boys

napped. The man's hopeless. I haven't seen more junk food in a month of Sundays. Want a cookie?''

"No, thanks." She snooped in the pantry and tilted her head. The cans and boxes were all ones she would have chosen. "How did he know what to buy?"

"He asked me about brands and stuff. He's pretty nice when he calms down."

"There's dim praise."

"Raffy dropped by and took care of the bathtub drain. He used some pretty colorful language in front of Ricky, so don't be surprised if he suddenly spouts off a few choice phrases.''

Marie sighed. "Thanks for the warning." A tiny surge of relief washed over her. The Blue Wall still stood strong, and Jack's friends on the force hadn't stopped watching over her and Ricky. Though she appreciated their help and knew they'd bailed her out of several costly repairs by doing the work as a favor, Marie still struggled when they dropped by. Often they came right after work, but if they were assigned to the beat with her tract, they knew she had an open-door policy. Two of the guys showed up and built the ramp for Sandy the day she arrived, just so she wouldn't have to come and go out the back door. A week later, during the first rain of the season, one of them had been on duty and stopped off to be sure the ramp wouldn't be too slick. The sight of a man in the same uniform Jack had worn made her miss him that much more.

Sandy broke through her sad thoughts. "Are you going to ask Peter to stay for supper?"

"I don't have much of a choice, Sandy. He's got a right to see Ricky. If I get prickly, then he won't let me see Luke."

"He and Luke are a package deal." Sandy glanced to-

ward the backyard where the boys both cheered about
something. "But it looks like he's a good dad, Marie. Not
many men are that clever with kids."

Marie dug through her freezer and took out another
package of pork chops. She'd already started thawing a
package this morning, before he and Luke pulled their
surprise arrival. *And it's turned out to be a pleasant surprise so far. Lord, I asked You to keep Your hand over
this. Please don't let go.*

A little while later, Marie returned to the backyard. She
couldn't stay away. As she walked toward the dirt pile,
Peter held his hand up and pushed his palm toward her.
"Better keep your distance, ma'am. Men at work here.
Grubby, filthy men."

"Mommy, I'm dirty!" Ricky brushed off the firefighter
emblem on his shirt and smeared the dirt more. He didn't
look repentant in the least; he looked downright proud of
his grimy hands.

"Me, too!" Luke held out his hands for inspection.

"I can see that. Your boss is almost as big of a mess
as you are."

Marie let Peter continue to play with them as she
weeded and pruned. He'd come over, swipe some of her
clippings and go "plant" them in the dirt pile to provide
landscape for the city and racetrack he and they boys were
making. Marie mentally corrected herself. He was con-
structing; the boys were wrecking havoc on whatever their
little cars and trucks encountered.

The very low-key ordinariness of the late afternoon
helped her tremendously. In the midst of such an upheaval, the fact that simple everyday play and chores still
carried on gave a measure of sanity to her precarious
world.

When the boys' interest finally flagged, Marie decided,

"Let's get you cleaned up." She held the hose while they all splashed, squished and rinsed. She swiped at a smudge on Luke's cheek. "You have dirt here."

"Do this." Peter demonstrated cupping his hands, filling them with water, and making a bubbling sound as he stuck his face in, then scrubbed his cheeks.

Both boys laughed.

Marie watched in amusement as both boys used Peter's technique to "wash" their faces. Both of them got more water on their shoes than on their faces.

As they headed into the house, Marie felt a flicker of hope. If this was a true example of how Peter and the boys got along, with a lot of time and effort, they might be able to arrive at a workable solution.

As they finished supper, Peter winked at Marie. "Luke likes bedtime stories. What about Rick?"

Clearly, he remembered what she'd said about him boring her son into nightmares with his bedtime stories. She called, "Ricky, get your book and take it to Aunt Sandy." *There. Took care of that.*

Ricky grabbed his Bible storybook and climbed onto Sandy's lap. Luke tentatively tiptoed over, and at Ricky's invitation, he scrambled up and joined them. She read to them as Marie and Peter washed the dishes. Luke nodded off before the story was over.

The way Peter snatched up Ricky after things were done almost shattered Marie's heart. He did it so naturally, but the move showed a thirst to make and foster a budding connection—a connection that would be for keeps. She closed her eyes at that thought. For keeps…he wanted his son. He wanted Ricky, not just for a few moments or a little pal, but as his very own, under his roof, in his heart and for a lifetime. She couldn't blame him, but she couldn't give in, either.

Marie opened her eyes again and watched Peter. Strong, yet gentle, he clutched Ricky to himself with a fierceness that defied words. The mixture of love and anguish on his face made Marie turn and walk away. In the few moments she'd held Luke, she'd fallen head over heels in love; so she knew she couldn't expect Peter to care any less for his own biological son, even if it caused her these moments of soul-deep torment.

Marie quietly slipped Luke into the upper bed of the trundle, then readied the lower mattress for Ricky. Peter's low chuckle blended with Ricky's delighted squeals. Airplane noises and more peals of laughter filtered through the door. "Do it again!"

Marie's head bowed in a moment of pain. Jack would have loved to hear those words. *I can't keep living in the past or wish for what might have been.* She finally summoned enough of a voice to call, "Bedtime, Ricky."

Peter held Ricky securely around the torso and legs and "flew" him into the room like an airplane. They came directly to the bedside. Instead of putting him down, Peter turned Ricky, gave him a big hug then settled him into Marie's arms. Smiling at her, he whispered, "Do you say night-night prayers, too?"

"Uh-huh," Ricky said, "Mommy helps."

Peter knelt down next to Marie and wedged Ricky between them. "Okay."

Marie slanted him a strained look and decided not to make an issue of his presence. He'd already handed Ricky back. As astute as he was, surely Peter intended it as a signal of his awareness that she was still in charge. She started the prayer, and Ricky quickly joined in, "Now I lay me down to sleep…"

After the usual prayer he'd said by rote, she'd taught Ricky to ask God to bless others. Tonight, his clear, sweet voice continued, "And God bless Mommy and Auntie Sandy and my fire truck. God bless Angel Daddy in heaven and—" he paused, cranked his head to the side and peeked with eyes rounded with adoration "—and God bless Mr. Peter and Brother. Amen."

Marie tenderly tucked Ricky in bed and avoided looking at the tall stranger, but she felt his eyes on her. Ricky's prayer knocked him for a loop, and she should have known it would happen, but the last part almost tore her apart, too. She turned on the night-light and made her way out to the hallway before she had to slump against the wall.

Peter came out, wrapped an arm around her and led her out to the patio. She melted almost spinelessly onto one of the battered lounge chairs. Before she could say anything, he asked softly, "When did you start praying for 'Mr. Peter' and 'Brother,' Marie?"

She stared at her hands. "As soon as I knew."

"We rated below his fire truck," he said ruefully. "I guess I have my work cut out for me."

"His fire truck is his all-time favorite."

"I noticed that when we played in the dirt today. He's a joy, Marie."

Nodding, she made no effort to converse.

He tested the webbing on the other lounger, then sat down. The plastic made an odd screech beneath him, but it held his weight. Silence swirled between them.

Leaning forward so his forearms rested on his knees, Peter stared at her intently. "Marie, let's make this work. You've been so gracious today. You even let me play with the boys all alone. You've even included Luke and me in your prayers. I scared you terribly yesterday. First impressions are hard to shake, and I don't blame you for being wary. Believe me—nothing is more important to me than the boys. By that, I mean both of them. Give me a chance to prove that we can work together for their sakes.''

''I'm not a gambler, Mr. Hallock. You want me to risk everything. I can't—'' her voice cracked, and she finished in a sickened hush ''—do that.''

''Maybe we need to think of this as gaining our new sons without losing our old sons. This doesn't have to be a loss—not if we're creative.''

''I don't believe in deluding myself. It's much less painful in the end if I face facts early on.''

''What facts?''

''You're wealthy and powerful. I'm poor and very ordinary. In the passage of time, you'll play those strengths against me.''

''What does that mean?''

''Luke is spoiled beyond imagining with every material thing a child could want. You'll be able to do the same for Ricky. You can hire others to do chores and manipulate circumstances to your benefit. I have nothing to offer but my love.''

''Nothing is more important than that!''

Tears streaked down her cheeks. ''True, but you can offer that, as well, Peter Hallock. You love those boys, too. In the end, the scales won't balance. I wish I wouldn't have ever pursued this mess, because I'm going to lose everything now.''

Chapter Seven

She'd sounded so bleak and hopeless. Peter sat on the sofa and stared at Marie's dilapidated home. The outside she'd dolled up with flowers and such, but the inside and patio showed the true age and wear. Though the cops from her husband's station obviously pitched in, the place needed renovation that would demand far more time, strength and money than Marie had.

The house was just like her—on the outside she seemed so composed and together, but inside she was only a prayer away from collapsing. How was he to reach out to her? After all she'd been through, he couldn't fault her for her fears. He'd made her feel that she had to give up everything. He'd pressed her too far, too fast. It made his heart ache to see how frightened she was, and he felt all the worse for having compounded the problem.

All afternoon he'd had such a great time with Luke and Ricky. When they were together, lost in play, the ache went away. But Marie kept a sense of perspective. At some point in the future, Peter knew he'd count that quality as a virtue. Right now, it was a barrier.

He'd called home as Marie napped. Luke chattered cheerfully with his nanny for a moment. Peter knew Anne treated Luke well. Still, he doubted she ever chased Luke around with the vacuum hose. Marie Cadant would open her heart to Luke and enrich his life in countless ways. She'd kneel with him to say those sweet, sweet prayers and sew him homemade pajamas out of flannel any little boy would covet. Peter wanted her in their lives.

But she didn't want him in hers.

He ached to help her. She wanted to live here for sentimental reasons, and he couldn't fault her for that; but one look let him know the place needed a lot of work—expensive work. Marie would be too proud to accept his offer to fund those repairs. Against his protests, she'd doggedly insisted upon paying him for the groceries; she'd never consent to accepting anything from him.

He'd never been in a stickier situation. If he offered assistance, he'd be wielding the financial power she already feared he'd exercise. If he didn't, he wouldn't be caring for his son and providing to the best of his ability. If he used that argument, then she'd counter it with the fact that she wasn't contributing to Luke's upbringing.

Love didn't have an economy. Who could assign a value to everything? *You make pajamas for Luke, and I'll...repair your car? Fix the plumbing? I'll trade you— a weekend together with the boys at my place for...what?* His head banged back on the wall. This wasn't business. Dickering over everything like a cold, hard transaction simply wouldn't work.

He shamelessly pumped Sandy for information that noon, and she'd been surprisingly forthcoming. Marie received Social Security benefits for Ricky and earned a pittance at the day care. Jack hadn't been on the force long enough to earn retirement or a pension. According to Sandy, men at the police station were wonderful about helping out—they fixed the leaking roof that winter, patched together the plumbing, even brought a tree at Christmas.

Marie brought an armful of sheets, a blanket, a brightly colored quilt and a pillow. "I'm sorry about the couch."

"It'll be great, Marie." He pressed on a cushion. "Comfy—but one blanket is plenty. Neat quilt. Did you make it?"

"Long ago. I'm starting to think even if this situation weren't so weird, you'd still ask half a million questions."

His mouth bowed upward into a sheepish smile. "Curiosity is one of my greatest failings. I drove my parents nuts when I was a kid because I always asked so many."

"Ricky's favorite word is why. Now I know who to blame."

"Speaking of the rascal, I can hear him." Peter grinned at the mumbled stream of gibberish coming from the boy's room.

"He talks in his sleep." Marie looked at him, silently inviting him to tell her about Luke.

He picked up on the cue and hastily provided, "Luke is a quiet sleeper. Real quiet. I don't think he's ever talked at all. Barely even tosses or turns."

"Ricky's worse than a top. He whirls and turns. About once a week, he gets tangled into the blankets like a little burrito and wakes up crying because he's stuck."

"So I'll be sure the boys don't share a double bed when we go on vacations. Luke'll be so black and blue he won't—" He stopped midsentence. "I did it again, didn't I?"

"We never said anything about vacations."

"No, we didn't. I'm full of ideas. Why don't Luke and I tag along to Yosemite? It would be fun. It'll also be safer with two adults to keep an eye on the boys.'' He nodded definitively. "When they turn six—''

"Your enthusiasm is nice, Peter, but it may be premature, if you think about it. We're not out of the woods.'' She sighed. "You and I don't exactly mesh perfectly, and the boys might not become close friends. At best, the weekend deal will only work for a few years. After that, school, ball teams and friendships will complicate it.''

"You're right. We need to give it time. Planning that far ahead is foolish.''

"Oh, no! Not foolish—every parent has dreams for his child. It's just that we aren't…like everyone else.'' Her gaze skittered to the side as she mumbled, "This is a unique situation. I think we'd better take things a week at a time.''

"Okay. For now, you're tired. Go on to bed.''

"Good night.''

He watched her pad down the hall and felt a wave of male admiration. She smelled vaguely flowery, and he couldn't help appreciating the gentle sway of her hips.

A little later, he heard Marie moving about in the bedroom. The chain on the trapeze over Sandy's bed rattled as the women exchanged a few sentences. Soon, things went quiet.

Peter lay in the dark and stared at the ceiling. *Lord, I don't understand any of this. I don't know why You allowed this to happen. Ricky is such a miracle. Thank You for bringing him into my life. But Father, I already love him. You know how fiercely I already feel about him. Even Solomon wouldn't have the wisdom to solve this. Help me. Help us. Show us Your plan.*

He turned his head to the side. The gold-edged pages of Marie's Bible gleamed dully in the dim room. He'd

been in such a hurry to pack and come down, he'd left
his own Bible on his nightstand. He didn't mean to make
any noise, but as soon as he stood up and a floorboard
made a faint protest, she rocketed out of her room.

"It's me, Marie. I just got up to borrow your Bible."

"Oh."

"I didn't mean to alarm you."

Marie made no reply. She took a glass from the cabinet
and dumped a few ice cubes into it before filling it at the
tap. "Would you like some water?"

"Sure. Thanks." He padded into the kitchen.

Taking care not to brush his fingers, she passed a glass
to him and took a jerky sip from her own. "If you're
hungry, there are apples in the refrigerator or cookies."

"No, thanks."

"Sleep well." She set down her glass, turned and left.

Peter sipped the water and listened. Her bedsprings
didn't make a sound. She was out of sight, but not in bed.
The woman didn't trust him one bit. Instead of reading
the Word, he decided he'd go lie down and pray. Maybe
Marie would relax once she decided he'd settled down for
the night. He set the empty glass in the sink, went back
to the couch and peeped at her as she crept past and into
Ricky's room. When she didn't come back out, he finally
went to the door.

She'd curled up on the floor at the bedside. The colorful
rag rug gave the room a cheerful air, but it hadn't been
comfortable at all as they knelt on it for bedtime prayers.
Lying on it had to be murder.

"Marie, this isn't necessary."

She sat cross-legged and pushed her hair off of her face.

Peter took his wallet out of his pants and placed it on
Ricky's dresser. He added the keys to the rental car. "I
can't go anywhere without ID or money. See? I'm not

going anywhere. I'm certainly not trying to swipe Ricky from you—yes, Sandy told me you misinterpreted what I said last night. I blew it, and I understand why you're nervous. At least you can see I've brought Luke along. That gesture should restore your peace of mind.''

She let out a mirthless laugh. ''I don't remember what that is.''

He cringed. ''You need to sleep. Can Ricky sleep in your bed with you? I'll carry him.''

Marie nodded and gracefully rose from the floor. Peter scooped Ricky from the bed. He padded after her until she stopped on the far side of the master bedroom. Sandy was asleep, so neither of them spoke. He laid down his son, lovingly ruffled the carroty curls on the pillow and turned toward Marie. Resting his hands on her shoulders, he leaned close. He didn't hear her gasp, but he felt it beneath his hands.

''I'm sorry I disturbed your sleep, Marie.'' He went back to the couch and knew he was in big trouble. He'd almost kissed her.

Chapter Eight

They went to church the next day. Marie wore an ordinary-looking cotton shirtwaist. Her figure did wonders for the style. The plum color of it accentuated the circles under her eyes, though.

After the worship service, Marie and Ricky waved Sandy off on her date. Peter picked up Ricky and popped him onto his shoulders. "I think we ought to take Mommy to lunch. What do you say, tiger?"

"Hungreee!"

Marie smiled. "He's always hungry."

A wolfish smile creased Peter's face. "I'd say it's hereditary, because I'm the same way, but then I'd have trouble explaining why Luke has a hollow leg."

Luke bent down and stabbed a chubby finger at his leg. "Hello, leg."

She laughed and held out her arms. Luke straightened and let her lift him. Marie watched as Peter swung Ricky down and blithely buckled him into his car seat. He hadn't even thought to defer to her for that small act of care. He'd helped Ricky comb his hair and brush his teeth for church, too. It was nice to have some help...but it made her feel uneasy. Peter plowed in and simply made himself part of whatever was going on.

Peter started toward home but made a wrong turn. Just as she opened her mouth to correct him, he shot her a smile. "I'm dying for Italian food. On my way to the grocery store, I spotted a place around here.... There it is!"

"We can't go there!"

"Why not?"

"Figaro's is—it's—we can't eat there!"

"Of course we can." He ignored her nonspecific protest and stopped the car. The valet smoothly helped Marie from the car, and Peter claimed both boys. Within moments, they were shown to a table.

Eyeing the snowy linen tablecloth, Marie swallowed hard. The last time she'd eaten at a fancy restaurant was on her first anniversary. It had been ages since she indulged in anything this frivolous—or expensive. Peter squeezed her hand. "So what if the boys spill? Do you think that's novel around here?"

"Yes! There isn't another child in the place!"

"Big deal. They're well behaved, and wine stains far worse than tomato sauce, so stop fretting."

"How would you know what stains worse?"

"I worked my way through college by doing any number of odd jobs. A linen supply place hired me one summer."

"It's hard to imagine you were once young."

"It shouldn't tax your imagination at all." Peter tilted his head toward Ricky. "Just look at him."

Peter was a great conversationalist. He entertained the boys as they waited for the meal and managed to put Marie at ease. She found herself smiling at him and ap-

preciating his sense of humor. At his request, the waiter
brought out large dish towels to use as a makeshift bibs
for their sons…and by the time Ricky decimated a plate
of spaghetti, Marie told him, "Good thing you asked for
that dishcloth! I would have had to toss out Ricky's
shirt!"

"Luke's just as messy when he eats." He wiped one
of Luke's hands as Marie grabbed Ricky's and tried to
clean off the sticky red sauce. "I have a video of Luke
eating chocolate pudding for the first time. It's guaranteed
to send you into hysterics."

"I'd love to see it."

Peter nodded. "I'll have it ready when you come up
next weekend. Do you have some films of Ricky stashed
away that I can take up with me?"

"No."

His brows knit. "Marie, I won't keep them. I'll just
have them copied."

"I don't have any videos, Peter." She hastened to explain, "We didn't have a camcorder."

"Oh." From his flummoxed expression, Marie gathered he was momentarily stunned that anyone wouldn't
own such an expensive item; but to his credit, he quickly
recovered. "Okay. While you were napping, Sandy let me
look through those memory albums you've made for
Ricky. You must have spent all sorts of time on them.
They're incredible."

"Thanks."

"If you remember to bring them up with you, I can
scan them and keep the reproductions."

Though Figaro's was the most expensive restaurant
around, Marie noted Peter barely even bothered to look
at the total on the tab the waiter slipped to him. With a
wave of his platinum credit card, and a flourish of a pen,

the bill was settled. A small twinge of regret hit as she reached for her purse. It had been years since she'd had such a nice time.

"This was a wonderful surprise, Peter. I enjoyed it—" she ruffled Ricky's fiery curls "—and I think you can tell Ricky did, too."

"Terrific. Luke and I loved the company even more than the good food." He stood and lifted Ricky into his arms as if claiming a father's privilege. Marie's heart beat faster. They looked so right together. She took Luke into her arms and felt a spurt of pure joy. Sharing the boys pulled her heart in opposite directions—she loved gaining Jack's son, but she feared loosening the exclusive bond she shared with Ricky.

When they got home, Peter winced as he consulted his watch. Marie waited until they walked up the wheelchair ramp to the door before asking, "Have to leave soon?"

"A little over an hour left."

"Was there anything special you wanted to do?"

"Would you mind if I rocked Ricky and put him down for his nap? He's about to conk out on us."

"Go ahead." She cuddled Luke close to her heart. "Shall we put him down in there, too?"

Peter thought for a moment, then shook his head. "Lie him on the couch. That way, we won't bother Ricky when we leave."

Marie and Luke stayed in the living room. The minute she sat on the couch and reached for him, he'd come to her and snuggled. The affection and trust he showed made her glow inside. He yawned. "Sleepy, honey?"

As he nodded, his head rubbed her shoulder and his soft baby curls brushed her neck. She wanted to memorize every second, every sensation. His chubby little hand came up, curled into a fist and he popped his thumb into his mouth.

Ricky seldom sucked his thumb. He was a bit longer, definitely lighter than Luke—but those comparisons didn't warrant more than a fleeting awareness and acknowledgment. Both boys deserved to be cherished just as they were.

Luke's body slowly went limp as he fell asleep. When he grew too heavy for her to hold any longer, Marie grudgingly slipped him onto the sofa and listened to the soft creak of the rocker in Ricky's room. Peter's low rumble sounded foreign. He spoke softly to Ricky, gentling him into his naptime. Long after the little boy's body went lax with sleep, Peter continued to cradle him. He didn't even look up when Marie slipped in.

She quietly took a few pictures. Ricky deserved to have a memento of the first days of his reunion with his father. When Peter startled at the click and whir of the camera, she gave him an apologetic smile. Her eyes filled with too many tears to see him silently mouth words of appreciation.

He gently laid Ricky on the small bed and drew a blanket over the boy. Bending over, he unabashedly placed a kiss on his son's forehead. "I'll see you soon."

They went back to the living room. Peter sat down on the edge of couch and patted the cushion next to himself.

Marie sat down in the chair directly opposite him. With no more than one day's acquaintance, this man had asked her to move into his home. Keeping distance seemed wise—even though it meant she couldn't reach over and touch Luke. She fiddled with the camera strap.

"May I have the roll of film? I'll have duplicates made and give them to you right away."

"I suppose so." She checked the dials. "There are two shots left."

"Good. We'll take snaps of one another. That way, Luke and Ricky can each have a picture of us." Peter mugged for the shot she took, then swiped the camera away. "Sit over there in the sunshine. It'll look pretty on your hair. Come on, smile."

"I'm nervous!"

"Luke doesn't have to know that. Turn this way a little more. I want him to see your dimples. There!" He smiled broadly. "I got it! I'll have them ready next weekend. You're coming up, aren't you?"

"I don't know...."

"Please, Marie. You know how important this is." He leaned toward her. "Sandy is already wild about Luke. I know you both want to spend more time with him. When do you get off work on Fridays?"

"Five-thirty, but I don't know—"

"Marie, please come. Why don't we have you fly this next time, until your car is repaired?"

"Fly!"

"I have so many frequent-flyer miles, we could go around the world six times. Ricky would love being chauffeured up on a fire engine, but I think he'll still enjoy flying, don't you?"

She relented because she wanted to see Luke so badly. "Are you serious about it being free?"

"It won't cost a single cent." Peter then pressed, "About your car, Marie—"

"It's running."

"But not for long. An oil leak can cause major engine damage. If you catch it early, it'll be nothing. I tell you what—I called my mechanic. His brother-in-law owns a garage not far from here. Let him have a look under the hood. I'd feel so much better if you did.''

"Is your past haunting you?'' she asked softly.

"Yes.'' He hadn't paused to even take a breath or think. The answer shot back with such conviction, she knew he'd been stewing over this.

"Then I'll get an estimate.''

He frowned. "Not an estimate, Marie. Get the work done. You'll drive up to see us for some of your visits, so the least I can do is pay for this.''

"No!''

"Marie—''

"I'm not a charity case!''

Chapter Nine

He paced back and forth with long, impatient strides, then walked to Ricky's bedroom door. Bracing an arm against the doorsill, he looked at his son, then drew in a deep breath. Without turning around, he said, "We'll compromise. I'll split the cost with you."

"No, I can rework my budget."

He pivoted sharply and snapped, "I don't want you to!"

Glowering at him, Marie said, "This isn't about what you want. This happens to be you trying to impinge on my private life."

His lips parted, then closed for a second. He came closer and rumbled, "Marie, this isn't about money—it's about keeping you, Ricky and Sandy safe."

"No, it isn't. Clearly you have vast funds and I don't, but I'm not going to allow you to do anything financial."

Peter groaned. "I'm not trying to buy my way into your lives."

"It feels like you are," she admitted all too promptly.

"Then I'll ask you to forgive me, Marie. I don't know what more to say."

"I believe in forgiveness, Peter, but I also know I have to exercise common sense and wisdom. I don't know you at all, and I don't know just how much trust I can put in you. People with wealth are inclined to try to buy their way out of problems or patch things up with money, but there are some things in life that don't have a price tag."

"I only want to take care of a few car repairs!"

"This time," she said. "But then where do I draw the line? It's a subtle form of control, and I'd be a fool to even think of it. I won't tolerate you tossing your money at me as if I were a charity case or a poor relation. Am I clear on that issue?"

His face stayed grim. "Will you at least go to the guy my man recommended? It's probably something minor, but mechanics see a woman like you coming and a cash register in the back of their brains starts *chinging*. At least we'll know he'll be honest." He'd scrawled the mechanic's name and address on a piece of paper and held it out to her.

Marie let out a rueful laugh. "If Ricky or Luke end up half as stubborn as you, I'm going to wear my knees flat, praying for patience!"

"Then we'll match," he countered as he pressed the paper into her hands.

She fingered the slip. "I guess we'll see you Saturday."

He tilted her face up to his. "No, Marie. Friday evening. The nice part about flying is that you'll be able to spend more time with us. My secretary will make the flight arrangements. She'll call you with the details and have the tickets waiting at the counter. Her name is Paulette."

She gave him a tentative smile. "We'll see you Friday."

* * *

Friday, Peter could hardly wait for them to get off the plane, yet a long trail of passengers came toward the baggage-claim area and Marie still didn't appear. *Did she chicken out?* He'd wanted to call her every single day this week—both to talk to his little son and to reinforce how much he anticipated their visit. It took all of his self-restraint to phone only twice. *Did I push too much? Did I act too casual so she decided it wasn't important?*

Luke rode his shoulders to keep from being mowed over by travelers. Just about the time Peter decided to ask one of the passengers if they'd seen Marie, Ricky and Sandy on the plane, they came into sight. Marie held Ricky in her arms and walked behind Sandy's wheelchair. Peter's heart sped up another notch. "There they are!"

Luke clapped his hands and shouted, "Ricky! Ricky! Marie!"

Peter watched Marie's reaction as he jogged toward them. The time he'd spent using the photos and teaching Luke to recognize Ricky and Marie had paid off in spades. Marie stopped in her tracks. Her breath caught and tears glossed her eyes.

Peter swept Luke into Sandy's lap. "Give Auntie Sandy a big hug, Luke." Luke wound his arms around Sandy as Peter gathered Ricky and Marie together in one, all-encompassing hug. He gave Ricky an extra squeeze, then smiled at Marie. "Luke recognized you from the picture. I got the film developed and have been showing your photos to him all week. Smart kid, huh?"

"Luke takes after his aunt," Sandy declared as she hugged her nephew. "At least in the brains department. He certainly took after you with his looks, Marie."

"Here, Marie. I'll take him." Peter eagerly curled his

hands around Ricky's ribs and tugged. "This little monster is too heavy for you to carry!"

Marie relinquished him and turned to get Luke. "Then I'll take Luke."

Sandy shook her head. "Nothing doing, sis. It's my turn to hold him. Besides, he weighs more than Ricky, and you still have a gigantic bruise from the lab drawing your blood."

Peter looked at the dark purple splotch at the bend in Marie's arm and frowned. "That looks sore. Luke bruised, too—but not like that."

She tugged at her sleeve to cover the mark. "Ricky wasn't happy at all about getting stuck. How did Luke do?"

"I bribed him with ice cream," Peter confessed. He noted how Marie redirected the focus to the boys. She wasn't one to want to be the center of attention. He didn't let on how seeing her held almost as much appeal as seeing Ricky. Instead, he directed them toward the baggage carousel and let the boys start up some nonsensical chatter.

The boys continued to prattle to one another the whole ride home. During one of the phone calls, Peter mentioned he'd gotten a car seat for Ricky, so Marie didn't need to lug one along. On the ride home, Peter pointed out a few sights and pulled into his drive.

"Wow. Marie told me you lived in a nice place, but she didn't say it was a mansion!" Sandy gawked at it.

Peter grinned at her. "I hope you'll be comfortable here." Peter had gotten advice from the rehabilitation department and rented a hospital bed for Sandy. When he took their luggage into the bedroom and Marie noticed that, she was pleasantly surprised.

"The bathroom is through that door." Peter handed

Marie her cosmetic case and indicated the way. He waited in anticipation of Marie's reaction.

"Oh, my word!" She stuck her head out of the door, and her eyes were wide with delight. "Sandy! Come look at this."

"What?"

"Peter put in grip rails, a handheld massage nozzle and a shower chair!"

Squeezing Sandy's shoulder, Peter said, "You're family."

For the next month, they traded weekends. True to his word, Peter gave Marie copies of the pictures she'd taken of him and Ricky together. He added an additional stack of carefully labeled snapshots of Luke. She'd pored over them as if she could recapture the lost years. The intensity of her love would have shocked him if he hadn't felt the same way about Ricky.

On the weekends when Peter and Luke went down to Orange County, Marie obviously fretted about him sleeping on the couch. Peter handled the matter with his usual forthrightness. "Stop worrying, Marie. In the overall scheme of things, this is small potatoes, so let it go, okay?"

She nodded and murmured about something she needed to do. Peter watched her walk away, then frowned at the door frame when he started to follow. Sandy showed a lot of skill, maneuvering her wheelchair around as she did. The scuffs and scrapes might have been from her first weeks in the chair, before she gained proficiency...but even that thought didn't hearten him. The reminder that Marie and Sandy were crammed into the bedroom of a house that offered neither of them any privacy or space—that bothered him plenty.

Even when Sandy left to live independently, she'd still
be a guest. Marie wouldn't do a thing to change the furniture arrangements. *She needs more space...space she'd
have in my home.*

Peter forced that thought away. It haunted him, but nag-
ging Marie wouldn't get him anywhere. He hadn't managed to keep his own wife happy and at home; why should
it be a surprise that Marie didn't want anything to do with
him, either? He'd have to accept things as they stood,
leave her in God's hands and do what he came down here
to accomplish—to spend time with the other half of his
family.

Things seemed to work out just fine until the week the
blood tests came back. Peter had arranged for all of the
specimens to be taken to the premier experts so they could
be confident with the results. Though the envelope had
arrived at his office via special messenger the day before,
Peter left it sealed and brought it down to Marie's with
him. While the boys played in Ricky's bedroom, Peter
took Marie's arm and led her to the living room.

"What's up?" Her bright expression clouded over. "Is
something wrong?"

"Have a seat, Marie." He wouldn't let her slip over to
the wing-back chair. He pivoted and pulled the envelope
from the side pocket of his suitcase. "The results are
back. I didn't open them yet. It didn't seem right for me
to without you."

She sank onto the couch and chewed on her lip. She
stared at the envelope with all of the anxiety and dread
he felt.

Peter sat beside her and left the results sealed. "No
matter what it says, Marie, both boys are special, and I
want us to share them."

For the first time, she initiated contact. Her fingers curled around his. "Can we pray before we open it?"

Peter clasped her hand tightly and bowed his head. "Heavenly Father, You are the first and best parent. You gave Your Son to us and knew the pain of separation from Him—but God, You knew He'd return to Your side. We feel like Abraham, walking Isaac up to the altar. Faith tells us You have a solution, but we don't see the answer. Lord, whatever Your plan is, reveal it to us. Give us the faith and love necessary to see this through. In Jesus's precious name, amen."

Peter urged, "Go ahead. Open it."

"I can't. You do it."

Nerves stretched taut, he crammed his forefinger into the edge of the envelope and tore off the flap. He'd botched it badly—a ragged, impatient rip that tattled on how little control he possessed at the moment. The single sheet inside crackled as he unfolded it, and the words leapt off the page.

Luke and Peter Hallock have no genetic markers in common. Ricky and Marie Cadant have no genetic markers in common. It is not possible for these boys to have been conceived by the respectively aforementioned adults. Further comparisons show an extremely high correlation of common genetic code between Luke and Marie, making the certainty of him being her son at 99.9987%. Peter and Ricky also share genetic code...

"Just as we suspected," Peter said in a hushed tone.

Marie compressed her lips and nodded.

"We knew it, but it still feels different, having the news actually written down in black and white."

She closed her eyes and nodded again. "Do we have to tell the boys yet? I don't know how to tell them."

"There's no hurry." Peter set the letter off to the side.

Since the envelope had come the day before, he'd had a chance to steel himself for the revelation. From her pallor, he knew Marie felt overwhelmed. Peter wasn't sure what to say or do.

Taking advantage of a few minutes of distraction, the boys decided to go exploring. A lot of giggling and an odd squeak jarred Marie out of her shock. She rose and went to investigate. Peter followed right behind, and they found the boys jumping from her dresser onto her bed. Marie stood in the doorway, frozen. Peter cupped her waist, set her off to the side and tucked a boy under each of his long arms.

"Hey, you rascals! You're in the wrong spot. You have a date in the backyard. Go race cars in the dirt. Ask Aunt Sandy to take you." He got them out of there and turned to face Marie. She'd turned hideously pale and wore a very phony, brittle smile. Peter spied a photo that lay on the floor, undoubtedly knocked off during the boys' she-nanigans. He knew he needed to acknowledge things, yet ease the strained situation. "That must be Jack. Do you mind if we take it out of here? It would be nice to see how Luke compares to his father."

"I'll get it." She hesitantly picked up the portrait and slipped from the room.

Peter steered her to the couch and sat next to her. One arm went around the back of the sofa and barely missed wrapping about her; the other hand helped steady the frame. He said nothing about how badly her hands shook. They both stared at the portrait. "You're right," he decided after a few quiet moments. "Luke does have Jack's mouth."

"He gets the same gleam in his eye, too," she whispered hoarsely.

Peter curled his arm around her shoulders and tipped

her head onto his chest. "Bittersweet, huh?" When she nodded, he murmured, "Go ahead and cry, sweetheart."

"I have to be strong."

"Sandy and the boys are outside." He gave her a gentle squeeze. "They won't get upset if they don't see you cry."

Marie folded the photo to her chest, let out a long, choppy sigh and shook her head. "It doesn't make any difference. Giving in to tears only makes matters worse."

Peter couldn't imagine how matters could get any harder. To his way of thinking, the situation was untenable. Each weekend, separating the boys grew more difficult. Luke and Ricky had grown attached immediately. For Marie and him, trying to ignore the tug of wanting to be with their biological children also tore at their hearts. The simple upheaval each weekend took its toll, as did the constant travel.

Peter had another reason he hated it.

He was jealous. Very few people knew Darlene had left him when she'd been in that fatal accident. He'd come home to a nasty, terse note informing him she no longer wanted to be his wife. Five frantic hours later, a phone call informed him of the birth of a son and the death of his spouse.

In the back of his mind, he'd sometimes secretly wondered if Luke was truly his son. Though Luke looked a bit like Darlene, he didn't look anything like the Hallocks. It bothered Peter that he couldn't see even the slightest bit of himself in his own flesh and blood.

Was it instinct that told him this wasn't truly his son, or was it disappointment in his failed marriage? Perhaps it was suspicion. Darlene had begun to grow disillusioned in the second year of their marriage. It didn't matter how much time he spent with her, where they vacationed, what praise he lavished on her. His gifts were unappreciated, his attention rebuffed. He didn't have any actual proof that she'd had an affair, but any fool could guess her actions weren't those of a faithful wife.

What Peter wouldn't have given to have a wife adore him the way Marie doted on her husband! She cherished his memory, loved his photo and had sentimental connections to the home he'd provided. Only once, in a dark mood, he'd tried to tell himself that she was no different than Darlene. Had Jack lived longer, Marie would have grown bored and unhappy, too. But then he remembered the withered stem he'd found pressed between the pages of her Bible. Jack and she had gone on a walk and plucked a dandelion. They blew the seeds off as they "wished" and she'd saved the stem. Marie told Peter she'd known that day that she loved Jack, and she'd added on that in the year and a half they'd been married, Jack fulfilled every wish she'd ever hoped to have. A wife like that wouldn't leave her husband.

He'd gotten lost in his own thoughts. When the corner of the picture frame started to dig into his thigh, he turned his attention back to Marie. Threading his fingers through her hair, he promised, "We'll handle it. With God's help, we can do it."

She tilted her face up to his and whispered in a shaky voice, "For the boys?"

"Yes, Marie. For the boys." *And for us, too.*

Chapter Ten

The sound of sandals on tiles in his entryway early Monday evening told Peter he was about to have a visitor. The emphatic, rapid slapping warned him that the visitor was on a mission. He straightened up. "Jill! What a surprise!"

His sister glared at him and marched across the room. From the fire in her eyes, he suspected he'd better brace himself. Jill never bothered to hide her feelings, and from the set of her jaw, he knew—

"Surprise? Oh, let's talk about *surprises,* dear brother. I dropped by yesterday. I hardly see Luke anymore, and I had a little time."

Peter had a sinking feeling, but his family had to find out sooner or later. He'd hoped for later, but—

Jill stopped directly in front of him and continued on. "Luke wasn't here. Neither were you. The two of you were down south visiting—let me quote the nanny precisely here—*your other son.* I think you'd better start explaining."

Peter groaned aloud. "I know I haven't said anything yet." He hadn't just remained silent around his family;

he'd been careful to close off the bedroom doors whenever they came over so they wouldn't see Marie's picture or Sandy's bed. He wanted to share the news with his parents and sisters, but he knew Marie couldn't withstand the pressure they'd put on her. Once they discovered a little Hallock boy wasn't under their wing, they'd have a collective fit.

"I'm waiting," Jill stated shrilly.

"Jill, some things—"

"Don't you dare try to put me off, Peter." She wagged her finger at him. "I'm not going to ignore this."

She was right. Once something piqued Jill's curiosity, she turned into a bulldog and wouldn't let go. He blew out a long, slow breath. "This is difficult—"

"Cut to the chase. You know better than to sugarcoat things with me."

"Okay. Here it is in a nutshell. Babies got swapped at the hospital. Luke isn't really my biological son." He watched Jill melt onto a chair, then he quietly continued, "He belongs to a widow in Orange County. She has my son."

Jill sat there and closed her eyes in horror. "I thought things like this only happened on TV. What are you going to do?" Her eyes opened wide and she cried, "We can't give up Luke!"

"I know. There isn't a chance I'd ever let him go." As the tension started to drain out of her, he quietly added, "Marie feels the same way about Ricky."

"His name is Ricky? What is he like?"

Peter spent a while sketching out details, then concluded, "Marie is emotionally fragile. She's been through too much for me to push her into doing anything just yet. I've purposefully left everyone in the family out of the loop on this because she and I need time to work out the issues.''

"Fragile? As in some kind of nutcase we could have declared mentally incompetent?''

"No!'' He half bolted from his chair. "Jill, that's terrible! She's someone very special. I don't want her to get hurt. She's already been through far too much. I need time to convince her to move up here.''

"If she won't come, will you move down there?''

He stared at the top of his desk. Distinct piles of forms, reports and letters demanded his attention. They represented his livelihood. Could he walk away from it all and live elsewhere if it meant he'd have both Luke and Ricky with him? He looked back at Jill. "I don't think it will come to that. If it does, my sons are more important than my job or anything else.''

"Peter!''

"Don't borrow trouble. I told you, she needs time. The blood tests from the lab finally confirmed our hypothesis just days ago. I'm thunderstruck, and Marie is, too. The last thing I need is for you to sic Mom and Dad on her. She'll dig in her heels or bolt.''

"All right, all right. Still, you have to tell the folks— and soon. I've already told Brianna and Kate what the nanny said.''

"Thanks a heap! Can't you ever keep secrets from one another?''

"Nope—at least, not up 'til now.'' Her impertinent smile didn't carry a hint of apology. "We all knew something was up. You're never around on the weekends, and we've hardly even seen Luke for the last month! The nanny's slip of the tongue just made us a bit more curious.''

"A bit?'' He gave her a censorious look.

"Okay. A lot. In our wildest imaginings, we didn't concoct this scenario. You've never been the type to sleep around, but we wondered if you'd had a fling on a business trip after Darlene died."

"Aw, come on, Jill! That's not my style. It goes against how a Christian lives."

She waved her hand helplessly. "I know, I know—but it was far more believable than this! This is totally outrageous."

"If you think it's outrageous, how do you think Marie and I feel? I'm barely coming to grips with it, and she's still in shock. You're going to have to keep this a secret."

The corners of her mouth tightened. "Okay. I'll finally keep a secret—for you." She forced a laugh. "Even if they're going to try to pump me unmercifully. My guess is, even with me keeping my big mouth shut, you'll be lucky to have twenty-four hours before everything breaks loose."

He didn't have twenty-four minutes. The phone rang. It was his parents demanding to know where their "other" grandson was.

Peter wanted to deal honestly with Marie. Okay, he'd gone behind her back with the auto mechanic. That car of hers had so much wrong with it, it was a marvel it moved at all. In fact, from what the mechanic said, the fact that the old thing withstood the long drive from his place to hers that night counted as nothing short of a miracle.

Peter paid for the mechanic to do the brakes, replace the compressor, muffler and carburetor, as well as overhaul the engine. Marie was charged for a simple tune-up and oil change. The mechanic truthfully told her the oil filter seal had been loose, causing a leak. She hadn't thought to ask if anything more was wrong. Peter breathed a sigh of relief when the mechanic reported back to him. Still, he'd vowed not to go behind her back any more, and he'd stuck to his word.

Much later that evening, after he knew she'd have Ricky tucked safely in bed, Peter called. "Marie, we have a problem."

"Luke's not sick, is he?"

"No, honey. Luke's fine." Her sigh of relief pleased him. "It's just that I haven't mentioned my family much."

"Uh-oh." Her reaction barely whispered across the line, but it carried a wealth of dread.

He hurried to reassured her, "We're real close, Marie. They know about Ricky. I tried to keep it from them for a while until you and I got over the initial shock, but the cat's out of the bag."

"Can you shove the cat back in?"

He forced a chuckle, but when she didn't laugh, he quickly shifted tactics. "You and I decided to still keep it quiet, and I didn't want them to find out yet, but my sister asked Miss Anne where Luke and I were. It hadn't occurred to me to swear her or my housekeeper to secrecy."

Marie said tightly, "Luke was bound to say something soon, anyway."

Grateful she wasn't condemning him for his oversight, Peter said, "At this point, we can either face them on our own terms this weekend when you come up, or we can plan on them crashing our party whenever they get wind of the fact that you're around. What do you think?"

"Couldn't you just be an orphan and simplify this a little?"

He chuckled. "Too late, I'm afraid."

"No, you have that wrong. *I'm* afraid."

Her admission made his heart twist. Marie rarely admitted to any weakness. She'd learned to bear up under extreme burdens, so for her to confess fear made his heart ache. He softened his voice and coaxed, "They're nice folks, Marie. They'll flip over Ricky. What are you afraid of?"

"How are they going to feel about Luke now?"

So that was it. Bless her heart, she'd worried one child might supplant the other! He doodled on his desk pad as he cradled the phone closer. He wished she were here so he could cradle and comfort her. "Marie, that's not an issue at all. I promise, they'll feel no differently than they already do. Mom stopped in the middle of our conversation today about Ricky and insisted that Luke was due to have his dentist appointment and demanded that I see to it. She insisted it was time for him to have a haircut, too."

"Whew."

"She also started spouting off wonderful ideas for redecorating so the boys could share a bedroom. Dad decided to see when the country club will enroll them in tennis lessons because they'll be great for doubles."

"Now wait a minute!" All of the relief he'd heard a second before evaporated in an instant.

"I know," he soothed, "they're getting a little ahead of themselves. They'll have to tone it down, but give them a bit of time to get used to the whole mess. They've been totally besotted with Luke, and that's not going to change at all. It's just that they have big hearts, and they'll automatically want to include Ricky in everything, too."

The line went silent for a long few seconds, then Marie said, "Part of me is glad Ricky will have grandparents in his life. That would be great, and I don't mean to sound nasty, but things are already complicated enough. You and I have to work hard to see eye-to-eye about several issues.

Adding their agenda to the relationship won't work. They have no say in what we choose to do, Peter.''

"I agree. Think for a minute—I kept this a secret for several weeks because I felt the same way." He heard her let out another sigh of relief and couldn't help smiling. "I'm just letting you know we're going to have to navigate around a few more people."

"Thanks for the warning."

He coiled the phone line around his finger. "So, what do you want to do about it?"

"Turn into an ostrich?"

He chortled softly. "We've been doing that for a month. What's plan B?"

"We pay a magician to make them all disappear?"

"No can do."

"So why can't we just let them peek at Ricky while he's napping?"

"They're too excited. Dad's voice will wake him, and a loaded gun wouldn't keep my mom from picking him up. She can hardly wait to get her hands on him." He let go of the phone cord, and the coil sprang free.

"Videotape? Can't we just video Luke and Ricky playing together this weekend?"

He had a camcorder, but he knew a tape wouldn't satisfy his parents or sisters. He countered, "Why not a good, old-fashioned pool party?"

"They'll drown me so they can keep both boys."

"I'll buy you a set of arm floaties so they can't."

"And I told you, you can't always buy your way out of a problem."

"There's a pity." He didn't like the way the conversation was going. The worry in her voice kept growing minute by minute. "Come on, lighten up. My family isn't going to eat you alive. They'll love Ricky, and they'll love you, too.''

"Give me a minute to try to believe that crazy story." Her wry tone carried more wariness than sarcasm.

Peter continued to play with the phone cord. "Ricky is a delight, Marie."

"I know that."

Peter jerked, and the cord tangled in his grip. "Marie, how could you possibly worry about whether they'll take to you? What's not to love? You're sweet tempered and patient. You're pretty as a china doll and love both kids to distraction. No one in his right mind would discount you."

"I'm not ready for any of this. You're catching me at a bad time."

Peter grimaced. "Marie, I tried to delay this. Honestly, I did. I know you're probably a little overwhelmed. I can't blame you, either. Still, try to turn it around. We ought to be proud to show off Ricky."

"That's the problem," she whispered sadly. "They're going to fall in love with him."

"And you're afraid of that? Aw, Marie—didn't you just say you want Ricky to have a family who loves him?"

"Are you implying Sandy and I aren't a loving family?"

"No!" he said without hesitation. He silently berated himself for the insensitive question. "You're wonderful with him. You're so great, I want you to be with Luke so he can thrive on your love, too. This isn't supposed to be a contest where the winner gets all. We all win when we love the boys."

Emotion choked her voice. "I'm not sure I believe that…about winning. I'm afraid I'll lose."

"Sweetheart, don't. Don't you dare say that. Don't you

think that for even one second. You're selling yourself short and insulting me all at the same time. No one can replace you in the boys' lives, and I'm not stupid enough to even entertain the notion that someone could."

"Peter, I'm not sure I can trust you yet. How can you expect me to trust your family?"

"We have to face the fact that my family is going be a part of Ricky's life. They're enthusiastic and affectionate, but I have to admit they tend to be on the forceful side, so I think it's best that we come up with our own game plan rather than let them barge in and run over us."

"Forceful?" She moaned. "Like you?"

"Worse."

"Impossible."

Chapter Eleven

That weekend, Marie felt absolutely sick to her stomach as she drove north. From the moment Peter told her his family was getting involved, she felt like she'd swallowed a carton of BBs. It was hard enough dealing with the distance between them and not seeing Luke each day. Handling Peter's innately forceful personality took all of her tact. She knew his wealth and social position gave him clout she'd never match, and though he'd never once used those against her, the threat he'd implied at their original meeting came flooding back. *You take good care of him until I can.*

He said his family was worse. Would they try to take Ricky away? Would they pressure her to move up here? There were so many of them, they could run roughshod over her desires and fill Ricky with thoughts and promises....

Promises. Today's promise from her Bible verse box ran through her mind. *Don't you be afraid, for I am with you; don't be dismayed, for I am your God; I will strengthen you; yes, I will help you; yes, I will uphold you with the right hand of my righteousness.*

Lord, I'm so scared. I'm more than just dismayed, too. You promise to strengthen me, yet I feel so weak. I don't even know how to pray. Please, just please… Regardless of the evening chill, she rolled down her window and gulped the fresh air to keep from being physically ill.

"Are you all right?" Sandy asked.

A hasty peek in the rearview mirror assured Marie that Ricky was still fast asleep in his car seat. She curled her fingers more tightly around the steering wheel and confessed, "I'm scared half to death."

"Hmm." Sandy waggled her brows and asked in a lousy Groucho Marx impersonation, "Want me to drive the rest of the way?"

Marie gave her a wobbly grin. "No, thanks. I haven't fallen apart yet, and I don't want you to get us in a crash before I have a full nervous breakdown."

Sandy laughed.

Marie forced her fingers to relax. She tried to rotate her shoulders to ease off on the tension. "It's good to hear you laugh. A few months ago I wondered if you'd ever be the lighthearted sister I once knew."

"I'm adjusting." Her sister didn't even pause a beat. "You'll adjust, too. You were a total basket case the first time you drove up here. If you're honest with yourself, you have to admit that it turned out fairly well. Peter's an okay kind of guy. He takes some getting used to, but once you get past the bulldozer exterior, he's all right."

"It's hard not to be flattened by a bulldozer. I'm facing a whole convoy of them this time!"

"Yeah, but they don't have a secret weapon—me!"

After she let out a tight laugh, Marie glanced at her

sister and whispered, "I'm so thankful you're coming along. I couldn't do this without you!"

"Yes, you could. I put in an unspoken request. The whole prayer chain at church is behind you!"

"They'd better be praying hard for a miracle."

It was just past midnight when they pulled into Peter's sweeping driveway. The lights blazed from nearly every room in the house. The front door opened before Marie even turned off the motor. Peter strode out to the car and opened the back door.

Peter grinned at Ricky. The sight of his son never ceased to fill him with a surge of wild love. "I'm glad you made it," he whispered to Marie, as he deftly got Ricky out of his car seat and carefully handed him over to Miss Anne without waking him. Miss Anne carried him into the house.

Peter pulled the wheelchair out of the trunk and opened Sandy's door. He knew she worked hard to become independent, but she looked tired. "You're undoubtedly feeling stiff after the long drive. I'll help you."

"Thanks."

After he smoothly transferred Sandy into her chair, she awkwardly patted his chest. He smiled. She winked, then her wheelchair whirred away. Marie started to follow her, but he reached out and held her back. "Wait a second."

Moonglow turned her hair a silvery color. Her features looked strained. He stroked his fingers down her grim cheek in a featherlight caress. "I was worried. I'm glad you're here."

"Afraid I was going to change my mind and stay home?"

"That, too."

Her features twisted and color filled her cheeks. "Oh, Peter, I'm sorry for being nasty. I'm a little road weary.

You were concerned that I might have fallen asleep behind the wheel, weren't you?''

''If you were tired, why didn't you stop at a hotel and call me?''

''I'm not sleepy-tired. I'm stiff-tired. I don't think I could've stayed behind the wheel for much longer.'' She sucked in a breath and quickly added, ''Please don't try to give me your if-you-lived-closer speech.''

Those exact words had been on the tip of his tongue. He gave her a guilty smile. ''Okay, I won't. I need to tell you something.''

The intensity of her gaze went up several notches. He'd sensed she felt strained, but the way her features went taut cued him in to the fact that her tension hovered at a critically high level. Peter hoped she'd understand.

''Brianna, Kate and Jill are dying to meet you and Ricky. They couldn't wait 'til morning, Marie. They're all inside. It's like a high-voltage slumber party in there. I couldn't calm them down. The last time they were this bad was when I brought Luke home from the hospital. I'd better warn you, they stayed for a month that time.''

''Is this your way of telling me they'll be here all weekend?''

'''Fraid so.'' He cupped her elbow and led her toward the door. After a few steps, he stopped. ''Marie, you're shaking. Believe me, my sisters are terrific. You have nothing to worry about. They'll love you.''

''I need to tuck Ricky in and help Sandy to bed.''

''Anne has Ricky well in hand. Sandy's not supposed to hide behind the scenes—they're eager to meet her, too!''

She vehemently shook her head. ''Sandy's exhausted. If they invite her to stay up, she's going to feel obligated to or embarrassed to turn them down.''

"Face it, Marie—Sandy's an adult and she handles herself and her limitations well. She can tell everyone she's tired. She can just about take care of herself, and you know it. I know you're nervous, but don't try to find excuses to avoid us."

"I didn't ask for this! You've set me up!" She pulled away from him and stared at him in disbelief. "It's hard enough, trying to live a double life. Then, you buttonholed me and decided to spring your family on me. I tried to be a good sport—after all, I came." She made a slashing gesture toward the car, then to the house, and her voice grew shrill. "Still, that wasn't enough! You have them all here, lined up to take my son and—"

"Hold on a second! They came on their own. I invited them for tomorrow, just as you and I agreed. They got excited and embellished the welcome a bit."

He'd hoped she'd understand. Clearly, she didn't. The stubborn look in her eye warned him he'd better not push too hard. Peter forced himself to calm down and appealed to her on a different level. He wheedled, "Take it as a compliment, Marie. They want to make Ricky their nephew right away."

"Oh, please! Let's forget that bit of deception! It's the middle of the night! Ricky's fast asleep. He wouldn't know if a nuclear bomb went off. Sandy needs my help, and I have to be sure the boys are all right. Once that's done, I'm going to bed."

She did just as she asserted. Though his sisters had a whole array of tempting snacks waiting in the living room and were eager to gossip, Marie gave them an icy nod, a plastic smile and went off to bed.

"I thought you said she was sweet," Kate complained.

"What got into her?" Jill wondered.

"I don't know," he grumbled darkly. "I don't understand women."

An hour later, Peter sat on the edge of his bed and wondered how he'd missed the fact that Sandy had slipped a note into his shirt pocket. She must have done it when he got her out of the car. He unfolded it and strove to subdue his emotions. "Marie's upset because this coming Friday marks the second anniversary of Jack's death. Please try to ease things for her with your family. She's lonely and scared."

He read the note again and tucked it into his dresser drawer. The last thing he needed was for Marie to accidentally see it. Still, he was grateful for that insight. No wonder she'd seemed so strained.

A small rustling sound caught his attention. Peter hastily donned his robe and went to check. He found Marie in the boys' room. He stood in the doorway and watched her. She knelt at Luke's bedside and tenderly filtered her fingers through his baby curls. At that moment Peter was glad he hadn't gotten them cut yet, even though his mother had been pushing him to. Marie should make that decision. A few seconds later she bowed her head. At first he thought it was in utter defeat, but then he noted her lips moved a bit. She was praying over his son. Peter wanted to go join her, but something held him back. He stood in the shadow and cherished the sense of rightness of her tending to his son's budding soul.

After a short interlude, Marie kissed the child, smoothed his blankets and moved over to Ricky. Peter grinned. True to form, Ricky flipped over and got so wrapped in the blankets, he needed to be untangled. She did so with practiced flair, never once disturbing his rest. She knelt beside him and prayed for him, too.

After she was done praying, Marie stayed at the bedside. Should he slip away and leave her this time alone with the boys, or should he go in and share it? Peter wasn't sure. Realizing this would be their only time alone together for the entire weekend, he decided to approach her. "Couldn't sleep?"

She shook her head and stood.

Peter gently engulfed her hand in his. "I'm not great at reading you, but I can tell something's bothering you. Want to talk it out?"

"No, thank you."

"If you change your mind, let me know."

She tugged her hand free. "Once I make a decision, I rarely change my mind."

"I'm willing to bet if it weren't for your iron resolve, you would have stayed home this weekend." Her eyes widened guiltily. "You're so tense, sweetheart. What about some time in the hot tub?"

Marie took an immediate, giant step away from him. Her arms wrapped around her ribs as she gave him an appalled look. "I'm not your sweetheart."

"Okay, Marie. I'm sorry." She'd never been demonstrative with him at all, but from the way she constantly snuggled and caressed the boys and made contact with Sandy, Peter knew Marie's reserve stemmed from a need to clearly define their relationship as platonic. They were standing in a bedroom while his sisters were in the house, so it made perfect sense that Marie would be hypersensitive about her reputation; but Sandy's warning shed a whole different light on why Marie acted so standoffish. Instead of taking it personally, he shrugged it off. "Sandy said traffic was a nightmare. Why don't you go get into your swimsuit and soak in the Jacuzzi?"

She shook her head. "I haven't worn a swimsuit since I had Ricky—I mean, Luke—I mean, oh, forget it!"

"Marie, how did you think you'd get through a pool party tomorrow without a bathing suit?"

Even in the dim room, her cheeks glowed with color.

"I have a supply of suits in the changing room off to the east of the pool. I'm sure there's something that'll fit."

She gave him a humorless smile and evasively whispered, "I'm sorry for waking you. I'll go back to bed now."

Peter stayed at the boys' bedside and listened to her slippered footsteps grow muffled as she padded down the hall. Seconds later, he heard her whisper a few things to Sandy as she helped her sister with whatever it was that qualified as her nighttime routine. When had Marie last slept all through a night? She woke up with Ricky at least once a night, and she also took care of Sandy. Peter decided to work something out so she could nap for the next two afternoons. The poor woman was ready to drop from sheer exhaustion.

Chapter Twelve

Marie woke as a loudmouthed baritone boomed, "Where's my other grandson?"

"Shh, Dad!"

"Don't make snake sounds at me. Go get him!"

"He's sleeping."

"It's seven-fifteen! Wake the tyke up! I've been waiting three long years for this!"

Marie carefully disentangled from the boys and slipped upward. She was in the embarrassing position of crawling off of the bed as the knob turned and the man's voice blustered on. "You didn't tell me *she* was in here!"

Marie hastily snatched her robe from the foot of the bed and held it up in front of herself. Heat radiated from her face, and she knew she had to be blushing virulently. She stared at the floor and stammered, "Please excuse me. I um… It was… Peter, please give me a minute!"

"Come on, Dad." Peter dragged him out as Marie dived into the belated coverage her robe yielded. She cinched the belt in at the middle and combed her fingers through her wildly tangled hair.

Ricky blinked owlishly and decided to make his demands known. "Mommy, potty. Hungreeeeee!"

"Men are too demanding at any age, my dear. I'm Lauren, Peter's mother." An impeccably groomed woman with elegantly coifed, silvering auburn hair pushed her way into the room. "Look at him! He's the spitting image of Peter! Geoffrey, you have to see him!"

Ricky took one look at the woman, screwed up his face and let out a terrified screech. He sprang to his feet on the bed and trampolined into Marie's arms. "Mommy!"

"Please excuse us." Marie sidled past the gawking woman and into the small lavatory. She made a distinct point of shutting the door.

While Ricky used the commode, Marie muffled a moan as she caught sight of herself in the mirror. Her hair looked like she'd stirred it with a stick. Her skin was pale, save the dark smudges beneath her eyes. Everyone would have been correct in taking one glance and finding her incompetent to handle another matter, however small it might seem.

On the other side of the door, a well-modulated voice singsonged, "Good morning, Mom! Don't you look fabulous!"

"Kate, honey!"

After a few seconds in which Marie assumed they hugged or kissed, she heard Kate ask, "If someone came bustling in on you at seven-thirty all dressed to the nines and caught you sleep tousled, especially for a first meeting, wouldn't you be mortified?"

"Why, yes, I suppose I would, but Ricky's just a little boy!"

"Yes, but his mother is entitled to her privacy and dignity. She slept in here last night, and we've put her in a terrible position."

"I'd resent anyone backing me into a corner like that," Peter's mother admitted.

"Let's go have a chat over coffee. I'm sure Marie will be out soon."

When she heard the bedroom door shut, Marie let out a gusty sigh of relief. So that was Kate. "God bless her," she whispered.

A few minutes later, Sandy zipped in. "Brianna helped me a little. Peter never told us she's a nurse."

Marie smiled at her. "You look great."

"I'll go hold down the fort. Want me to take Ricky?"

"I'd rather be with him when we do the reunion thing." Marie glanced at herself in the mirror and frowned. "But I need to make myself presentable."

"Okay. We'll see you soon. By the way—if his folks and other sister are as nice as Kate and Brianna, you don't have a thing in the world to worry about."

After a quick shower and shampoo, Marie had Ricky change out of his pajamas and into his favorite firefighter shirt and boots. She gave serious thought to skipping her usual wave of a mascara wand, swipe of blusher and lip gloss. The sin of vanity won out. She wasn't going to face everyone without looking decent. She'd chosen her apple-green sundress with appliquéd flowers on the bodice. It always perked up her spirits, and she desperately needed any boost she could get.

The skirt made a light swishing sound as she walked down the hallway where the bedrooms were located, past the elegant-looking beige-and-toast formal living and dining rooms and toward all of the voices in the sunny breakfast nook. Ricky clutched her hand tightly and carried his fire truck.

Everyone went silent. Peter and someone who had to be his father both shot to their feet. The man gaped.

Peter sensed Marie's uncertainty the second he spotted her. He gave her what he hope was a bolstering look and extended both hands. He drew her toward himself with one large hand and took Ricky's free hand with the other. It was hard to keep from staring at her. She looked so fresh and pretty, so utterly feminine, that he wanted to sweep her into his arms and inhale the flowery fragrance of her hair. Concocting a smile was no burden. "I'm glad you're here."

"I'll second that!" his dad agreed heartily. "Son, you didn't tell us Ricky's mother is—"

"Probably starving while we all chatter like brainless twits," Kate inserted, cutting her father off before he gave an appraisal of her appearance.

"Twits!" Ricky echoed the word with glee.

Peter threw back his head and laughed at Marie's dismayed expression. He steered her into the seat directly next to himself as Kate tickled Ricky and popped him onto the booster seat between herself and Marie. "Ricky's got big ears, just like Luke," he warned.

"My ears isn't big!"

Kate studied him and announced, "You're right, tiger. Your ears are just right! Do you want cereal or eggs for breakfast?"

"Cereal, please." He let go of his fire truck when Kate lifted it onto the table as if it belonged there.

"Such nice manners," Lauren Hallock purred. She then gave Marie a rueful smile. "I'm afraid his are far better than mine. I owe you an apology for bursting in on you this morning. I'm so thrilled to meet my grandchild, I overlooked simple courtesy."

Peter noted Marie managed to manufacture a wan, albeit polite, smile. He patted her hand. "If everyone would sit back and relax, I think we'll all appreciate the breathing space. There'll be plenty of time to get to know each other. For now, let's fill up. These little guys are enough to wear you out in nothing flat!''

Sandy giggled. ''Anyone want to borrow my wheel-chair?''

Peter made quick introductions, then kept passing food to Marie and tempting her to eat. She barely nibbled on anything. She usually had a fair appetite, so he knew she was trying valiantly to put up a polite front. She answered questions, but didn't initiate any conversation.

Ricky rested his fist on his fire truck and pointed. ''Who's that man, Mr. Peter?''

''I'm Grandpa, and we get to go swimming later. Luke likes to swim. Do you?''

''Mommy said no boots in the pool.''

Peter chuckled as he reached around Marie's back and rumpled Ricky's hair. ''In case you all can't tell from the fire truck and his firefighter badge and boots, Ricky loves the fire department.''

''Marie, more milk, please.'' Luke held his cup up to her, and she promptly filled it. Peter secretly cheered for his son. He'd asked Marie for help even though there were others at the table he'd known far longer. She had to know that meant a lot.

Peter's father drummed his fingers on the table. ''Ricky, why are you calling your daddy Mr. Peter?''

For a second, everything at the table stopped. Just as suddenly, his sisters all started a jumbled exchange. ''I'd like more milk, too.''

''Please pass the bacon.''

''Ricky needs a napkin.''

Ricky ignored all of the intended damage control and cocked his head to the side. ''I had a daddy, Grandpa. He died and lives with Jesus.''

"Yes, that's right," Marie said firmly. Her eyes blazed, but she didn't have any color to her cheeks whatsoever.

Peter saw his father open his mouth, and he immediately cut him off. "Dad, let it go."

"But Luke calls Marie Mommy," Peter's father groused. "It's only fair."

Peter said, "Enough, Dad."

Ricky's fingers tightened around his fire truck. "She's *my* mommy!" He turned to Marie. "You're mine!"

"Luke called her—"

"Marie," his mother said very distinctly, silencing her husband.

Peter lifted Luke into his lap. His son, the introvert, had popped his thumb into his mouth—a sure sign he was upset. Likewise, Marie had Ricky wrapped in her arms. The four of them made a tense little knot. Luke pulled his thumb out of his mouth and grabbed a fistful of Peter's shirt. The moist brush of his thumb against Peter's collarbone echoed the vulnerability in his voice. "You're my daddy."

"Yes, Luke. I'm your daddy."

"You not Ricky's daddy."

Peter couldn't lie to his son. He clutched Luke to his heart and looked Ricky in the eye. "Yes, I'm Ricky's daddy, too. You're both my boys."

Chapter Thirteen

Marie's chair careened backward and crashed against the wall as she stood up. "Outside," she gritted. Her eyes glowed with anger. "We need to talk right now, Peter."

"Mommy?" Ricky whimpered.

"Sandy, please take Ricky to the other room." Marie pressed a kiss on Ricky's forehead, set him into her sister's lap then marched to the French doors leading to the backyard and gave a doorknob a vicious twist.

Sandy's chair bumped a cabinet as she took Ricky from the room, and Kate reached for Luke. Luke wouldn't loose hold of him. "You're *my* daddy!"

Torn between the need to comfort Luke and the obligation to honor Marie's "request," Peter hesitated a moment. He'd blown it. Royally. He dipped his head, pressed a swift, hard kiss on Luke's head and said, "Of course I'm your daddy. I'm going to go out on the patio and talk with Marie for a little while. You be a good boy for Aunt Kate."

Those brief seconds comprised a delay he figured was essential to allow Marie to control her temper, but he wouldn't blame her if she wanted to roast him alive. What a miserable mess. He felt like he was tiptoeing through a minefield. Any step he took held lethal potential. Peter carefully shut the door behind himself.

Marie stood at the far edge of the patio with her back to him. She didn't turn around to face him, underscoring the level of betrayal she must feel. The way her shoulders were hiked clear up to her ears warned him to brace for a hefty blast. "Marie?"

She didn't respond, so he walked around the pool, past the brick barbecue, and leaned against the sun-splashed tile nook. When they'd been out last time she and Ricky visited, normal sounds filled the backyard—bird chirps, the breeze rustling leaves on the avocado tree, cheerful voices. Now everything stayed completely, eerily silent.

Marie continued to face away from him. Her voice vibrated with fury. "How could you do that?"

"I didn't—"

Marie wheeled around. Her eyes shot fire as she interrupted, "We agreed not to tell the boys yet. You just took an impossible situation and made it worse! I didn't think this could be any more catastrophic than it was, but you managed to complicate it even more. Why didn't you wait? Why couldn't you just—just—" she shook her head in angry frustration "—keep this between the two of us for now?"

A soft answer turneth away wrath... "For what it's worth, I'm sorry. It's important to be honest with the boys, and after Dad blurted out the truth, I figured it was more important to be forthright than to lie now and confuse the boys even more later. It's obvious he blundered, but we can't change it."

In utter exasperation, Marie raked her fingers through her hair in one brutal sweep. She took a deep breath, let it out slowly, and said in a voice she obviously strove to modulate, "I thought we'd ease into things more slowly."

He waited silently, unsure if she'd finished.

"Kids this age pick up on things, but they are also blessedly oblivious. I wanted to spare them the truth as long as—" her voice broke "—we could." She turned away and buried her face in her hands.

She needed to be held and comforted in the worst way. From the things she'd said, he knew her faith had sustained her thus far, but she still deserved consolation and someone to share the heavy burdens she carried.

Peter slowly pivoted her around and tugged down her hands.

Tears glazed her eyes. She tilted her head back a bit and blinked like crazy to keep them from falling. "I know we have to share the boys, but I wasn't ready...I hadn't thought—" Her words turned into an anguished cry. "*Jack* was Ricky's daddy."

For an instant, Peter felt a flare of denial at her proclamation, but the Lord vanquished it. Peter folded her in his arms and held her as she wept. Unable to sleep last night, he'd had one thousand thoughts about this mix-up. One thing he decided after praying for wisdom was to do his best not to be defensive when Marie brought up Jack. It would be a foolish waste of energy. Now, as she cried, Peter realized her tears somehow vented the awful ache knotting his own heart. Marie and he had only God and each other to help them through this catastrophe. Peter held her tightly. Together, they made a little island of helpless misery, facing a tidal wave that washed over them with relentless cruelty.

Marie finally sucked in a string of choppy breaths. She tried to wiggle free and mumbled an apology. Self-contained as she seemed, she probably didn't know how to behave after such a storm.

Peter didn't want her to be embarrassed. As he turned her loose, Peter murmured, "Earlier, I told you, you don't have to be all controlled and strong around me."

She wouldn't meet his eyes. "I haven't been. I need to go check on Sandy and Rick."

Peter watched grimly as she walked away. A few minutes later, Kate came out. "Luke's stacking blocks with Mom in the playroom. I told him he and Ricky get to share both of you, and that seemed to satisfy him."

"I don't think that'll satisfy Ricky or Marie."

"I can't imagine how I'd react if I were in Marie's shoes."

Peter nodded. "If it weren't for her faith, she'd shatter into half a million pieces."

Kate was the listener in the family and had recently opened a Christian counseling center. Peter respected her input. "Where do we go from here?"

Her brow furrowed. "Sandy said something about Marie's husband's death, and Marie's clearly got more than enough to deal with getting Sandy through her recovery and being a mother. With the switch and Dad jumping the gun, she's completely overwhelmed."

When Peter confirmed her assessment with a curt nod, she said, "We'll still have family time today. We can't very well cancel the pool party without making the boys think something's wrong."

"True," Peter agreed. "But only if Dad doesn't say anything more."

"He's never been good at nuance. He knows he blew it. I don't think you need to worry about him opening his mouth again."

By noontime, the boys seemed to accept the news. Luke

gladly jumped into Jill's arms in the shallow end of the
pool. Ricky screeched and didn't even balk for a second
when "Grandpa" or "Grandma" called to him. He trust-
ingly leapt into their arms. Brianna splashed by on a raft
and enticed him to go for a ride. Peter readjusted a mov-
able portion of the patio awning so Marie was under complete shade and walked over to her. "I'm going to lower
your lounger a bit, Marie."

"Please, don't. I'll probably fall asleep!"

Squatting down, he murmured, "That was the general
idea, Marie. You're exhausted. I know better than to ask
if you'd go inside. Sandy's here to keep an eye on Ricky.
I'll watch him like a hawk, too. Mom and Kate each
claimed a boy to be sure he's never unattended. Dad's
clear across the yard, getting ready to man the barbecue.
Believe me, our sons are safe."

His mother swam over to the edge of the pool. "Marie,
do I need to put some sunblock on Ricky?"

"Thanks for asking, but I already slathered it on. What
about Luke?"

Lauren laughed. "I got him, then Brianna swiped at
him, too. He's slippery as a seal."

Marie gave her a wobbly smile. "You make a terrific
grandma."

"Gramma!" Luke shouted.

"Coming!" Lauren swam off.

Peter gave Marie's hand a gentle squeeze. "That was
so kind of you. It may not show, but she's nervous, too.
Now you go ahead and rest."

Though she clearly fought her weariness, Marie fell fast
asleep all of fifteen minutes later. In spite of the kids'
squeals and shouts, she slumbered on. An hour later, as
the sun shifted, Peter moved the awning, but her slim feet
and ankles still caught sun. He took a beach towel over

to cover her and went still. She turned onto her side and wrapped her arms about her torso in an unconscious move of self-comfort. Tears trailed down her face.

"Just cover her," Jill whispered.

"I can't." He knelt and quietly murmured, "Marie?"

"Hmm?" She turned her face into his cheek.

The temptation to kiss her almost killed him. As her eyes fluttered open, the unguarded look in them let him see how truly vulnerable she felt. He tenderly brushed away her tears. "The sun's about to fry you to a crisp. I'm taking you inside."

She cringed as he slid hands under her knees and shoulders. "Peter—"

"Hush, Marie. I'm not about to let you drive home tomorrow if you're still this fatigued. Do you want to eat lunch then nap along with Ricky and Luke, or are you going in to lie down now, and I'll bring them to you after they've dried off and eaten?"

She shook her head, as if to clear a muddled brain, and blinked. "I can't think with you holding me."

"Funny, I think much better when I'm close to you. Since I'm the clear-minded one of us, I'll decide. You're going to bed now." He straightened up, smoothly hefted her fully against his chest and ignored her gasp. "Sandy, Marie's going to go lie down for a spell."

A few seconds later, Peter felt Marie's damp lashes sweep against his neck. From the moment she came awake and he'd brushed away her tears, she'd exerted her customary iron control and stopped crying. Damp lashes meant she'd begun to cry again. He could imagine several valid reasons for her to weep. There, in the middle of the hallway, he stopped and clutched Marie more tightly, as if the strength of his arms would be a barrier against the fears and troubles she bore. "What's wrong, honey?"

"Ricky," she said in a tear-laden voice, "he's having s-such a good time."

"Yeah, he is."

"He...he—" she gulped "—he really likes your p-parents and your s-sisters."

Peter detoured toward the front of the house where his study was located. She needed comforting, and he knew if he took her to the guest room, she'd never allow him to stay and simply hold her. He sat on the big leather couch and gently cradled her. He couldn't let go of her. "He's precious, Marie. They love him right back."

"I d-don't know w-what to do."

"We don't have to do anything right now, Marie." Part of him wanted to press for her to move in with him. He certainly had an advantage at the moment, but Peter couldn't do that to her. He bit his tongue and settled her more securely against his chest. Slowly, tenderly, he coiled his fingers in her soft curls.

Silence swirled around them. She continued to take choppy breaths in an effort to keep from weeping. Courage was a fine quality—but not to this point, not when it robbed her of the release tears could bring. "I have sisters, Marie. I don't come unglued when a woman cries," he invited.

She slumped more fully into his arms and confessed thickly, "I come unglued when I cry. I completely fall apart. It's stupid, and I don't want to do that." A few seconds later, she shifted and started to pull away. "Really, I—I'm okay."

"Sure, you are." She was as far from fine as he ever imagined, but refuting her assertion seemed cruel. Dignity was all she had left. Even if she did come completely undone while weeping, he wouldn't think less of her; nonetheless, Peter admitted it wasn't what he thought of her that counted at the moment. She desperately needed to control something, so if she wanted to clamp down on her emotions, the least he could do was support her and give her a safe escape. "You just need a bit of sleep to knit up that old raveled sleeve of care."

"I just napped out by the pool." She stood up and self-consciously straightened her sundress. Peter noted how she avoided meeting his gaze.

"You barely even closed your eyes. The guest room's window overlooks the pool, so it'll be pretty noisy. This room is much quieter." He stood and gestured toward the couch. "Go ahead and lie down. I've been known to nap here a time or two, myself. It's almost as comfy as your sofa."

Her gaze darted toward the door. "But—"

"The boys have half an army watching them, Marie." He took her by the shoulders and guided her back to the couch. "No one could ever love them like you do, but we can keep them safe and show them a good time."

She made a small, indeterminate sound, and the panicked look on her face spoke volumes.

"No one's going to say anything about relationships. I know it felt like a catastrophe earlier, and all of the adults are on edge, but the boys seem to be fine—and that's what counts most, isn't it?"

She nodded tightly.

The small nudge he gave made her sit on the edge of the cushion. He guided her stiff shoulders downward. Every last inch of her screamed of ambivalence. Clearly, she needed the rest, but her maternal instincts still demanded she mind the boys. Peter resorted to a truth he'd hoped to not have to speak, because he didn't want her to feel as if he were manipulating her. "Marie, if nothing else, take a nap for my peace of mind. I'm worried about you driving home in this condition. You're teetering with exhaustion.''

''You promise no one will—''

''I'll be sure either Sandy or I are with Ricky all of the time. How's that?''

To his relief, she twisted and reached for a throw pillow. As she tucked it under her head, she mumbled, ''Just for a little while.''

''For a while,'' he echoed. In his heart, he wished she'd stay in his home forever.

Chapter Fourteen

Sunday, they went to Peter's church for the first time. They'd avoided attending because Kate was a member there. Had they gone, Peter couldn't keep the secret and shield Marie. Afraid to miss a single moment of time with Ricky, the rest of Peter's family attended services, too.

After the service, Peter deftly fielded a few introductions and questions. Jill and Brianna helped Sandy into Jill's car. Kate ran interference with a nosy older man while the pastor exchanged pleasantries with Marie, then Kate yanked her parents over to introduce them to the inquisitive pianist so Peter could sweep Marie and the kids in a perfectly orchestrated getaway.

"God bless your sisters," Marie said under her breath in a heartfelt tone.

"Amen!" Peter drove off and took them to a nearby park. Everyone met up there for a picnic.

Lauren brought a picture-perfect red-and-white checkered picnic blanket and spread it out on the grass. Peter's father opened up a low-slung beach chair and Peter slipped Sandy down onto it so she'd be at everyone else's level. In no time at all, a fried chicken, potato salad and lemonade lunch tumbled out of a large wicker basket.

Marie squinted at the ground. "This spread looks like it belongs on a magazine cover, but we're missing the ants."

"We gots aunts," Ricky disagreed. He pointed and said, "Aunt Sandy, Aunt Jill, Aunt Anna and Aunt Date."

Brianna laughingly poked Kate in the side. "He got that right. You're always the one out on a date!"

Sandy and Kate compared dating notes while Jill and Brianna cleaned up after lunch. Peter's parents took the boys over to the toddler playground. Peter drew Marie off to a shady bench where they could still easily watch the boys. He confessed, "After Lisa got taken, we've always been on guard."

"You haven't said much about her."

He stared into the distance and said, "We were at school. Lisa was only two. Mom put her down for a nap. Someone jimmied the lock on the bedroom window. We got ransom notes, but no one ever picked up the money. Mom's never stopped blaming herself. We were all kind of relieved that I had a boy, because I think having a little girl would have been too hard for Mom to handle."

"Peter, that's so sad. It's not your mom's fault, but if I were in her place, I'd never stop blaming myself, either."

"Kate took me aside yesterday. She told me that from the moment Mom found out about Ricky, she's been terrified you wouldn't trust her, but when you told her she was a terrific grandma, you gave her hope."

"Should I say something directly about it?"

Peter stared at his mother. She looked up and waved, then quickly turned back as Luke pulled at her. "Mom doesn't talk about it. She occasionally makes veiled references, so I'd suggest you wait until she opens the door. She picked up the pieces and went on with life for the rest of us, but I sometimes see that faraway look in her eyes and know she's still hurting.''

Marie watched Lauren catch Ricky as he came down the slide. She spun him around and hugged him close. The joy on her face was unmistakable. Marie's heart wrenched. Before she could help herself, her thoughts tumbled out of her mouth. ''And I'm driving away with her grandson today.''

Peter turned and looked into her eyes. His gaze was steady, yet his face went grim. ''Yes, you are. But, Marie, this is a different situation.''

She closed her eyes and moaned, ''This just keeps getting worse.''

''Worse?'' He laid his hand over hers. Warm fingers curled around hers. ''Marie, we've each connected with our biological sons. We both now have a son of our heart and a son of our flesh. We're richer, not poorer.''

''For richer, for poorer.'' She opened her eyes and looked at him sadly. ''It sounds like a wedding ceremony.''

He sucked in a deep breath, then said, ''My timing stinks. I was going to wait, but since we're on the subject…''

Marie's heart lurched. *Surely he wouldn't…he couldn't dare…* From the look in his eye, she knew he was going to, but Marie couldn't say anything to stop him from continuing on.

''I don't want to rush you, but I want you to think about something—''

No, Peter, no. Don't do this.

''—about us,''

Lord, please don't let him say it. Please, God—

"—getting married." Peter's fingers tightened painfully around her icy hand. "From the very beginning, we agreed whatever we did, the kids would always come first. Often, in custody situations, adults use kids as pawns. We haven't done that, and we don't want to. Ever. We have to face the fact that, sooner or later, it will all boil down to one thing—either they are our pawns, or we are theirs. Either we continue to separate them and haul them back and forth, or we give up our independence for their sakes."

"Oh, Peter," she said in a strangled tone.

"I know I'm not being romantic in the least. I'm not good at this kind of thing. It's…not a marriage of two besotted hearts, Marie. It would be a marriage of two adults who willingly sacrificed for their sons."

She shook her head in mortified disbelief. "People marry because they want to be together forever. They become one in the eyes of God. I've had that kind of love—"

"And you were incredibly blessed, Marie. I know you and Jack had a fairy-tale life. You've already said you'll never love like that again. Very few people know the truth about my marriage. Darlene wasn't happy. No matter what I did, it was never good enough." He paused and admitted in a tone that resonated with distress, "She'd left me the day she got into the accident and had Luke. I don't plan to ever love and experience rejection like that again."

Each heartbeat thudded painfully. Breathing hurt. Marie stared at him in mute anguish.

"Marie, we could make it work. For the boys."

"Marriage is sacred."

"So is family, Marie. This is a way we can all be a family—both boys, you and me—all together."

She shook her head. "Marriage is for life. What happens if you meet a woman—"

He threw back his head and snorted. "Don't even bother going there."

"What about fifteen years from now when the boys go away to college?" Marie stood and yanked free of his grasp. "No. Absolutely not. This is wrong. I can't."

His shoulders lifted and fell with a deep sigh. "Marie, if it's because of the intimacy issue, I won't push you. We could have separate bedrooms."

Shocked, Marie babbled, "It's time for me to go. I have a long drive—"

"Marie—"

"I don't—"

He stood and rasped, "Stop it. I knew my timing stunk. I know you're upset, and I'd give anything to miraculously solve this whole thing. I don't expect you to answer me today."

"I've already answered you! No. Do you hear me? No!"

"I heard you," he said in a flat tone. "But it's the only workable solution to an otherwise insurmountable problem, and I want you to think about it."

She couldn't help herself. Marie turned to the side to keep from looking at him any longer. It was a belated and futile attempt to block out what he'd said. Desolation swept through her. Jack had courted her, gently taken her beyond her doubts after having suffered a childhood of bitterly divorced parents and made her feel safe about placing her heart into his care. Their marriage was a slice of heaven on earth, and his death had been a descent into emotional purgatory. She'd never give her heart to a man again…yet, the idea of a loveless marriage was a travesty.

"If you're afraid you might meet a man in a few years," Peter began.

She wheeled back toward him. "No!" Her voice went hoarse with emotion. "When Jack died, he took my heart with him. I'll never fall in love again!"

"Okay. It's an open invitation, Marie. Think about it. You refuse to move in without being married. I gave you the only other option. There's nothing else I can do, because we can't go on like this."

They returned to his house in utter silence. Peter picked up the suitcase Marie slid out into the hall. He carried it to her car and hastened back into the house. He hoped maybe he could have a few more words with her—reassure her, reinforce that he wasn't pressing for an immediate decision, help her calm down a bit. She looked thoroughly rattled. The minute he spied her, Peter knew Marie wasn't going to give him that opportunity. She walked directly ahead of Sandy. By now, Marie knew him well enough to predict he'd exercise discretion and refrain from saying anything in front of an audience. She held Ricky tightly, and his sleepy head drooped onto her shoulder. He was ready for his nap.

Peter didn't want to embarrass her, but her shocked pallor alarmed him. He chose his words carefully, then said in a subdued tone, "Marie, I know this weekend has been pretty overwhelming. Don't you think it would be best for you to have a little time alone before you got on the road?"

She shook her head and managed to avoid his eyes.

He let out a long, slow breath and mentioned in what he thought sounded like a mellow and calm tone, "Luke and I will be down Friday night."

Her head shot up as she croaked, "No!"

Peter's guts knotted. In his haste, had he shattered the

fragile bridge they'd started to build between their families? From behind her, Sandy motioned wildly. It wasn't until Marie was occupied clipping Ricky into his car seat that Sandy whispered urgently, "Marie will be at the cemetery or church all day. Remember? It'll be exactly two years since Jack died."

"Ahhh," he whispered quietly. Though sadness for Marie's loss tugged at him, relief also coursed through his veins. His proposal wasn't solely responsible for her vehement reaction. "Thanks."

Marie said nothing to him as she slid into her seat. Peter caught the door and leaned in. "Will you please call me when you get home? Just to let me know you've made it?"

He had to be satisfied with a nod, just as he had to settle for Sandy's phone call. "Marie is busy with Ricky. We made it home just fine."

Chapter Fifteen

Marie worked Monday through Thursday. Sandy stayed with Ricky all day Friday, freeing her to go to the graveside alone. She'd been stunned when a florist's truck pulled up at her curb in the morning. The deliveryman handed her a bouquet of pink roses and babies' breath, tied with a blue ribbon. She sat down to read the card and bit her lip. "In memory of a wonderful man, one Luke would have been proud to call his father, and one I could have considered a great friend. Our love, Luke and Peter."

"Why is he acting so nice?" She looked at Sandy with tear-filled eyes. "I gave him ample material last weekend to prove I'm mentally unstable!"

"You didn't. Besides, you deserve to be treated well. Call and thank him."

"Sandy, are you nuts? After the way I behaved last weekend, I'm just waiting for Peter to plow in and serve up a sheaf of papers that enable him to take Ricky away."

"Get serious! You didn't do anything weird at all. You were tired. You napped. Big deal."

Oh, Sandy, if only you really knew what happened…that he'd asked me to marry him for the sake of the children…and I came off looking like a neurotic mess instead of a mature woman.

Sandy didn't know what she was thinking. Her sister blithely continued on in a gratingly cheerful tone, "Besides, if Peter tried anything like that, he'd have to give up Luke in the exchange, and we both know he'd never do such a thing!"

After the day passed, Marie knew she should call, but she just couldn't. On Saturday, she started to dial the phone but slammed down the receiver at the last moment. Had the flowers been a tribute to Jack, or a sneaky first step in a belated courtship? Was Peter using circumstances and tweaking situations in an effort to maneuver her into marriage? In her heart of hearts, she didn't want to believe so. He'd been straightforward with her so far. *But he wants Ricky badly—badly enough to take me in the bargain.*

After Sunday evening service, Marie summoned what little courage she had and prayed Peter would be out someplace so she could leave a message on the answer phone and be done with it.

He answered.

"Um, Peter?" She closed her eyes. *Why did he have to be there?* She steeled herself with a deep breath, then blurted out in a single breath, "This is Marie. Thanks for remembering Jack. That's all I wanted to say. Goodbye."

"Wait! Marie? Marie, are you still there?" He paused for a second, then went on, "I'm sorry things are so tough for you right now. I want you to know I'm not trying to pressure you into a commitment. We'd already swamped you last weekend, and I'm to blame for letting them all try to do the 'Gregarious Hallock' routine. My proposal was poorly timed and caught you off guard. I promise I won't pressure you.''

Lord, why did You have him pick up the phone? I really didn't want to have to talk to him. This is so awkward!

He seemed to accept she was having a hard time responding to him, so he filled in the silence. ''Let's continue on with our weekends together—just quiet time as parents and children together. Would you rather have Luke and me come down there for a few times in a row until you're more comfortable, or do you maybe want to meet halfway between? You know, that might be a nice change, and the weather is perfect for it. I can check into hiring a beachside cottage.''

''Um, we have a little problem....''

''We do?''

''Sandy's going to an independent living apartment complex next week. Since she's not here with me anymore, it's not acceptable for you to spend the night here any longer. We won't have anyone with us at the cottage, either.''

''Marie, come out of the Dark Ages! I've promised I'm not going to try to have my wicked way with you. What's the problem?''

''It still sets a bad example. I can't do it.''

''We aren't even in the same bedroom!''

''I care about my reputation.''

In a voice heavy with frustration and resignation, he asked, ''How far away will Sandy be? Can't she come home for weekends?''

''That defeats the nature of her program. Besides, it's out in San Bernardino. Her boyfriend is a trucker, and his route takes him by there almost every day. I have a feeling they'll be seeing a lot more of each other, and she's so happy, I don't want to interfere. It would make me sick, thinking she might give up her romance because she feels obligated to stick around here for my benefit.''

He grimaced and grasped at straws. ''We can have Anne accompany me. She's the boys' nanny. Won't she count as a suitable chaperon?''

''Can I mull it over a bit?''

''I don't think I'm supposed to give an honest answer at the moment. It would probably come across as controlling and selfish.''

''Think for a minute. *Is* it controlling and selfish?''

After a prolonged silence, Peter said thoughtfully, ''Marie, I told you from the start that the boys have to come before any other consideration. My desire is for them to be together and for each of us to be with both children at once. I ache to be with Ricky every bit as much as I think you ache to be with Luke. If that makes me selfish, so be it. I think life is pretty tough for you right now, and worrying about what someone else might say or think is one burden you shouldn't have to carry.''

''I'm uncomfortable.''

''I'll reserve two hotel rooms. I'll even stipulate they have to be across the hall instead of adjoining. How's that?''

''It sounds like a lot of trouble and expense.''

''Not really. I have close friends who needed some highly specialized surgery for their daughter. I did the research and connected them with a world-renowned pediatric cardiologist. I have a standing invitation to stay at their place. They happen to own a nice beachside resort about twenty minutes north of Malibu.''

''It's midsummer, Peter. A place like that is undoubtedly booked solid!''

''I'll give them a call. I'll get back to you in about fifteen minutes.''

"Good news," Peter said fifteen minutes later.

She could hear the excitement in his voice, and that made guilt spear through her for her lousy attitude.

"The Reccauts were so excited about you and Ricky, they blocked out a pair of suites on the third floor for us every weekend for the next month!"

"I'd rather take it one week at a time."

"That's fair. Anne is willing to come along, so the proprieties are taken care of. Assuming we'll continue to do this, I'm sure my sisters will clamor to come along for the other weekends. I'll meet you there on Friday evening. It'll be about a two-hour drive for you. I'll send a map so you can find it easily."

"So the map was all right?" he asked as he met her in the parking lot that Friday.

"Yes." She looked at the truly unique building behind him. Huge plate glass windows reflected the palm trees and ocean, and multicolored tiled turrets with fairy-tale cupolas appeared in whimsical locations along the walls— as if a child had been playing with enchanted blocks. "Peter, this place is—"

"Great. You'll love it. Won't she, Luke?"

Luke was riding on Peter's shoulders, and he squealed several excited phrases of welcome to both Marie and Ricky.

Peter set down Luke, then hugged and kissed Ricky. "Here, Marie. I'll get your suitcase."

"We're right on the beach!" She pulled Luke and Ricky together as she stared at the stretch of sand that glittered in the late-afternoon sun while automatically ordering, "Boys, hold hands."

Peter pulled her battered suitcase and Ricky's small bag

from the trunk, then smiled at her. "So I see you brought Ricky's, uh...*h-o-r-s-e* along, too."

Marie cast a glance at the stick horse and cowboy hat she'd smuggled into the trunk. "Your mom and dad—"

"Don't worry, Marie. Mom checked with me first, and I figured it was okay for them to send Ricky a little gift. Luckily, they've given Luke a lot of their love and time, but they've never gone overboard on spoiling him with junk."

"Okay." She sighed in relief. "I only brought it up if the boys got bored, but since it looks like we'll have plenty of fun in the sand, I'd rather leave it in the car. After seeing how fantastical this place is, I'm afraid he'll swing around and break something!"

"I thought the same thing. Luke's is still in my trunk, too. I just didn't want him to need *h-o-r-s-e-y* if Ricky brought his along."

Marie traced the painted line on the asphalt with the toe of her sandal. "In a funny way, it's an answer to prayer. I've been asking that we'd be of like minds."

"Amen," he agreed softly. Peter then changed topics. "I have a feeling you're going to go nuts over your view."

Marie guided the boys as they wended through the parking lot, over a charming bridge and crossed the lobby. She didn't say a word until she got into her suite because she was too busy trying to absorb the elaborate surroundings. Once she nudged the boys into the room and crossed the threshold, herself, she stopped and sucked in a noisy breath. "Peter! This is huge! It's decadent!"

"Not too shabby." He tilted his head to the right. "Anne is in that room. She's got this evening off. I hope you don't mind sharing the suite with her."

"My house isn't this big! Of course there's room. Besides, as old fashioned as it sounds, it's not seemly for her to share your suite.''

''Exactly.'' He turned a bit, winged his elbow to the door next to Anne's and said, ''That room is for the boys. The one straight ahead is yours.''

''And I've been standing here, gawking while you held the cases! I'm so sorry, Peter. Here, let me get the door.'' Marie hurried across the plush beige carpet and opened the door. She'd been put in a corner room, so both a side and the back walls were comprised of floor-to-ceiling windows. With the curtains open wide, she got a panoramic view of the ocean and a blazingly beautiful sunset. ''Oh, my gracious!''

''Almost as beautiful as you are,'' Peter said under his breath as he passed behind her to put her suitcase on the bed.

Marie gasped and wheeled around.

He tossed the case onto the mattress with ease and took in her surprised expression. ''Oh, come on, Marie. Your husband had to tell you how lovely you are. A man would have to be blind not to appreciate such a pretty woman. I'm not trying to seduce you. I'm merely stating a fact— you're easy on the eye. I have three sisters, and I don't think any of them ever objected to a honestly given compliment.''

''I'm not one of your sisters.''

A slow smile lit his features. ''Thank heavens. I'm already sadly outnumbered.''

Marie headed for the window, as if she could walk straight out into the view. Entranced, she watched the sun-gilded waves undulate. ''I seriously doubt your sisters ever succeeded in ganging up and beating you at anything important.''

''Ha! That shows what you know. Because we were a

secular family and my parents instituted a majority-rules vote, I had to suffer through a whole year of family folk- and ballroom-dancing lessons. Kate is the only one of the three sisters who didn't clobber my feet so badly that I didn't limp for the remainder of each week!''

"It's a shame you didn't grow up in a Christian family, but I gathered that Jill and Kate are believers now, too.''

"Praise God, yes. The three of us are praying for Brianna and my folks." He glanced down at his feet. "But don't you pity my poor toes?''

"With your big feet?''

He gave her a look of mock outrage. "Hey!''

"Oops." She gave him an owl-eyed look of innocence. "Was I supposed to feel sorry for you?''

"That would be nice. If you can't summon up com- passion or even pity, at least tell me you don't dance and won't try to manipulate matters so the boys have to un- dergo that particular agony."

She abruptly turned back around and gave Peter a stunned look. "Do you think I'm manipulative?''

He gave the thought a moment of consideration. "I'd label you stubborn a whole lot sooner than I'd tag you as manipulative."

In light of the fact that she'd refused his marriage pro- posal, she decided he was soft-pedaling the issue. She didn't want to press it, either, so she opted to take a light- hearted approach. "Thanks a heap, and for the record, I don't dance. I have all of the grace of a wounded buffalo, so you can rest assured your toes are safe from me."

"I don't believe you for a second. I've seen you do some pretty fancy footwork to catch stuff the boys have dropped."

"That's reflexes, not recreation." She glanced down and wrinkled her nose at a smudge on the back of her hand, then at her son. "Ricky and I need to wash up. Would you like me to watch Luke so you can have some time alone to relax?"

"Why don't we take the boys for a walk on the beach before supper so we can all unwind? They're restless from the drive, and you and I probably could stand to let the sea breeze clear out some of the cobwebs."

Marie glanced out the window again. "Is the beach safe?"

"The stretch down there is well lighted. We'll stay close to the hotel, too. I saw the sand buckets in your trunk. That was a nifty idea."

"We'll use them tomorrow—that is," she hurriedly added, "if you don't have other plans in the wings."

"Afraid of being manipulative?" He winked to let her know he was teasing and calmly set Luke on the floor after catching him bouncing on the bed.

"Perhaps." She caught a touch of his playfulness and waggled her brows. "Then again, perhaps you'd better start worrying that I might be plotting something. This place seems like a set for one of Hollywood's medieval fantasy series. I might find a nefarious knight or a dragon."

"That's some imagination you have."

"Another quality mothers develop." She looked about the room and said, "Really, Peter, this place is awesome."

"I'm glad you like it. Did you want to unpack anything before we take the boys on that walk?"

"Not particularly. I expected one of those sleepy seaside cottage-type places—not this upscale resort. I'm afraid I just threw everyday clothes in the suitcase."

"You'll practically live in your swimsuit, Marie. Other than that, all you need is one dress. I'm sure you managed that.'' When she didn't reply at once, his features twisted into a scowl. ''Didn't you?''

''Just about.'' Marie coasted over to the sink and busied herself by scrubbing off that smudge. The task seemed amazingly interesting and complex, for all the effort she put into it.

''Marie,'' Peter growled, ''tell me you brought a bathing suit.''

A quick glance in the mirror let her know guilty color filled her cheeks. She tried to play word games. ''Okay. You brought a bathing suit.''

''Woman! What were you thinking? We're by the ocean. What person in their right mind wouldn't bring a swimsuit?''

''I never pretended to be in my right mind. In fact, there are plenty of days when I think I'm probably certifiably nuts. Sandy would undoubtedly second the opinion.''

Peter strode over to her and rested his palms on her shoulders. The weight of his hands made it clear he wasn't going to brook any further nonsense. He spoke in a deceptively soft tone. ''If you don't own a swimsuit or you're self-conscious around me and don't want me to see you in a swimsuit—''

Marie sucked in a sharp breath and tried to twist away. His hands eased, but he slid them down her arms and clasped her hands. ''Marie, we have to be honest with one another. We're going to spend lots of weekends here. You can't plan to—''

''You're wrong, Peter. You can't plan. I agreed to one weekend here. You're making assumptions. I—oh, Ricky!'' Ricky turned and gave his mother a guilty smile. He'd climbed onto the bed. So had Luke. Between the two of them, they'd managed to open her suitcase and get into her makeup. They were merrily drawing on each other with her lipstick.

Peter swiped Luke from the bed. To his credit, he kept from laughing outright. He strode toward the door and tossed Luke over his shoulder. "You clean up your clown, and I'll clean up mine. Luke and I will meet you by the elevator in five minutes for a walk on the beach."

The evening breeze felt brisk and invigorating. "You little rascals stay out of the water," Peter said with mock sternness.

The boys wistfully looked toward the waves and protested.

"Tomorrow, after breakfast, I'll take you in the water," Peter promised. "It's too cold tonight."

As if to punctuate his declaration, Marie zipped Luke's fleecy jacket clear up to his throat and pulled the hood over his ears. She glanced at Peter and murmured, "I worry about him getting another ear infection."

"Yeah, me, too. They're miserable. He runs a nasty fever and whimpers all night long with them."

"None of that, young man," Marie admonished Luke as she tapped his nose gently with her fingertip. Luke giggled back.

Ricky grabbed Peter's hand and tugged insistently. "C'mon! C'mon, Daddy!"

He'd never stop being delighted and a touch astonished that this little redheaded boy called him "Daddy." The wonderment was every bit as great as when Luke had done the same. The feel of a little hand in each of his big hands felt so right. Peter grinned at Ricky and said, "Okay. What do you see?"

Luke and Ricky dragged him toward a heap of kelp. Marie knelt in the sand by him and oohed appreciatively at the smelly pile. Her enthusiasm over the commonplace never ceased to amaze Peter. Over the weeks they'd known each other, he'd seen her admire bugs, draw pictures in the mud with her toes and accept a bouquet of weeds with pure appreciation. She didn't act like the kelp was a castoff from the sea; she acted like it was a gift from God.

Feeling impish, Peter lifted a strand of kelp, grabbed a pod and squeezed. It popped, releasing a loud, snapping sound. Marie fell backward and laughed. The boys tried to copy his trick, but their hands were too small and weak. Peter helped each of them, and Marie continued to laugh.

Charmed by her reaction, he asked, "Why is it so funny?"

"Sandy always loved the beach, and she'd probably know all about popping kelp—but I had my nose in a book so much, I missed out on that!"

"Here. You do it."

Marie curled her hand around a pod. She squeezed, but nothing happened. She pursed her lips and tried once again.

Peter felt a strong temptation to take advantage of her pursed lips. He'd gladly plant a kiss on them. *No, I wouldn't. She wants nothing to do with me. It's not just the thought of a platonic marriage, either. She avoids even casual touch, like I'm a leper. I already lived through that once before.* Her hands shook as she squeezed the pod. He teased, "Are you a weakling?"

Chapter Sixteen

"I'll do it. Just give me a minute."

She flashed him a smile, and he knew she hadn't picked up on the bitterness that swelled for that moment. Peter shook off the old memories. Marie wasn't anything like Darlene. He nudged Luke, and playfully whispered all too loudly, "Mommy thinks she's as strong as Daddy."

Luke nudged Ricky and passed along the supposition. He giggled the whole while.

Marie changed her hold and tried once more. Her hand shook with the effort, then suddenly, the kelp pod popped. It held a bit of water, and it squirted out and hit Peter on the chin. Marie waved the pod in the air and teased, "Gotcha!"

He looked at her and said very quietly, "I'm yours anytime you say the word."

Quick as a whip, Marie jumped to her feet. She tugged down the hem of her jacket and declared all too brightly, "I thought we were going to go for a walk!"

Peter allowed her to change the subject. He'd promised himself he wouldn't push her. They walked along the dark, damp sand where tide was going out. The boys tripped along, admiring their footprints, picking up bits of shells and poking their fingers into sand crabs' bubbling holes. Marie accepted each bit of shell with a word of praise and slipped it into her pockets.

"Your pockets are going to get awfully gritty," Peter warned.

She shrugged. "Clothes wash. Childhood isn't forever. They deserve to gather treasures."

"I like the way you think."

"I think we're getting pretty far away from the hotel," she countered.

"Hey, sports, this lady here says we're going too far."

The boys looked longingly a bit farther down the sand and begged to continue on. Peter brushed a strand of Marie's windswept hair behind her ear. "If we were voting, you'd be outnumbered, three to one."

"Now wait just a minute. You didn't like getting outvoted when it was about dancing!"

Peter smoothly turned her to face him. He loosely placed a hand on her waist and took up her other hand in a ballroom-dance pose.

She went stiff. "What are you up to?"

"My sisters all told me every little girl dreams of being Cinderella at the ball, just once in her life. We're staying at a castle, so the stage is set." He winked. "Just for a minute, pretend I'm charming, even if I'm not a prince."

There, by the early light of a full moon, he traced the steps of a waltz on the shore with her. She hesitantly followed, but soon her natural grace shone through. Her moves were supple, and he drew her a bit closer. He smiled down at her. "I didn't know how much I'd appreciate being outvoted someday."

Marie took a step away, but he twirled her back into

his arms. "Don't," he whispered into her hair, speaking to himself every bit as much as he was speaking to her. "Don't forgo the simple pleasures of life or cheat us out of innocent joys, Marie. Sometimes, you take life a moment at a time. This moment, this time, just let the wind blow, the children laugh and our feet sketch the sand. Let this instant be the once-upon-a-time in the little girl dreams you had."

She sighed her acquiescence. He tucked her closer still then continued to take a few more steps. He caught himself before he kissed her hair. She was a soft armful of woman and it seemed so very natural to kiss her. The pull of attraction grew each time they were together, yet Peter knew she didn't return the feelings. Especially now, after he'd practically scared her into a full panic with his ill-timed proposal, he'd have to monitor himself carefully.

Marie giggled. She whispered, "Look at the boys."

Peter started to chuckle at the sight. Luke and Ricky were in a clench and attempting to imitate the dance—but just then they tripped over each other and fell into a sand drift. Marie's arms tightened around his waist as she threw back her head and laughed.

He chortled along with her, then gave her a quick hug before letting go. They both dusted the sand off the boys, and Peter decided, "It's a good thing you're not a prissy woman. These two boys are grubby as can be, and they're that way more often than not."

"It's biblical."

He shot her a quizzical look. "Oh?"

"God made Adam from dirt. The boys are just getting back to basics."

The boys were exhausted by the time they got back to the hotel. "They're too sandy to put to bed," Marie declared.

"So, let's sluice them off." Peter headed toward the bathroom. He sat Ricky down on the counter, then took Luke from Marie and put him beside Ricky. As Marie started the water, he peeled off gritty little shirts and shucked off Luke's shoes. Marie knelt on the closed seat of the commode, and their shoulders brushed as she finished undressing Ricky.

"Great teamwork," Peter murmured later as he helped her rise after they said bedtime prayers with the boys.

"We don't do half-bad."

"I arranged for a late snack to arrive at eight-thirty." Peter glanced at his bare wrist and frowned.

"You took your watch off to bathe the boys. It's on the counter."

He went and got it. As he reappeared in the small sitting room, she tried to excuse him. "I'm not all that hungry."

He grinned as he slipped his watch in place. "I didn't play fair. I know how much you love chocolate."

A knock sounded at the door. Peter grinned. "Chocolate torte, Marie. I know it's your weakness."

She groaned.

The next morning, Marie groaned again when Peter handed her a box and announced, "I got you a swimsuit."

"You expect me to fit into this after you stuffed me with chocolate torte and half a box of truffles last night?"

Peter glanced down at the swimsuit she'd dropped back into the gift box. She'd acted like it was a viper. "I called Brianna. She advised me. Mrs. Reccaut opened the gift shop early just for this, and she promises it'll fit. There's even a cover-up in the next box, if you're worried about getting a sunburn."

"I'm comfortable in what I have on." She perched her hands on her hips and gave him a disgruntled look.

"Shorts?" He eyed her denim cutoffs and sunny yellow T-shirt as if he were really trying to give the outfit a second chance, then scowled, "Oh, come on, Marie. We're taking the boys into the water! You'll get soaked, and those shorts won't dry off. A picnic is ready for us to pick up, and the Reccauts made sure to reserve a cabana in our names, so I'd like to spend the whole day down there."

"What about naps? The boys get impossibly crabby when they skip their naps."

"They can sleep on towels in the cabana. The swimsuit is even a one-piece—you can't get any more modest than that. Hurry and go change. Anne and I will take the boys down to the lobby and pick up the picnic."

"Pick up picnic!" Luke echoed the words gleefully.

"I have sunblock, so don't worry. Oh—why don't you give me your keys now, so we won't forget to get the sand buckets out of your trunk?"

"Now who's being manipulative?" she muttered under her breath as she put the keys in his palm.

"I'm not being manipulative." He caught her look of disagreement and hastened to add with maddening playfulness, "I'm orchestrating fun."

"You're incorrigible!"

"And you, dear lady, are stalling." Peter pocketed the keys and looked to Miss Anne. "Let's get these boys downstairs. We have some serious beachcombing to do!"

If she'd gone shopping herself, Marie would have selected a suit like the one Peter got for her. The black looked sleek and would slenderize. The legs weren't cut high on her thighs, and the neckline came to a modest vee. She slipped into it with marked reticence, but a critical look in the mirror told her she wouldn't make a complete spectacle of herself. She pressed her hand on her not-quite-flat tummy and scolded herself, "No more choc-olates!"

She hastily grabbed the cover-up from the other box and slipped into it. Peter had chosen a lightweight green dress with a hem that ended modestly above her knees. A pair of deep pockets for the boys' shells proved Peter had made a good choice. Marie glanced in the mirror again, critically assessed herself and told her image, "I'll just leave this on all day. He can't complain."

"There's Mommy!" Ricky announced as she got off the elevator.

Peter studied her from unruly curls to pale pink toenails and nodded. A smile tinted his voice. "Yes, that's Mommy, all right."

Miss Anne walked to the cabana with them, then Peter said, "Why don't you go enjoy yourself? Marie and I will play with the boys." She went off. Peter and Marie romped with the kids, and Luke tugged on her cover-up. "We's going in the water."

Ricky wiggled as she slathered more sunscreen on him. "Mommy, you don't lose my shells."

"I won't."

"My shells," Luke reminded her. "Don't lose my shells."

"Of course I won't." She stood.

Peter tugged her back inside the cabana. His eyes twin-kled. "You need to leave your cover-up in here. The boys' shells are in your pockets."

"I'm going to have to teach our boys to start laying up their treasures in heaven." She took off the cover-up.

Peter winked at her, then growled, "I'm going to get the boys little bags so they can carry their treasures. I refuse to give you an excuse to wear that thing anymore."

"You and your money," she hissed.

He gave her a purely masculine smile. "You and your treasures."

She groaned. "Let's go swimming."

They played in the shallow waves, enjoyed a delightful lunch basket and tucked the boys down inside the cabana for a nap. When Miss Anne returned, she watched over their sons while Peter invited Marie to go for a stroll.

Clearly, Marie didn't want to be alone with him. He sensed her fear, saw the wariness in her eyes. *She thinks I'm going to urge her to reconsider the proposal.* "It's beautiful here, Marie. Let's take a break. Just saunter along and soak in the atmosphere. Relax." Peter picked up the cover-up and held it out so she could slide her arms into it. He knew she was too mannerly to refuse his gentlemanly gesture in front of an audience, and he was making a definite concession, letting her wear the cover-up.

As they walked along the sand, they kept a discreet distance between themselves. He asked about Sandy, and when it became obvious he wasn't going to coerce her, Marie slowly relaxed. As they turned back, he looked at the footprints they'd been leaving behind. They matched, stride for stride. If only everything else would fall into cadence....

After the boys' naptime, they built sand castles with the their sons, rinsed off in the water to the shrill screeches of excitement and finally headed back to the hotel. "I'll return the picnic gear to the kitchen if you drop off the towels over at the gym," Marie suggested.

"Anne, we'll meet you and the boys in the lobby," Peter finished off the plan. They all separated. Five slim minutes later, Peter and Marie met in the hallway and headed for the lobby. When they got there, Anne was smiling and chatting with a tanned hunk.

Marie looked around. Peter frowned and did likewise. Their steps picked up pace. Panic welled up as they asked Anne in unison, "Where are the boys?"

"Oh, over on the step—" her voice died out as she turned and pointed toward the staircase.

The steps were empty. The boys were nowhere in sight.

Chapter Seventeen

"Luke! Ricky!" Their voices formed a strained duet. His voice was hoarse with concern, hers started out coaxing and soon turned shrill with panic as they looked around the furniture and potted plants. Everything stopped in the lobby. "My sons," Peter said in an urgent plea for help, "they're missing. Both of them. Three years old. A blond one and a redhead."

"Boys!" Marie cried out.

"Where?" Peter wheeled around.

She shook her head frantically. "I'm calling them. Boys! Ricky! Luke! You come to Mommy right now!"

"I'll go up the stairs and look," Anne said tearfully.

The man she'd been flirting with grimly said, "I saw you earlier. I know what they look like. I'll go check the beach."

"The beach!" All of the color bled from Marie's sun-kissed cheeks. Peter braced her arm as the horror of the situation rolled over him, too.

"Come with me," the young man smacked a few of his friends on their shoulders. "Let's get out there.

They're just little squirts—they couldn't have gotten very far."

From behind the registration desk, Mrs. Reccaut ordered, "Bob, go block the driveway. No one leaves. Victoria, call every department and have them institute a search."

She came around and took Marie's hand. "The boys probably just toddled off. Come with me to the dining room. We'll look under the tablecloths. They may think they're big white tents and are hiding under one. You can call them. Peter, try the game room."

All around them, guests and hotel employees searched for the boys. As each second passed, Peter's horror skyrocketed. "Not again. Please, dear God—not again!" He dashed to the game room, but it was empty. He tried the men's room and found it vacant. His heart nearly beat out of his chest.

A woman exited from the ladies' room. Knowing they sometimes went there with Marie, he asked, "Were there two little boys in there? My sons are missing."

The woman shook her head.

Peter continued to search. *It's all my fault. I brought them here, even though Marie wasn't delighted with the idea. I pressed and cajoled—and this happens. I should have never left them with Anne. Luke and Ricky are my sons. I should have kept them with me. Lord, please let them be safe!*

A small wedge propped open a housekeeping closet. Peter's hopes soared. He burst into the closet, fumbled for the light switch and found nothing but cleaners, mops and supplies. Afraid the boys might sneak inside later, he kicked the wedge out of the way as he left.

The bridge and the bushes—the boys were so impressed with the bridge from the parking lot. They might have gone there. Was there water under that bridge? I didn't even pay attention! My sons, God, please keep them safe. Peter dashed toward it. He could see the parking lot was blocked off, and people were searching between the cars, calling for the boys. Peter scanned the bushes as he headed for the bridge. He got down on his knees to look beneath the bridge. Nothing. No water, to his relief—but no boys, either.

The acrid taste of fear flooded his mouth, and his heart twisted.

God, please, please, give my sons back to me. Don't let anything happen to them.

Mr. Reccaut came outside as Peter stood up. "Marie said she's taught Ricky to go to a policeman if he gets lost. I have all of the security guards standing in conspicuous locations."

Peter nodded. "I taught Luke that, too."

"My wife's staying with Marie. They'll keep looking inside while you and I search out here."

Peter raked his fingers through his hair as he scrutinized a man carrying a blond boy. "It's not Luke."

"I expect them to be together," Mr. Reccaut said as he pointed toward a bronze castle sculpture gleaming in the sunlight. "There's a maze in the hedges just past the castle we ought to check out. The boys probably just wandered off, and they could get stuck in there."

"Lisa—" Peter's voice broke off.

"This isn't Lisa. Those little guys are like greased lightning. I'll bet they just streaked off."

"We found them!" someone shouted.

Peter raced toward the sound of that voice. A doorman held open a gold-framed, etched-glass door, and relief flooded Peter as he burst into the lobby. "Where? Where are they?"

"The elevator," a clerk shouted above the celebratory din. "They crawled on the bellhop's cart and hid between the garment bags and luggage. The bellhop is bringing them back down."

Peter elbowed his way to the elevators. He could see Marie frantically dodging furniture to get there, too. He plotted a course to intercept her and wrapped his arms around her shuddering frame. "They're okay. We found them, and they're okay."

Folks cheered when the elevator doors opened. Peter didn't give the bellhop a chance to take the boys off. He swept Marie into the car, and they each grabbed for a boy. As the door swished closed, the bellhop asked in a sheepish voice, "What floor, sir?"

They sat in a knot on the sofa—Marie glued to Peter's side so she could still touch Luke. Ricky sat on her lap, and Peter's arms enveloped all of them in an unyielding hug. She couldn't stop shaking.

"Mommy, don't cry," Ricky chirped.

"You scared Mommy."

Peter took a deep breath and repeated again, "You boys are to never leave us. That was very naughty and dangerous."

"We was bad," Luke said.

"Very bad," Marie whispered.

"Sorry."

They'd already gone through this litany half a dozen times. Peter finally said, "You boys go sit in time-out on your beds. No talking."

Marie hugged Luke and Ricky and cried even harder when they both kissed her and toddled away. She burrowed into Peter's shoulder and confessed, "It's all my fault. If I hadn't turned you down, we'd never have to be here.''

"Marie!''

''I can't ever let anyone else watch our boys. Never. Never again, Peter.''

"Honey—''

''I'll marry you. I will. For the boys.''

Peter scooped closer still, cradled her head on his shoulder and took a deep breath. Could this finally be the chance he'd been praying for? It nearly tore his heart out each time Marie drove away with Ricky. Though she fought the truth, Peter knew deep in his heart that they were all meant to be a family—*one* family, not two.

Still, he couldn't take advantage of this debacle. In time, she'd resent him for it. It went against all he wanted and needed, but still, he said, ''You're distraught, Marie. So am I.''

''You can't tell me it's not the right thing to do.''

He took a deep breath, then let it out slowly. ''Of course I can't. It's the only thing to do, the best and right thing. I wouldn't have proposed to you if I didn't believe it with all my heart. I'm afraid you're letting the emotions of this moment carry you away and say something you'll regret later.''

She burrowed closer and borrowed some of his strength. ''We should get married. I mean it. I do.''

''I do,'' Marie said almost inaudibly. She stood in the judge's chambers and stared at the small leather manual as he read off the civil vows. Acting as her maid of honor, Sandy sat to her left. She held Ricky on her lap. Peter's dad stood to his right and clasped Luke's hand. Peter's voice sounded deep and sure as he spoke his vows.

He'd refused to marry her the awful day after the boys

were found. Marie knew he was being honorable enough not to take advantage of a terrible mishap. If anything, his integrity reinforced her decision. She couldn't bear to be away from Luke. It wasn't just that Luke was the only link she had to Jack—though that, alone, provided enough cause. She adored the little boy and had to be with him. As for Ricky—he was the child of her heart. She could never relinquish him, and he needed a father's steadying influence. After thinking the matter through, she decided no man would ever do a better job as a father than Peter Hallock.

The Old Testament was full of arranged marriages— ones made not for love, but for practical purposes. She and Peter had solid reasons to combine their families. God had blessed the unions in the Bible; she prayed He'd keep His hand over their arrangement, too—unique as it would be.

Peter stood beside her, steady, caring, gentle. He'd given her every chance to back out. Repeatedly he advised, "Don't let fear rule your decision, Marie. If you do, you'll regret it later. Take a bit of time."

"I told you once before, I rarely change my mind," she said. "It's the right thing to do. I know it is."

Since she'd been so adamant, he agreed. He'd allowed her to determine what kind of ceremony they'd hold. She asked for something very private and subdued. Today, of all days, she wanted no reminder of the time she'd worn romantic white satin and lace and pledged her love to the man of her dreams. She couldn't make sacred vows in a church; she asked for a civil ceremony since this wasn't going to be a true marriage. It was a partnership. A businesslike agreement. Signing the certificate would be the same as signing a contract—nothing more. Taking off Jack's ring nearly tore her heart asunder. She carefully tucked it away in her jewelry box next to the one Jack had worn.

Now the boys each clutched a ring. Ricky climbed down from Sandy's lap and leaned against the wheelchair. Marie took the ring from him. Peter took the ring from Luke. They exchanged the bands. Peter had chosen the rings—and he'd been wise enough not to get her a solitaire since that was what Jack had given her. Instead, Peter graced her shaking hand with an eternity band. "Diamonds are the boys' birthstone," he told her just before the ceremony. She stared down at the glittering piece and promised herself she'd make things work out. She had to—for the boys.

"You may greet your bride."

The judge's words jarred Marie. Peter promised a platonic marriage. She knew she couldn't ever sleep with a man she didn't truly love. At the judge's direction to kiss, she gave Peter a startled look.

Peter eased the bouquet of pink roses he'd given Marie out of her hands and barely gave it a little flip through the air so it would land neatly in her sister's lap. "Let's hope tradition holds true and you're the next bride, Sandy," he said.

Marie smiled at him. He'd said just the right thing. He smiled back at her, then stepped closer. She couldn't quite believe he was really cradling her face in his hands. His hold felt tender, his hands incredibly warm. When his head dipped, she let out a small gasp, but he caught and silenced it. His lips pressed against hers in a chaste kiss that lasted long enough to satisfy their audience. When he lifted his head, a keen sense of loss struck her. A flush of warmth stole over her. *She'd liked him kissing her!* If he ever found out, she'd be terribly embarrassed.

Peter's deep brown eyes sparkled with more warmth

than Marie had seen there before. He slowly let go of her, then slid his arm about her waist and nestled her into his side. Family crowded around to give their congratulations, and for a few moments everyone pretended like this was truly a love match.

Lauren had arranged the use of the private dining room in a local, five-star restaurant. Peter's mom and dad took the boys and his sisters took Sandy to an intimate family reception. Marie felt self-conscious being left alone with her husband.

Husband. Even the word seemed strange. Wrong. Partner or friend, yes—but husband? She couldn't bend her mind around that concept.

Peter laced his fingers with hers and strolled to the car as if nothing were amiss. As he tucked her into his luxury sedan, he praised, "You look beautiful."

Marie mumbled an embarrassed, "Thank you."

Peter hunkered down, took the seat belt from her nerveless fingers and tilted her chin so she'd have to look him in the eye. "Marie, take things at face value. I'm not trying to seduce you. You're my wife. You're an attractive woman. I'm going to compliment you and buy things for you, just as I'm probably going to lose my temper and get moody. You take the good with the bad."

"For better or worse," she whispered.

"Yeah. Let's hope there's more better than worse." He winked. "Here. Your hem is going to get caught in the door." He scooped the skirt of her blue voile dress and tucked it next to her thigh. He tenderly trailed his fingers down her cheek, then stood and closed the door.

As the door shut, Marie let out a shaky breath. Her cheek and leg tingled. Her breathing was jagged—all from a few words and the brush of his hand. She pressed her head back into the padded rest and asked, "What have I done?"

Chapter Eighteen

Peter did his utmost to make their move go well. Kate had pulled him aside before he, Marie and the boys drove down to see to matters. His sister had given him a few pointers about how he needed to be "sensitive during this transitional time." Following Kate's advice and instituting plans of his own, Peter strove to streamline things for Marie.

He'd sent a van for Sandy, had her taken to Marie's house then allowed the sisters to go through the whole place. Whatever Marie no longer wanted could be used in Sandy's new place. Before her accident, Sandy had lived with a roommate, so she needed several things. Peter watched the boys while a few of Marie's friends from the church helped pack.

While the boys napped, he took Marie for a slow walk around the house. "We can take all of it, none of it— some of it. Most of my place was done by a professional decorator, so I'm not overly attached or stuck on any of the furnishings. We can trade anything you like better or scrap everything from both houses and get all new stuff."

"Could we trade my couch for the one in the playroom?"

"Sure." He cast a look at the brown tweed one and smiled. "Yours is a lot more comfortable. What about that picture you have hanging over it? It matches well, and I've never been crazy about that abstract thing I have right now."

"Okay."

Peter tried not to shadow her too closely in her bedroom. He hoped she'd leave all of this behind. There was something impossibly intimate about the bedroom furnishings she'd chosen and shared with another man. Marie slowly ran her fingertips over the polished cherrywood dresser. Her touch was gentle, loving…. Peter looked away. Kate had warned him he'd feel spurts of possessiveness and jealousy—and at the moment, her warning made perfect sense.

Marie sighed. "The knobs on this are easy for Sandy to work. I ought to let her have the bedroom set."

Peter tried to hide his elation. "I'll have the movers deliver it to her place with her boxes." Feeling a bit guilty, he decided to be mature and do as Kate had suggested—to accept and move ahead rather than fight the inevitable. He purposefully picked up Jack's portrait. "I'd like to be sure this makes it in one piece. The boys need to grow up knowing about Jack. He was important to both of them."

Marie's eyes welled up with tears, but she blinked them away. "Could we put it on the shelf in their room?"

"Sure, we can." Peter slid an arm around her. The way she shook troubled him.

She took a big gulp of air and bravely whispered, "I won't keep it in my room. I know I'm not being a real wife to you, but I won't insult you by clinging too tightly to the past. I'll try. Honestly, Peter, I'll try."

He set the frame down and turned her into the full shelter of his arms. "You're doing fine, sweetheart. I'm really proud of you." He kissed her hair, then rested his cheek on her crown. "There's no hurry, Marie. We can just take clothes and toys this trip."

"No. This is it. I have to have closure. I—I'll need to put the house up for sale, too."

"I can take care of that for you." He gave her a gentle squeeze. "I was thinking, though…"

"Yes?"

"The youth pastor at your church is living in an apartment. They're really strapped for money and have two little boys, too. We don't have those concerns. If you'd like, you could quit claim the property to them, and they could just take over your payments."

"Jack would have liked that. He and Brad were good friends."

It only took two days to take care of everything. Peter arranged for them to take a "family honeymoon" on the way home. They spent a day at Disneyland, then spent a night on the *Queen Mary*. They went to the Monterey Bay Aquarium and splashed in a hotel pool.

So much had happened in such a short time. Marie was glad they had a few days to decompress. Peter tactfully got suites so there was never an awkward situation regarding hotel beds. Since they weren't on his turf or hers, they could simply enjoy the bright summer days and the boys' boundless enthusiasm over simple things.

Peter seemed surprised at several of the things Marie did, but he didn't interfere with them. He'd made a funny face when she dumped pudding onto a paper plate and let the boys "fingerpaint," but a few moments later, he'd gotten two more plates and insisted she and he join along in the fun. In truth, he'd shown a remarkable propensity for getting involved, and she admired that.

Even honeymoons end. The melancholy thought went through her mind, and Marie tried to quell it. *You knew,* she scolded herself, *this was the way things were going to be. It was a good trade. Wise. Give it time and work on it.*

She did her best to settle into her new life. Try as she might, she didn't feel at home. The beige-and-toast living room felt far too formal and stiff. Her room seemed cavernous after she'd gotten used to having Sandy's bed and possessions crammed in with hers. She no longer changed menus on a whim or did the cooking. Peter was unfailingly polite and attentive—but that made her feel like a guest instead of a family member. She kept telling herself, *"It'll take time."*

To her embarrassment, the housekeeper immediately took the snapshots they'd taken of each other and had them enlarged. She put them in lovely pewter frames and set the one of Peter on Marie's nightstand and the one of Marie on Peter's dresser.

"Leave them be," Peter soothed when Marie fussed.

"But—"

"We don't care what other people think, Marie. We did the very best thing possible. We're partners, and we'll make this work."

"But it's humiliating to have Mrs. Lithmas know our private business."

"She's not a gossip, so you don't need to worry that she'll say anything to folks in the community. My parents and sisters all know we've done this for the boys' sake, so they'll turn a blind eye to the way we've set up our

home. What we do or don't do is no one else's business.
If we're happy and the boys are safe and content, we're
fine!''

"Fine," she echoed in a thoroughly unconvinced tone.

Nothing felt fine. She was used to walking around the
house barefoot and propping her heels up on the coffee
table. Because of the way Peter studied her feet the first
morning she padded into the kitchen, she'd started wearing shoes. The bathroom cleanser Mrs. Lithmas preferred
made Marie sneeze. Peter nearly scared her out of her wits
when he bumped into her in the hallway the first night
when Ricky cried out in his sleep. She was accustomed
to a double bed and felt lost and strangely bereft in the
big queen-size one in her bedroom. No, nothing felt fine.

As if he could read her mind, Peter smoothed her hair
back from her shoulder and said, "It'll take time to settle
in, Marie. I want you to do whatever makes you happy—
rearrange furniture, select menus, go get your nails
done...."

She glanced down at her bare nails. "I've never in my
life had a professional manicure."

His mouth tilted up in a grin. "Your toenails were pink
that first morning."

"Yeah, well..." Surely, her cheeks had to be pink now,
too.

"You always went barefoot at home," he persisted.
"Now you don't."

*I dodged from the bathroom to my bedroom in nothing
more than a towel—but that doesn't mean I'd ever do that
here, either!*

"Seriously, Marie, you can't act like a guest here. It's
your home, too. I fully expected you to still hum in the
shower and pick flowers from the garden, but you aren't."

"You knew I hummed in the shower?"

He chortled softly. "Yep. Sunday mornings, getting ready for church. It always struck my funny bone when you chose a hymn that said something about water or a fount or the ocean."

"You're one to talk! You whistle between your teeth whenever you can't find your car keys." She paused, then added, "And you never set them down in the same place, so you're always doing a musical scavenger hunt for them!"

They looked at each other, then broke into laughter. Peter winked at her. "We've got a good start, Marie. We'll make great partners."

Miss Anne had resigned as soon as the boys were found. Aware she'd been remiss in her duties and endangered the boys, she'd quit tearfully and left the hotel at once. The fifth day back at their home, Peter sat at the supper table and asked, "When will you start interviewing for a new nanny?"

Marie's fingers curled into a fist around her fork. She stared at him with nothing short of horror and said, "I'm not!"

"Marie, surely you'll want help with the boys. They're energetic."

She shook her head adamantly. "All over the world, women have several children and manage without domestic help. We still have Mrs. Lithmas. I do nothing but play with the boys all day long. I need to do something."

"Being with the boys is the most important thing you can do. We're agreed on that, but—"

Face pinched with strain, Marie whispered, "I came so I could mother both of them. If you want to replace me—"

"No! No, Marie. It's not that at all!"

"I won't let anyone else watch them. Never again."

"Uh-oh!" Luke's sound diverted their attention. "Milk."

Peter reached over and belatedly righted the now-empty glass. Before he could say anything, Ricky tattled, "Luke made a big mess!"

"Yes, he did." Marie started sopping up the spill with her napkin. "We all do sometimes."

Peter said nothing to her as he got up from the table, though her obvious regrets cut him deeply. He grabbed a dish towel to absorb the white puddle on the floor. *Lord, You are in control. Please work a miracle in this marriage so she doesn't go on feeling it was a mistake.*

After supper, Peter excused himself and went into his study. There, where he'd comforted Marie on the couch, he sat and prayed. Things were going so well with the boys, and he enjoyed Marie's sweet presence. The pastor's recent sermon came to mind... *Don't ask God to change others. Ask God to work on your own heart and life first.* He humbly prayed in that vein, then emerged in time to read the Bible story and share bedtime prayers. He and Marie each kissed both boys, then she turned on the guardian angel night-light as he turned out the light.

As they slipped into the hallway, Peter startled Marie by wrapping his arm around her shoulders. She looked up at him, wide-eyed. "Things are going well." He grinned. "Brother Luke and I rated ahead of Ricky's beloved fire engine tonight during prayers!"

"That's tight competition."

"Speaking of tight..." He curled his hand over her shoulder and started to gently knead. "You're knotted up worse than the rigging on a yacht!"

"I'm okay."

"And I'm the tooth fairy."

A smile quirked her lips. "Actually..."

Peter chuckled. "You got me there. Seriously, though, Marie, you need to relax a bit. Let's go for a swim or have a soda out in the Jacuzzi."

"I really don't—"

"Yes, you do have a swimsuit," he interrupted. "I'm not taking no for an answer."

Her brows lowered in consternation. "Now I know from whom Ricky inherited his stubbornness."

"It's called persistence, and it's a great trait, not a flaw." He waited a beat. "I've instilled it in Luke already. We men have to stick together, or you women would run the world!"

"This isn't fair. I'm outnumbered!"

"Aw, come on, Marie." He jostled her lightly and continued to rub her neck. "You love a challenge!"

"There's a difference between a challenge and a demolition."

Peter merely chuckled, led her to her room and nudged her inside. "You have five minutes. Meet me out at the pool."

She'd felt self-conscious that day on the beach—and she'd managed to keep on the cover-up most of the time. Tonight, that wouldn't be the case. Marie skimmed out of her clothes and wiggled into the swimsuit. As she snapped the elastic on the right leg downward for better coverage, she muttered, "No chocolate and no more ice cream."

In a move of pure vanity, she decided to run a comb through her hair before she went out. "Why am I doing this? The minute my hair gets wet, it won't make a hill of beans' worth of difference!" Her heart whispered back, *You want to look nice for Peter.* She slammed the comb down onto the dresser top and abruptly came to her senses.

In the past days, she'd grown increasingly comfortable

with Peter—maybe too comfortable. What she felt went beyond a simple partnership or friendship: those impish winks he gave her, the way his hand reached for and held hers when they walked with the boys, the way his voice dipped into a lower register as he wished her a good-night before they retired to their separate bedrooms....

Marie sucked in a sharp breath. *This isn't that kind of relationship. I can't feel that way about Peter. Merciful heavens, I'm going to make a mess of this whole deal if I let myself fall in love with him. Lord, Your word says we set our affections. Help me guard my heart, or I'll ruin everything if I—*

A light tap on her door made her jump. "Marie? Ready?"

Chapter Nineteen

She looked around the room, frantically trying to concoct an excuse. She wasn't about to go out there with him—not after she just figured out her heart was traveling down a hopeless road! "Um, Peter? I changed my mind. I think I'll pass tonight."

"You can't do that to me! Not after what I've been through!"

Intrigued and a bit worried by his tone of voice, Marie steeled herself for the sight of him in his swim trunks and opened the door. *His shoulders are so wide…his arms so muscular and strong… Good grief, get a grip on yourself! Look up at his face and—* The sight jolted her. "What happened?"

His lips puckered toward her in an outrageous parody of a fish. He tried to speak with them that way. "The compwezzor bwoke. I bwew up da air maddrusses odd by mysoff!"

Giggles spilled out of her. He snatched her hand, and she didn't pull away. Peter chortled softly, then yanked her through the house and out to the backyard. Two bright orange vinyl air mattresses floated in the pool. The late summer night air felt warm and velvety. Night-blooming jasmine filled the yard with its own special, sweet fragrance. Peter inhaled and declared, ''Ahhh. Paradise.''

''Let's hope we're not raising Cain and Abel!''

Peter grinned at her. ''No, we're not. The boys get along amazingly well.''

''They do, don't they?''

''We all do,'' he replied as he led her to the steps of the pool where the lights turned the water an enticing shade of aquamarine.

She forced a smile. ''Yes, we do.'' *Oh, Peter, I think I'm getting along with you a little too well!*

''What are we waiting for? Come on.'' His fingers squeezed her hand a few times as an encouragement to join him. Together, they slowly descended into the warmed water and stopped when the level reached Marie's waist. ''Want to swim a little while before we float?''

''I could use the exercise.''

Peter's gaze dropped from her face, downward and slowly back up. An appreciative glimmer lit his eyes. ''You're already in beautiful shape.''

Marie stepped backward and said his name in a low, warning tone. The last thing she needed was for him to tempt her into making an utter fool of herself. Feeling as she did, that wouldn't take long.

''Aw, come on, Marie. You're lovely. I already told you I'd pay you honest compliments. Don't get all bent out of shape.'' He punctuated his words with a quick, playful splash.

Marie let out a surprised squeal.

''Afraid of a little water?'' His hand hit the water at a sharp angle and sent a spray over her.

''How can you ask that?'' She laughed. *Playful. If I'm*

playful, he won't read too much into this. "You see me after I bathe the boys each night!"

"Uh-huh. You look like a drowned rat."

Marie let out a shriek and used both hands to shove a wall of water at him. A water fight ensued. Marie gave just as good as she got. He went underwater, grabbed her legs, and dragged her below the surface. Marie tickled him to make him let her go, and she sprang to the surface. Finally, after they were both breathless from the horse-play, she took one final lunge at him. Peter opened his arms wide, caught her and twisted her in a weightless twirl all the way around before he came to a halt. They were heart to heart and stared at each other for a long, stunned moment. Marie slowly unwound her arms from his neck. *What in the world am I doing?*

"Okay," he rasped hoarsely. "I won that one. Let's float for a while." He scooped a hand behind her knees, walked through the water and lifted her onto the bobbing raft.

It took a moment for Marie to catch her breath and find her tongue. It had all been in fun—but it had been so very long since a man held her. It felt good. Peter felt good—his strength, his gentleness. She'd begun to form more of a connection with him than she imagined she could. It scared her to discover she'd begun to open her heart to him. "I—um—I've had enough. I ought to go inside."

"Not a chance." Peter hovered over her raft. He pointed at his lips and puckered them up again. "We-member? I bwew up dis waft fo you."

His face looked so comical, she smiled. "Far be it from me to hurt your tender feelings."

Peter snatched his own raft, hopped aboard and caused a minor tidal wave in the process. He chuckled at Marie's gasp as her raft bucked. "Sissy girl. Betcha you're a chicken on the roller-coaster rides!"

"It's a good thing you're not putting your money where your mouth is," she shot back. "As far as I'm concerned, the bigger the chill, the better the thrill. The difference between those and your pool madness is, on roller coasters, I get a safety bar or harness."

"Ahh." Peter sculled over next to her. "Then I'll hold you and keep you safe." He reached over and claimed her hand. Marie didn't know whether to pull away or leave things as they were. She never knew what to do when he sneaked under her defenses. Was he just being a nice guy, or did he have ulterior motives? Unsure of where she stood, Marie remained quiet.

"Look up there," Peter said after they'd bobbed next to each other in silence for a short while. "Just for us. God gave us a blanket of stars."

"Just for us?"

"Absolutely." He turned his head and winked at her. "He whispers His love on the wind, too."

"Mmm," she hummed. "I like that."

"You know, after Darlene left and I spent sleepless months with Luke, I came out one night and lay here. The pool lights went out, and all I had was the starlight and a sliver of the moon to see by—and that night, I decided if God could surround me with that kind of majesty, He'd also cloak me with His love."

"That's beautiful, Peter."

His eyes held hers. "That realization filled an aching void inside of me. No matter how hard I tried, I hadn't been able to make my marriage last, but God's love for me didn't depend on situations or circumstances. It just was. I thought about how nothing Luke did would ever stop me from loving him, and I figured the Heavenly Father had that kind of love for His children, too. From that night on, I knew I could count on it, just as Luke could always count on my bottomless love.''

Marie turned away from his gaze and stared back up at the heavens. Peter's words were eloquent. He often spoke of his love for the boys or his family—but this was a glimpse of a part of himself he usually kept closed off. Rarely did he mention his marriage—and only out of necessity.

Marie wordlessly squeezed his hand.

''I like that about you, Marie.''

''What?'' She turned her head on the raft pillow. It squeaked beneath her.

He stared straight back at her. ''You don't rush in to fill silence with meaningless words. You listen—really, truly listen. Sometimes, I watch how you take things in and wonder what you're thinking.''

The last thing I need is for you to know what I've been thinking! She tried to interject a flippant tone to her voice, ''You could ask—but that doesn't guarantee an answer.''

Peter chuckled. ''Oh, so you're going to hide behind the old feminine mystique?''

''It's a woman's prerogative.''

''I thought changing her mind was a woman's prerogative.''

''That changability is one facet of the mystique. We have to keep men guessing.'' She disengaged her hand from his and looked at her fingers. ''I'm getting pruney.''

''Stay a while longer and relax.''

''If I do, I'll fall asleep, roll off the raft and drown.''

''I'd catch you.''

Marie cocked a brow. ''Horrors, no! We don't want the boys to be orphans!''

Peter pretended to think on it for a moment. He rubbed

his chin and drawled, "Well, let's see. Mom and Dad would rush in and claim to be their guardians, but Kate, Brianna and Jill would pitch royal fits and scramble to get their hands on the boys, and Sandy would come in—"

"And mow everyone over in her wheelchair," Marie inserted lightheartedly. "She'd grab both of them and ride off into the sunset."

Peter's chuckle rippled around her. "Guess we'd better be careful so the 'survivors' can avoid an ugly scene like that."

They floated under the balmy star-shot sky in companionable silence for a while. Peter trickled water through his fingers. It splashed softly into the pool. When Marie yawned, he towed her raft to the steps and they got out.

As they dried off, Peter asked, "You used to keep that cool little holder with the Bible promises on your kitchen table. I liked seeing the promise each day when I came down to visit. Where are those?"

"By my bed."

He used the edge of his towel to catch a drop that slid from the hair at her temple. "Marie, this is your home, too. Those little things make a difference. I also like having reminders of God's faithfulness around the house. Do you mind bringing them out to the table?"

"If you'd like me to."

"There's no time like the present."

She went to her bedroom and brought out the box. It fit easily in her palm, yet Marie carried it cautiously. So often, God had spoken to her through those little strips of papers. The promises on them gave her hope and peace.

Peter met her in the kitchen. Once she set the box on the table, he asked, "Do you take the next one out of the front, or the back?"

"The back. That way, yesterday's is in the front so I

can still remind myself of it and today's is always a surprise.''

''So what was today's?''

Marie handed him the paper, and he read aloud. ''Psalms 32:8—'I will instruct you and teach you in the way which you shall go. I will counsel you with my eye on you.''' He looked at her and nodded somberly. ''That's good. I like knowing He guides and leads us, and He keeps watch over us.''

''Yes. Well, I think I'll turn in. Good night.''

As Marie lay in bed, she wondered about Peter's words. Did he mean ''us'' generically because God watched over all of His children, or did ''us'' mean them and the children? *What's wrong with me? Why am I hoping ''us'' could just mean the two of us?*

Chapter Twenty

Melway General Hospital had been notably silent for some time, when their attorney contacted Peter. Marie was passing by his study when Peter motioned for her to come in. He hit the speakerphone button so she could hear everything. "We will, of course, handle each of the cases separately," the attorney said. "I'll settle with Mrs. Cadant. As a hospital administrator, I'm sure you'll understand part of the settlement is that you will not reveal to her any offer I place on the table."

Marie's jaw dropped. Peter pressed a finger to his lips and motioned for her to sit down. He asked, "Why don't we all meet together and discuss this?"

"We'd rather not."

"I'll have to get counsel on this."

The man on the other end of the line cleared his throat, "Do you have representation?"

"Marie and I plan to share the same attorney."

A sigh slithered across the phone line. "I see." He paused, then said, "In that case, I need to deal with him. Could you give me his name, please?"

The next week, their attorney called. Marie invited him over that evening. After the boys were tucked in, she, Peter and Stuart Penny sat in the living room and pretended to sip the coffee Mrs. Lithmas had left for them.

"They're offering two and a half million for each parent/child pair," Stuart said without preamble. "In return, they admit no blame. They want to make this go away quietly."

"But what if they've done this with other babies?" Marie looked down at her hands.

"Nightmarish as it is, on very rare occasions, babies are mistakenly given to the wrong parents. I sincerely doubt this was an intentional, malicious act. In no way do I mean to excuse what happened. I'd never admit this in a court of law, but the simple truth is, both boys were born under extremely tense circumstances. Their emergency deliveries occurred within fifteen minutes in a very small community hospital. Frankly, my medical expert read the charts and says he's amazed they managed to spare Marie's life."

Peter wound his arm around her and snuggled her closer. His lips brushed her temple as he murmured, "Thank God they did."

She shivered.

"Reconstructing this is an imperfect science. Our best guess is it happened in the mad scramble right after the deliveries. There was only one nurse in the nursery. Both babies reached her almost simultaneously—one from the maternity operating room, the other from the emergency room where they'd delivered the Hallock baby as a last-ditch effort."

Marie quietly asked, "Where is that nurse now?"

"I wanted to interview her. By all rights, we can depose

her, but there's a problem.'' Stuart grimaced. ''She's got end stage lung cancer.''

''Upsetting her won't change what happened,'' Marie said. ''This can't be altered. It would be cruel to burden her. If it's okay with you, Peter, I'd rather leave her alone.''

Peter cleared his throat. ''Actually, I'd really like this whole matter to be kept quiet. The boys are both happy. That's what's most important. If the press gets hold of this they'll sensationalize it, and the boys may not come away emotionally intact.''

Marie nodded in silent agreement.

''You could,'' the attorney said, ''stipulate in any settlement that the boys receive counseling. Certainly the two of you are entitled. Do you have any other concerns?''

Peter stared out of the window. His expression went bleak. ''Most of all, I'm worried that if this ever went public, the media would make suppositions about the size of the settlement. There is a world of greedy people out there who target rich families for kidnapping.''

The way his voice dropped to a hushed horror on that last word jolted Marie. She twisted and stared at him. ''You never said anything!''

He grimaced. ''I hate to think about it, but it is a consideration. I worry the boys would become targets.''

She studied his austere features and rested her hand on his arm. Pressing it firmly, she declared, ''We don't need the money. We can forget it all.''

''Actually, they low-balled the offer.'' Stuart shrugged. ''I told them I'd present it, but only as a formality. They know full well it is only a fraction of what they should put on the table.''

''That kind of money would fund worthwhile charities,'' Peter mused. He looked at Marie. ''What if we were to get Sandy set up in a place close by here? She's made major strides and she could live alone if she had an attendant. We could build or buy a place with a dozen customized apartments and hire a few of the physical therapy students at the college to live in as personal attendants.''

''I'd love to have her closer. Ricky misses her something fierce. But what about a job? She's been looking for work—''

''A nationally recognized center for kidnapping and related problems is about five miles north of here. I'll bet with proper funding, they could stand to hire Sandy and a few others. Most of their work is on computers or phones.''

''So we can pull the boys off the altar, like Isaac, and use the ram in the thicket?''

''Exactly.''

''I don't get it,'' the lawyer said.

''In the Bible, Isaac was going to be sacrificed, but God provided a way out so he was kept safe,'' Peter explained. ''I don't want our sons put in any jeopardy with any media coverage. The potential danger of any attention whatsoever would always put them on the block, so to speak.''

''So we could make this all go away quietly,'' Marie added, ''and try to turn it into some good.''

Peter flashed her a smile. ''We'll do it and call the complex Isaac's House.''

''There could be problems with the fact that a portion of that money is intended for the boys,'' their lawyer pointed out.

''We can donate our share to the Isaac's House, Marie. The boys' names will be listed as property owners. The property is in trust and property appreciates. Would that suffice, Stuart?''

"If we draw up the papers, we can present them to a judge for approval."

Marie's hand curled around Peter's arm. "If it's God's will, it will work out."

"Families were meant to be together, Marie. Because He worked a miracle and brought us together, I can't imagine He'd refuse something as minor as this."

Days passed. Marie continued to ease into her new life. Saturdays were family days, Sundays were church days and the rest of the time Marie tried to concentrate on doing things to blend their family and make things run smoothly. The boys were young enough to be flexible. They acted as if they'd been together all along. She cherished the time she had to devote to them.

Sandy came up for visits, and when she was back home she used the video camera equipment attached to her computer to have "face-to-face chats" with Marie and the boys. She'd even started teaching the boys the alphabet song, which they managed to botch in several creative ways.

Though Peter's father still worked, his mother didn't. She frequently dropped in for a few hours to play with the boys. Marie knew she wasn't a believer. Still, Marie refused to change things. Even when Lauren came over, Marie led the boys in prayers at meals and bedtime. If the boys singsonged part of "Jesus Loves Me," Marie sang along. She prayed the Holy Spirit would woo her mother-in-law.

One afternoon, after they put the boys down for their nap, Marie caught Lauren giving the window a strained look. Marie's heart twisted. *Sweet Holy Spirit, she needs Your comfort.*

Lauren joined her in the living room for a glass of iced

tea and stared at the small gold cross Marie wore about her neck. "I grew up in a family that went to church every Christmas. I never really understood why it was supposed to be such a big deal. After Lisa…" Her voice trailed off.

Marie sat quietly. *Lord, give me wisdom.*

"After Lisa was taken," Lauren rasped, "I decided I couldn't understand a God who gave His Baby away."

"It was divine love. Because sin separated all of His children from Him, God sacrificed His own Son to regain all of us. As a mother, the magnitude of His gift overwhelms me. As His daughter, I'm thankful He was willing to give all He had to forgive me."

Lauren shook her head. She set her glass down on a coaster. "I can't accept that. He let them kill His Son. Don't tell me God is love if He did that. No matter why He did it, the fact that He did tears my heart out. I want nothing to do with a God like that."

"Lauren, my son was taken from me and restored to me…and I got the bonus of a second son. God gave His Son so all of us could become His children again."

"You don't understand. No one can. My daughter was taken. I never got her back. He got His Son back. You got your son back. I never got Lisa back."

"The pain of that is immeasurable," Marie empathized. "But I think of how God has the ability to comfort you and meet you where you are because He also endured the pain of separation."

Lauren twisted the glass back and forth on the coaster in a show of agitation.

"When my husband died, I struggled with similar feelings," Marie confessed. "How could God rob me like that? Then I finally came to the point where I started being thankful for the time I did have with Jack. I realized that because he'd been in my life, I received a blessing—a child. Since we were both believers, I know I'll see him again someday in heaven. That could be your one true hope—that if you find God, you'll see Lisa in heaven.''

''That's the difference between us. You can be thankful. Me? I'm still just angry. I'm not about to give myself to God when He let a kidnapper rip out my heart and soul.'' She let out a brittle laugh. ''You must think I'm a horrible person.''

Marie reached over and squeezed her mother-in-law's hand. ''I'm not here to judge you. It's okay for you to be honest with me. God is big enough to handle your anger, and He's patient. If you ever want to talk about it, Peter and I are both willing to listen.''

Lauren lifted her glass with the other hand and took a quick sip of her tea. She then flashed an all-too-bright smile. ''Hearing you say 'Peter and I' really does my heart good.''

Marie didn't push the topic. She'd prayed for wisdom, and her heart told her to head on toward the new topic. ''I have to give you a lot of credit. You reared a fine son.''

The boys giggled in the other room. Lauren grinned, and some of the tension melted from her shoulders. ''It looks like you'll have your hands full, rearing those two.''

The judge was impressed with the plans Marie and Peter drew up for Isaac's House. He'd given approval, and they spent an evening driving around the area to look at existing places that could be retrofitted and adapted. After viewing the third place, Peter tucked Marie close to his side and told the real estate broker, ''Let's forget about retrofitting and remodeling a place. Widening doorways and lowering counters is only a part of the requirement, and I think all of the places you've shown us would end up looking too crowded and clinical.''

''What do you have in mind?'' the agent asked.

''Land.'' Peter smiled at Marie as he said, ''Show us all of the good-size lots that are available.''

''There are only four possibilities.''

The fourth place was perfect. They put in a bid, and the sale closed within days. An architect conferred with a disability expert before he started drawing blueprints. Sandy expressed her delight with the whole concept. Peter gave her a fax machine so she could send information, pictures and ideas to them. Her boyfriend continued to drop her off and picked her up for short visits when his trucking route took him by. He'd volunteered that he was going to change routes because seeing Sandy was important to him.

''The preliminary blueprints and specs will be ready soon,'' Peter told Marie one morning before he left for work. ''If you get a chance, could you ask Mom or one of my sisters to mind the boys so we can sit down and look at them carefully? Either the tenth or eleventh would be best for my schedule.''

''Will do.'' She wiped an orange juice mustache off of Luke.

''What's today's promise verse?'' Before he went to work each morning, Peter took time to read the new slip or asked Marie to. They'd made it a little family devotion time—just a quick read, then a sentence or two of prayer. He'd come to relish those few moments when his family came together spiritually.

''Here, Daddy. I help you.'' Ricky fumbled to grab the next slip from the holder, then handed it to him.

''Thanks, tiger.'' He turned his attention to the little blue paper and began to read aloud. ''Romans 5:8—'But

God commends his own love toward us, in that while we were yet sinners, Christ died for us.'''

"I love that verse." Marie smiled. She looked at the boys. "It tells me even when I did bad things, God still loved me so much, He sent Jesus to die on the cross."

They held hands in a quick prayer, then Peter kissed all three of them on the cheek and headed out the door. He'd worried about whether Marie was happy, but in the past several days, she seemed to smile more. He often heard her laughing with the boys. She was accustomed to working. Having her help with Isaac's House was a stroke of good luck. She'd been creative, considerate and insightful. Maybe this was God's way of giving what she needed—an outside interest.

In the past, Peter had often worked on weekends to handle business matters that couldn't be put off until Monday. Ever since he'd met Marie and Ricky, he couldn't do that. He'd gotten behind on several matters. His vice president was taking over more of the load, but Peter wanted to be scrupulously fair. He'd started doing more in the late evening after Marie and the boys went to bed. He looked at the stack of files on his desk and grimaced. He ought to take them all home tonight. Tomorrow was Friday, and he didn't want anything interfering with their weekend.

The partnership worked well. He'd go home, they'd have supper with the boys, have family time and bedtime prayers then he'd slip off to his study and work or do whatever he wanted. Marie never asked or expected anything from him.

Indeed, odd as it was, he believed theirs was a match made in heaven. He had no heart to give to a woman; her heart still belonged to Jack. Two wounded souls, neither with the ability to love again—but still able to forge this union for the boys' sake. He felt thankful for how much Marie gave to make it all work.

That afternoon, his intercom buzzed. As he hit the button, he looked at the picture he'd taken of the boys building a lopsided sand castle. That day had been every bit as golden as the sun glowing all around them. His secretary's voice broke through that fleeting memory. "I've put this call straight through as you asked, Mr. Hallock. It's your wife."

Marie hadn't ever called him at work. Peter was astonished. He'd made provisions with his executive secretary to interrupt whatever he might be doing if ever Marie called, but this was a first. She'd already called and left a message with Paulette regarding a date for the blueprint appointment, so that couldn't be why she'd called. He grabbed the receiver. "Marie! This is a surprise. Are the boys all right?"

"Yes."

The butter-soft leather of his desk chair squeaked slightly as he leaned back. He couldn't imagine why she called, but knowing her, she'd tell him in a second. Marie always thought for a moment before she spoke. His gaze went back to the photo, and he suggested, "Marie, how would you like to take off for a little mini-vacation this weekend?"

"I...um, need some help."

"Sure, I'll help. Want me to make reservations and—"

"No."

Something in her voice struck him as odd. His seat thumped forward. "Marie? What's wrong?"

Chapter Twenty-One

When she didn't respond right away, his concern sky-rocketed. "Marie? Marie! What's going on?" He'd ask to speak to Mrs. Lithmas, but she'd taken a few days off for a root canal.

"I tried to get Brianna, but she's not home."

"Why do you need Brianna?"

"To watch the boys." She paused again, and when she spoke again, her voice came across the line in a mere whisper. "I think I might need stitches."

Stitches. Blood. She's hurt. "Do you need the para-medics? An ambulance?"

"No, Peter. Who's your doctor?" Her strained laugh came across the line. "You're surrounded by doctors every day, but I don't even know who ours is."

"Where are you bleeding? How bad is it?"

"It's just my arm. I'm okay. Really, Peter—the big problem is, I can't strap the boys in their car seats. If you can come watch them, I'll drive to the doctor."

Fat chance I'd let you drive. "I'll get home in ten minutes. Will you be okay for ten minutes?"

"Yes."

He let out a sigh of relief. As he dashed out of his office, he called over his shoulder, "Marie hurt herself, Paulette. Cancel the rest of the afternoon appointments."

Traffic was light, but time seemed to drag. *How bad is the cut? She sounded calm. Maybe it's not so bad. But Marie wouldn't call if it weren't severe...* He stepped on the gas. He used his cell phone and reached his parents. "Mom, can you meet me at my place? Marie hurt herself. I need you to watch the boys."

Peter skidded into the driveway, raced into the house and hollered, "Marie?"

"In the kitchen."

Both boys sat at the kitchen table. They were wearing more cookies than they were eating. Marie had her back to him as she grabbed something out of a cabinet. "Marie! What are you doing?"

She turned around. With almost no reaction, she wrapped the dishcloth atop a sizable wad gracing her arm. Peter's eyes narrowed. The cloths she covered were dark. He glanced down and noted the red trail on the floor. "Let me see that."

She pulled her arm close to her ribs. "It'll be okay. Just tell me where the doctor is."

"You have to go to the emergency room for stitches, Marie." He covered the distance between them as he spoke. "Trust me—I'm an expert on the finer details of where to go when, and who does what. Now let me see."

She gazed up at him. Her eyes were bigger than usual, and her face looked pale. Though she made no complaint, Peter knew her arm hurt.

She whispered, "I haven't looked at it yet."

"I'll take a peek. You sit down." He hooked his foot around the leg of a chair and dragged it over. From the way she looked, he expected her to melt into it, but Marie gracefully lowered herself onto the edge. "Scoot back," he said gruffly.

"I don't want to ruin the upholstery on the chair."

He cupped his hands around her hips and slid her deep into the seat. "I don't care about the upholstery, and it makes me feel better for you to be back here."

"The boys are a mess."

It's got to be bad if she hasn't looked at it and doesn't want the boys to see. Peter played along with her. "Boys, you've had enough cookies. Get down and go wash your hands and faces. Use your bathroom."

"Keep your hands together and don't touch the walls," Marie added.

Once Luke and Ricky started down the hallway, Peter's patience evaporated. He opened the dishcloth so he could assess the damage. Peter strove to act nonchalant. Marie stayed so incredibly calm, it seemed ridiculous for him to lose control if she was handling this so well. He gently peeled away three more dishcloths and sucked in a sharp breath.

"It's not too bad, is it?"

He looked up at her. She'd trained her wide eyes on the ceiling. They glistened with tears that she kept blinking back. He didn't have the heart to tell her the full truth. "You're right. You need some stitches. I'll wrap your arm with a makeshift dressing. How did you do this?"

"Out on the patio, by the barbecue. Luke pedaled full tilt on his trike, and I realized he was going to hit the nook. There's aluminum flashing underneath it. It's pretty sharp."

There's an understatement! Peter didn't want to leave her to go get a first aid kit. If Marie looked down at her arm, she'd probably faint. Dishcloths were handy—he used them to make a replacement bandage.

"You spared Luke quite a bump. I'll get someone out to work on the nook right away."

"Please," she agreed.

Peter inched closer and cupped her head to his chest. His other hand soothed back and forth across her shoulders. "Mom is coming to watch the boys. I'll take you in as soon as she gets here. Why don't we have you lie down on the couch?"

"No, I'll get it stained."

She nestled into him more fully. Actually, he wasn't sure she hadn't simply slumped or fainted until her left arm slid behind him and curled loosely around his waist in a silent bid for more support and closeness. It was the first time she'd even initiated any contact, and he liked the feel of her in his arms. Peter dipped his head and lightly kissed her soft, fragrant hair. He could tell her he wasn't worried about the couch—but he'd already told her that about the chair. If they stayed right here, he could continue to hold her. She seemed content enough.

"Be sure to tell your mom not to let the boys go out there," Marie whispered into his shirt. "Not 'til it's fixed."

"Okay." He heard the boys playing gleefully at the sink.

"Luke's forehead looks all right."

He gently rubbed his thumb back and forth over her temple. "You spared him, Marie. I'm really mad at myself for not realizing the nook had a sharp edge. I should have—"

"Shh," she cut him off. Her hand patted his hip in a lulling cadence. "It was an accident. The boys are fine."

"But you—"

"Just a few stitches, Peter."

His mother sailed in. Peter simply scooped Marie out of the chair and into his arms. "Thanks, Mom. The boys are washing up."

That evening, Marie pretended not to notice when Peter slid his arm around her and coaxed her to let her head rest on his chest. He'd been terrific.

Until she got into the emergency room, she'd actually managed to fool herself into believing the cut wasn't very big. When Marie saw how the deep cut sliced from just above her wrist clear up toward her elbow, she let out a cry. Peter gathered her close then, too. Just like now. He was comforting, protective...and she was thankful for the strength he shared so freely.

Peter arranged for an expert to examine her. He'd made sure she didn't have any nerve or tendon damage. She hadn't thought about the fact that anything else might be wrong, and Peter's clear thinking reassured her. Once the doctor evaluated her, things moved quickly.

She'd whispered tightly, "I hate needles!"

"Everyone does. You're just a tiny little pincushion, too." Peter kept her face turned toward his as the doctor started to suture her. "Speaking of needles, those jammies you made for the boys out of the race-car-print flannel are pretty spiffy."

"Do you—" she paused and winced as another needle pierced her arm "—want me to make you a pair, too?"

He winked. "I'll get back to you on that." He didn't even take a breath as he addressed the doctor. "Sam, she felt that last stitch. Numb her up a bit more, will you?"

Peter babied her while they put in nearly thirty stitches. His voice kept her calm, and his hold kept her anchored. Now the TV flickered. She wasn't really watching the movie. Content, Marie rested in Peter's arms. They remained like that—a pocket of comfort—for some time. She wasn't in any hurry to move, and he seemed at ease with her. He finally rubbed his jaw in her hair. "You're about due for a pain pill."

"They make me woozy."

"So we'll put you to bed."

When Marie emerged from her bathroom, Peter was waiting with a glass in his hand. As she accepted it and the pill, she said worriedly, "What if the boys wake up?"

"Stop fretting." He pulled back the covers and scolded, "I'm perfectly capable of seeing to them. I'll wake you up at about midnight for another dose to keep you ahead of the pain."

"Aspirin is fine."

He gave her a sardonic look. "And you thought I gave Ricky his stubborn gene?"

She laughed weakly, but her laughter stopped short as Peter casually tugged the crisscrossed ends of her robe's sash. His grin faded, and his features went wooden. She still slept in Jack's old police academy T-shirt.

Do I say something? Do I stay silent? He looks so upset.

"Take the pills, Marie," he growled.

She swallowed hard to get them down—but the lump remained in her throat. She'd hurt his feelings, and it bothered her. *I have to do something, say something...* Peter wordlessly took the glass from her hand. Just as he turned to go, she blurted out, "I don't think I can get out of the robe without your help. I was stupid to put it on, but I knew you were out here and—"

"And you didn't want me to find out you can't give up your other husband's shirts any more than you can relinquish his memories," he cut in harshly.

A soft answer turneth away wrath. She stared up at him in silence, then quietly explained, ''It hadn't even occurred to me. It's a habit. Jack's T-shirts are all I have.''

''You've got to be kidding.''

She shrugged her left shoulder sheepishly. ''It seemed silly to go shopping for a trousseau, and I didn't have time or money to do it, anyway.''

He looked at her intently, as if to read her mind. She stared back at him, willing him to understand she hadn't meant to insult him. Almost imperceptibly, he nodded and put down the glass. ''Tomorrow. We'll get you new stuff tomorrow.''

Marie pivoted to the side and tried to shrug out of the robe. All of the sudden, she felt incredibly self-conscious. He held the back of the collar and tugged on her left sleeve. ''Take your good arm out first. That way, it won't pull on your sore one so much.''

''Good idea. Thanks.''

Half of the robe's weight hung in his hand. He hovered behind her and ordered softly, right next to her ear, ''Slowly straighten your arm and let the robe slide off. Don't tug.''

The feel of his breath brushing against her sent a shiver through her, and the bandaging caught on the chenille. Peter reached down and patiently freed it. ''There you go.''

''Thanks.'' She fought the crazy urge to turn into his arms.

''Lie on your left side—I'll tuck a pillow next to you.''

He moved, and she didn't know whether to be relieved that she hadn't thrown herself into his arms or disappointed that she'd lost the opportunity.

''You can elevate your arm, and it won't throb as much.''

"I guess I can try." She wrinkled her nose and confessed, "I usually curl up on my right side. It's going to feel funny." What really felt funny was telling him those oddly personal quirks. Strange how she never realized she had them—and they were the sorts of things *real* husbands and wives knew about one another. The awkwardness of the situation kept growing. She stammered, "I ought to go check on the boys."

"They're fine." Peter curled his hands around her waist and twisted. The action carried her right to the edge of the mattress. The pressure of his hands forced her to sit.

I sleep on the other side, closer to the boys' room....

"Brace your arm while I help you with your legs."

Peter slipped a big, warm hand under her knees, lifted and effortlessly slipped her onto her side. He leaned over to put the extra pillow next to her body. When the back of his hand bumped her knee, he let go of the pillow and casually tugged downward on the hem of her nightshirt. Gratitude and embarrassment both washed over her.

She carefully positioned her aching arm on the pillow and sighed in relief as he drew the bedclothes up to her neck. "Thank you, Peter. Good night."

His fingers slid through her hair from temple to tips just once, as he hummed, "Mmm, hmm." He hovered over her for a silent moment like a guardian angel, then the comfort of his presence was gone. The carpet must have muffled his tread as he left.

From her shoulder clear down to her fingertips, she throbbed unmercifully. She hoped the medicine would start to work soon. Marie lay there and told herself she had a good deal. Peter was an excellent partner. He'd been very compassionate and helpful today. He was attentive and undemanding—but most of all, he truly loved their boys. So why, when this was a simple, straightforward, chaste partnership, had she really wanted him to kiss her good night?

Chapter Twenty-Two

Peter walked down the hallway and slowly let out his breath. He'd wanted to gather Marie in his arms, bury his face in her hair and comfort her. She was a real armful of woman. She sure wouldn't appreciate knowing he felt that way about her. Marie didn't even like it when he paid her simple compliments. He'd wanted to brush kisses on her face and give her get-better kisses on her fingertips. Instead, he'd made as hasty a getaway from her room as he could without seeming rude.

At midnight, he gathered up his nerve and went into Marie's room again. It took a bit of doing to shake her awake. Finally, her eyes opened to a sultry half-mast. "Huh?"

"I have your pills, sweetheart. Let me help you sit up."

He sat on the edge of her bed and slipped his arm behind her shoulders.

She wiggled and settled into his side with a small, kittenish sound.

"How are you feeling?"

"Arm burns."

He pressed his lips to her temple, then across her forehead. He'd hoped she was just warm from having been burrowed beneath all of the covers, but he discovered otherwise. "Marie, honey, you're running a bit of a fever."

"'Sokay. Gave me an'biotic shot at the 'mergency room."

"Let's wash you up and have you take some aspirin. You'll feel better if you do."

"Need to take the boys—"

"I'll go take care of them." He nudged Marie into her bathroom. "Can you manage by yourself?"

She gave him a wide-eyed look and actually blushed. He couldn't attribute the color to fever because it didn't just ride on her cheeks—it tinted her entire face. "I'm fine."

"Honey, if you get dizzy or faint, call me."

She didn't agree, but she didn't protest, either. Peter decided not to press her. He left the bathroom door open just a crack and went to see to Ricky. When he came back, Marie was leaning against the bathroom doorsill.

"Beddy-bye time, Mrs. Hallock."

"Mrs. Hallock is thirsty. She didn't drink anything because you said she needs to take an aspirin."

"Ahhh. I knew I married a brilliant woman." He noted how she managed to cradle her right arm with her left—a definite giveaway that she was hurting. "I'll pop aspirin and pain pills into you. What would you like to drink?"

"Just water, please."

She'd washed off a bit. The scent of her soap clung to her. Before they'd gotten married, she wore one certain perfume all of the time. He'd liked the fragrance—it reminded him of sunshine and wildflowers. She'd stopped wearing it, and he suspected that was her subtle way of making sure he didn't suspect her of having any seductive designs on him. He knew he ought to appreciate her integrity and motive, but it bothered him that she'd given up on it—just as she had stopped doing so many other things.

On occasion, she used to band her curls back with a satin ribbon—but she didn't now. She used to have breakfast before she put on makeup; now she appeared at the table with her "face" on. Marie did her utmost to be the bandbox, perfect image of a wife—but at the same time made it clear this was all smoke and mirrors. Tempting him was the least of her motives.

Pathetically, none of that mattered. He couldn't think of another woman on the face of the earth whom he found half as intriguing, yet honor demanded he ignore the ever-increasing pull he felt toward her. He'd tried to convince himself at the office today that all he felt for her was a simple partnership, but the wild drive home and worrying about her in the emergency room disabused him of that notion. He'd started to develop feelings for her—feelings he never thought he'd have again.

Her steps were unsteady as Peter led her to the bed and nudged her to sit on the edge of the mattress. She obediently swallowed the pills he slipped to her, then blinked at him. "Sorry I'm keeping you up. You look tired."

"Tomorrow's Saturday. We'll all sleep in."

At seven the next morning, Peter woke abruptly. He'd come conscious at once, thinking the sharp jarring and shaking of his bed meant they were in the midst of an earthquake. He bolted upright, only to discover Luke and Ricky scrambling across his mattress with all of the enthusiasm only two preschoolers could muster at such an hour. "Sport! Tiger! What are you doing out of bed so early?"

"Hungreee!" Ricky announced.

"I should have guessed," Peter muttered. "It's not breakfast time yet." He raised the covers in a silent invitation. The flannel pajamas Marie made for the boys rubbed against his ribs as his sons crept under the blankets on either side of him.

"Mommy sleeping."

"Yes, Ricky, she is. We're going to let her sleep in late. Do you both understand? Leave Mommy alone today. Her arm hurts."

Peter wasn't surprised the boys went to her room first. It came as no wonder that she hadn't awakened, either. At five, he'd slipped aspirin and another pain pill into her. Hopefully, she'd wake up in better shape late in the morning. In the meantime, he'd keep the boys relatively quiet and under control.

Resting with the boys bracketing him was as realistic as expecting to stay dry while walking through a car wash. Peter soon gave up. For the first time ever, he was going to play solo parent to both boys.

Marie emerged from her bedroom at eleven o'clock. She half staggered into the playroom and slumped onto the tweed couch she'd brought from home. Once there, she closed her eyes to stop the dizziness that assailed her. "I don't care what those pills are. Don't give me any more of them."

Peter tossed a soft acrylic throw over her legs and lifted them onto the couch. Marie automatically grabbed for him since that motion sent her world reeling. Marie thought he brushed a kiss on her temple and murmured, "I like what those drugs do." It must have been the drugs. He'd never do that.

Washed out as she felt, Marie spent most of the day

lying on the couch. She loved watching Peter with the boys. An odd mixture of intensity and careless abandon characterized his interactions with them. Though a big man, he never towered over them. He spent most of his time lying or sitting on the floor. They made a tent out of a blanket and the trestle table. To the boys' delight, Peter dug out flashlights. They "camped" and had a picnic lunch under the dark cloth folds.

Brianna showed up in the late afternoon. She brought a casserole. As it baked, she started to draw a bath for Marie. Marie gave her a whimsical smile. "Okay, so I already thought you were a cool sister-in-law. The supper you brought smells great, but this—well, it just might make you my favorite person. You're a blessing." Marie gave her a quick, one-armed hug.

"So are you." Brianna turned off the water. "Can you get in and out okay?"

Marie didn't bother to muffle her laugh. "I'm a mom— I'm used to doing things one-handed!"

She felt far better after her bath. Though she would have liked to wash her hair, she couldn't manage that feat. Getting dressed posed some problems, but Marie managed and arrived at the supper table just in time for prayer.

Jill came over after dinner. "I volunteered to do night shift with the boys. In the morning, I'll take them to church. Mom and Dad will take them home and bring them back on Monday or Tuesday."

Marie gave Peter a startled look. "But—"

"Thanks," he said. He patted Marie's left hand and whispered, "You need to rest. This is what family is for, and it'll get Jill and my folks to go to church!"

How am I supposed to argue with their plan? I can't imagine being without the boys for that long. "I don't know if Ricky is ready to be away from me."

"Mom said if there's a problem, she'll bring them back and stay here. I happen to know she's been concocting all sorts of schemes to get you to let her have the boys for a weekend, so this isn't an imposition."

Marie looked at Peter. He subtly winked. She let out a long sigh. "Okay. We'll try it."

The next morning, she accepted the boys' sloppy kisses and looked at Peter. "Go on to church."

"No, sweetheart. I'll stay home with you. If you're feeling better later, we can go to the evening worship service."

"I'd like that."

Jill grabbed the boys' hands and said, "I'm taking Marie's car. It has the car seats in it."

"The transmission is stubborn," Marie mumbled. "You'll need to double-clutch."

"I'll talk with you about that later." Peter scowled as he strode toward the door. "My car has car seats in it, too. Take it, Jill. I'll grab my keys for you."

Peter hovered all day. He insisted on pouring fluids into her even though the fever had passed. After lunch, he led her to bed, tucked a blanket over her and firmly declared she needed to nap. Marie stared up at him. "I'm not sleepy."

He toed off his shoes and surprised her by lying down on the other side of the bed. "Then we'll talk a while. With the boys underfoot, we don't get much time just to converse."

"Do you think they're all right?"

"Yes." He stacked his hands behind his head and looked over at her. "Mom's been worried that you wouldn't trust her since you found out Lisa was kidnapped. Asking her to mind the boys means the world to her."

"My hesitance isn't because of Lisa—it's because Ricky and I are nearly inseparable."

"The two of you are practically joined at the hip," Peter agreed. He said the words in such a kind tone, she took no offense. He grinned and continued, "Luke's about caught up on that, too. He clings to you every chance he gets."

"They're good boys."

"And you're a good mommy. We did the right thing, getting married."

"I'm glad you think so." She wiggled onto her side.

Peter turned to face her and carefully arranged a pillow under her hurt forearm.

"Thank you."

His fingers trailed down hers slowly. His eyes went darker than usual, and his voice took on a husky tone. "You're more than welcome."

"I feel so ridiculous about this." His touch felt so reassuring, so comforting. She didn't want him to leave her. "Talk to me about Isaac's House."

"Sure. The owner of the lot next to where we bought contacted me this morning. If we want to buy his land, he'll sell it at the same cost as our current lot."

"Which side? The one with the neat, old trees?"

"Yes, the one to the east. Due to space constraints, the architect had to pare down our original plan from twelve apartments to ten. If we buy this extra land, we can build mirror image complexes, and I'm almost sure we can keep the trees as a central common."

"Oh, that would be wonderful. Can we afford it? Could we still keep the therapy pool?"

"They're taking measurements. We already know the city zoning code will let us do it. Finances aren't an issue. The only thing is, if we do this, it'll set back when we break ground because we'll want to resituate where the buildings are located on the lot.''

"Sandy might need to live with us for a while."

"Fine by me. You know she's always welcome." He glanced downward. "How's your arm?"

She shuddered. "I don't want to talk about it."

"Why won't you take something? I know you hurt."

"I'll just nap."

His knuckles slowly trailed down her cheek, then he carefully pulled the blanket up to her nape. "You make it hard for me to respect your wishes when I know there's more that can be done."

"More isn't always better," she whispered.

"If I let you win this disagreement, you have to let me win the next three."

"Not a chance."

"Okay, the next two. But I'm warning you now, that's the best deal you'll get out of me."

"Shush." She closed her eyes. "I'm trying to sleep."

Chapter Twenty-Three

Peter made grilled cheese sandwiches, burned the first batch, and gamely made more. Marie tried not to laugh at him—he'd blithely ignored the skillet the first time, and now he hovered over it like a tiger ready to pounce on... *Well, it is his next meal,* she admitted to herself.

No one could have ever put plates on a table with more pride and glee. Marie smiled up at Peter, then watched as his brow furrowed. "What's wrong?"

"Well, maybe we ought to have other stuff with the sandwiches. You know—round it out, make it nutritious."

She started to stand. "I'll get—"

"Stay put." He glowered at her. "I'm making supper."

Entertainment of this variety came only once in a lifetime, Marie decided. She leaned back in her chair and watched Peter root around in the cabinets and refrigerator. He plopped a fistful of baby carrots on each plate, added some chips, wrinkled his nose and an aha! smile tilted his mouth as he dived toward the freezer.

Marie prayed over their meal and asked the Lord to bless the hands that prepared it. The sandwich was cold, the ice cream was hot, and the chips were stale—but no meal had ever been better.

"I think you need to rest tonight," Peter decided as he drank the last of his ice cream from the bowl.

"I can sit in a pew just as easily as I can sit on the couch." She smiled. "I really want to go to service tonight."

He sighed. "Luke gets that same 'pretty-please' look on his face. It's irresistible."

Peter watched as she emerged from her bedroom fifteen minutes later. Though the early-autumn evening was warm, she'd chosen a dress with loose-fitting long sleeves to hide the bandage on her arm.

"Um, Peter?"

"What is it?"

He hadn't noticed she'd kept her left hand behind her back until now. She brought it around and smiled sheepishly. A pair of strappy black shoes dangled from her forefinger. "Daddy, will you peese hep me with my shoes?"

Lord, it's a good thing I'm going to church, after all. My mind is heading toward things of the flesh. She's my wife, and it's not supposed to be a sin...but Father, I don't know how to handle this attraction and still honor my promise to her!

Once he walked her into the sanctuary, he realized the spiritual renewal she found here was every bit as important as the physical refreshing she got from sleep.

Folks who had been away on vacations heard through the grapevine that he'd married, and a few came over after the service to meet his bride. To her credit, Marie carried off her role as wife beautifully. She didn't fawn over him or put up any pretenses, yet she stayed close and smiled freely as she mentioned the boys and made it clear they were all enjoying family life.

As he helped her into the car and leaned over her to latch the seat belt, Peter murmured, "I'm glad we came."

"So am I. I like your church."

"It's *our* church now."

The corners of her mouth rose. "Is this the first disagreement I'm supposed to let you win?"

"No, we're not disagreeing at all. It's an undeniable fact. In your own words, 'The music here makes me feel right at home.' You can't argue with that."

"Your debating skills leave my head spinning."

"Then I'd better get you home and tuck you into bed. I have a busy day planned for you tomorrow."

"Busy? Life is going to be quiet as a tomb with the boys at your mom's and you at work."

"I'm taking the day off."

To Peter's relief, Marie wasn't running a fever the next morning. He took her out for breakfast, then insisted, "We're going shopping."

He'd called his folks and let Marie get a report on how the boys were doing, then swept her into several boutiques. Peter knew she'd lived frugally, but her reaction to the price tags was far from amusing. He inched closer and murmured in her ear, "Sweetheart, stop looking at the tags and start looking at the merchandise. You deserve some new stuff."

She gave him an appalled look. "This robe costs more than Sandy and I paid for a whole week's groceries!"

"I see we have a problem." He waggled his brows. "Whenever I see you in it, I'll have cravings for meat and potatoes."

Marie giggled. "You're outrageous."

"Me?" He gave her a wounded look.

She hissed under her breath, "And so are these prices!"

"I'd pay ten times that so you wouldn't wear that ratty old T-shirt."

She squared her shoulders. "It's not ratty. It's broken in." .

"I've always heard wine and cheese are the only things that improve with age."

A twinkle lit her eyes. She rocked to and fro from toes to heels and back. "You're wrong. Definitely wrong. Blue jeans improve dramatically with age."

"Ahh, you have me there. I'll have to pay a forfeit for losing the bet." He snagged three nightgowns from the display and marched toward the sales associate.

That was only the beginning. Peter calmly handed over the garments and said, "My wife needs to replenish her supply of intimate wear."

"I'm sure we can take care of her."

Marie stared at him. He wasn't sure whether she was angry or embarrassed. Peter strode back to her, gently pulled her into his arms and whispered in her hair, "I know you don't want me to see what you end up getting. I brought you here because this is where Mom always comes with my sisters. Promise me you'll get some pretty stuff. Enough for two full weeks, and I'll step outside while you shop."

"Two weeks!"

"Okay. I'll make a better deal." He leaned back and tried not to smile at her flushed cheeks. "Two weeks for you, and two weeks for Sandy, too. Get her some pretty nighties and stuff. She could probably use a little boost."

"You don't play fair."

Peter lightly kissed her forehead. "Do it, Marie. If you don't, I will."

She gasped.

"Promise, and I'll step outside. I'll even go into the shop next door, so I can't see whatever you choose through the window."

"I could sew—"

"No!" he hissed. Visions of her in flannel decorated with silly cats or cartoon cars flitted through his head.

"Can't we just go to a discount department store? This place is outrageously expensive."

"You're worth it. Do it for yourself. Do it for me, because I want to provide for you. If neither of those matter, do it because you know Sandy would enjoy some pretties."

"You're my husband. How you feel is more important than my sister."

"You're some woman, Marie." He caressed her cheek with the backs of his fingers.

"I must be insane. I'm putting a blackmailing husband before common sense."

Peter chuckled. Mindful of her arm, he gave her a careful hug then cruised toward the door. He paused a second, then came back. He handed the sales associate his platinum card and tilted his head toward Marie. "She might need a bit of help since her arm is hurt. Thank you in advance for all of your assistance."

While Marie got her lingerie, Peter went into a little boutique next door. He cruised around the clothing racks and realized he didn't even know what size his wife wore. "Do you have the phone number for the place next door?"

"Probably. If not, I could get it for you."

A smile lit his face. "Better yet, can you estimate a woman's size? The blond—"

"I'd be happy to." The clerk left, then returned a few

short moments later. "The blond lady with the huge blue eyes and dimples?" Peter nodded. "Six petite. Definitely a size six."

"Thank you. I'm going to ask a little favor…" He quickly selected a wide variety of dresses, shirts and slacks. Before the woman put them in the dressing room, she followed Peter's instructions and cut off the price tags.

Peter claimed Marie and sat on a plush couch as she was ushered into the dressing room. Bags of lingerie lay at his feet, but he resisted the temptation to peek. He insisted, "My wife is to come out and let me see each outfit."

"Peter!"

He laughed and turned to accept a cup of espresso from one of the employees. Moments later, Marie timidly emerged. He lifted his forefinger and rotated it in a silent entreaty for her to turn. She did. "No, sweetheart, that dress doesn't do you justice."

Her lips parted in surprise.

He winked. "Try on that blue one next. You wear a lot of blue. Is it your favorite color?"

Her left shoulder hitched a bit and she flickered a tiny hint of a smile at him. "I guess so. I never really thought about it."

When she reappeared in the dress he'd suggested, he again motioned for her to turn. He nodded his head once, emphatically. "Yes. It's a perfect match to your eyes. That'll make a nice church dress for you."

The storekeeper did an excellent job of cajoling, shepherding and prodding. From hushed whispers, Peter knew she zipped, unzipped, buttoned and moved with cheerful efficiency to make sure each garment hung right before she'd let Marie out of the dressing room. He was glad of the clerk's assistance. The timing was bad—Marie certainly couldn't do much for herself. He should have taken her shopping long ago. At least Marie was in the hands of a woman who seemed to treat her with the right combination of matter-of-factness and fun. He'd be sure to slip her a sizable tip. Commission, alone, on these things would be hefty; but Marie required and deserved extra help, and Peter wanted to show his gratitude.

Marie continued to reappear in new combinations and ensembles. He'd never seen anyone so transparent—when she liked something, her eyes lit up. When she didn't like it, her lips pressed together in a prim, tense line. She emerged yet again. Peter took his cue from her. "I don't care for that one. What do you think the problem is? I've never seen you wear that shade."

"I look bilious in this color green." She glanced down and made a hopeless gesture. "Peter, you've gone way overboard. This is far too much."

"We're just getting started."

"You already said yes to six things!"

He patted the cushion next to himself. Marie came over and hesitantly sat down. Peter wrapped his arm around her and held her for a few silent moments. He eyed her bandage. "Is your arm hurting?"

"Only when I bump it."

"Would you feel better if you got to rest a bit before we continue?"

"Peter, you're not listening to me. I don't need all of this!"

He ran the blunt edge of his fingers back and forth very slowly along the shallowly scooped neckline of the yellow-green dress. "Gifts aren't supposed to be only what you need. They're supposed to be 'just because.' I want to do this for you. I want to do this *with* you. Please, honey, stop being practical and just enjoy yourself."

She let out a deep sigh, but to his delight, she nodded. She gave him a game smile, then whispered, ''All of this stuff is so pretty.''

He grinned. ''Pretty things for my beautiful wife.''

He took her to two more stores, out for a quiet lunch then stopped at a white building graced with pink awnings. ''It's too hard for you to wash your hair. Mom suggested I bring you here.''

''Harlan's! Peter—this isn't just a little corner hair salon.''

''Do me a favor—stop having a hissy fit.'' He got out of the car before she could formulate a response. Peter took her inside and glanced at his watch. ''I'll be back in three hours,'' he told the receptionist. ''Remember what I said—only a trim. I don't want her hair cut short.''

Three hours! Marie gaped at him.

Peter smiled at her and slowly ran his hand down her hair. ''Your hair is beautiful, sweetheart. I hope you don't mind if I got a little bossy about that. Now tell me—if I gave you a choice between a station wagon and a van, which would you prefer?''

''Peter!''

''You can't keep driving that old car. You're double-clutching. That means the transmission is ready to go out. We'd be silly to repair it. You can count this as one of the arguments I get to win, so which is it—a van, or a station wagon?''

She gave him a hopeless look.

''Okay. I'll do some legwork. Enjoy yourself.'' He brushed a kiss on her cheek and left.

Three hours later, Marie didn't know whether to strangle Peter or kiss him. She'd been pampered outrageously. The stylist fidgeted with one last strand of her shining hair, then the flamboyant cosmetologist spritzed her with a decadent fragrance. "Marvelous, darling. Marvelous!" she oozed.

Marie smiled at her. "Remember that scene from *The Wizard of Oz* where Dorothy goes to the beauty shop? I feel that way."

One of the women from their congregation was having a manicure. She laughed, "With a man like yours, you can certainly click you heels and say, 'There's no place like home!'"

Uncertainty swamped Marie as she stepped out to the reception area. What would Peter think? He sat over by a leafy palm, thumbing through a magazine. The moment he caught sight of her, he set aside the magazine and stood. He didn't smile, and that made her even more nervous than if he would have. Marie wasn't sure how she expected him to react, but he wasn't behaving along any line that she might have concocted.

He walked around the small, lacquered coffee table and stopped almost a yard from her. He scanned from her crown to her sandaled feet. When he'd finished that slow once-over, a smile lit his face. "You had your toenails painted."

Embarrassment streaked though her. "Yes." *Please, can we go? Everyone is standing here, staring at how you're reacting!*

"I want you to come back here every week."

"We'll talk about it later," she whispered. Dollar signs danced in her head. Peter was nuts if he thought she'd squander money like that! She turned and thanked everyone, then left.

Peter tucked her into the car and sniffed. "Whatever that is you're wearing, I hope you bought a big bottle of it.'' When she didn't answer, he clucked his tongue. ''I'll be right back.''

He strode into Harlan's and reappeared a few slim minutes later. He carried the glitzy gold-and-black net bag with the careless disregard only a man fully assured of his masculinity could display. Once he got in the car, he tucked the bag next to her and didn't say a word. From the chinking sounds and the way it bulged a bit, Marie knew he'd filled the bag with more than just a single bottle of that outrageously expensive perfume.

''That's it, Peter. You've won your arguments.''

He winked. ''No, I haven't. We didn't argue about that at all. It's a man's privilege to pamper his wife. Think of it as something you do for me. That scent is great. Wear it because you know I like it.''

''I don't want to sound ungrateful, but—''

''Then don't say anything,'' he cut in smoothly. He steered into traffic, deftly changed lanes and said, ''I've found a few cars. Would you like to see them now, or do you need to go home and rest?''

''I don't need a new car, and I'd like to go get the boys.''

''While you were at Harlan's, I called. Mom and Dad promised to take them out for pizza and a movie. We'll get them back tomorrow.'' He glanced at the lane adjacent to them, merged and entered a left-turn lane. In a careless tone, he revealed, ''I test drove a van and a station wagon. They both maneuver smoothly, but I'm not sure which will be easier for you in terms of handling the boys and their car seats.''

''Peter!''

He chuckled. ''I'm winning this argument, Marie.''

''You're taking advantage of the situation!''

"I grew up with a bunch of sisters—I learned to do that to survive."

"I'm the one who is outnumbered in our home!"

As he pulled into a car dealership, Peter countered, "Then I need to be extra careful to spoil you."

Marie shook her head. "Stop. Peter, I need to talk to you."

He glanced at her. "Okay."

"No, really talk."

"Fine. Shoot."

"Not here—someplace else."

Something in her tone got through to him. "Fine. Where?"

"I don't know. What about a park?"

"Sure." He drove around the block to the park where he'd proposed. Marie wondered if it was an intentional choice, but she didn't ask. Once he parked under the shade of an old magnolia, he turned in his seat and raised his brows. "What's so important?"

"Peter, you can't buy me."

"What's that supposed to mean?"

Marie knew she was treading on sensitive ground, but she couldn't let this go. She put her hand on his and quietly said, "I remember you saying Darlene wasn't ever satisfied with you or your gifts or vacations. I'm not like her, and I don't want you to feel like you have to jump through hoops so I'll stay in this marriage."

His brows knit. "All I wanted was to give you what you need."

"I have all I need." She gave him a tender smile. "Sooner or later, you'll finally learn I have simple taste. I married you because it was the right thing to do. Don't you think we're building a pretty good family?"

"Absolutely." He didn't pause for even a split second, and his smile reinforced his opinion.

"Then do me a favor and stop acting like money or things will make us better. Stop insulting yourself—you're a terrific dad and a solid husband. You don't need to buy our affection or allegiance."

"I'm not!"

Marie let out a sigh. "Okay, Peter. If that's what you believe, I must have been out of line. Please forgive me."

He started to chuckle, and his eyes twinkled. "It'll cost you."

She leaned back against the headrest and groaned. She'd married the ultimate gamesman. Barely peeking at him from the corner of her eye she asked, "What is it going to cost me?"

"Gracious acceptance of a new van."

Mrs. Lithmas came back from her time off and took over the kitchen and housekeeping once again. The timing was perfect, since Marie was supposed to be mindful of her arm. Peter tapped on her bedroom door that morning. He assigned himself the job of combing her hair. "It's too hard on you."

"Really, Peter, I can do it."

"Take it easy." He snatched the brush.

Marie didn't want to admit it, but the way he drew the brush through her hair over and over, filtered his fingers through the strands and toyed with the curls felt wonderful. He didn't hasten through the task. Instead, he drew it out. When he set down the brush, he slid one hand beneath her hair. As his thumb stroked back and forth on her nape, he asked, "Where are your ribbons?"

Startled, she looked at his reflection in the mirror. "I

didn't bring them when we moved here. Sandy—her boy-friend likes her hair in the ribbons.''

"I like your hair, too. It always looked soft and feminine when you wore ribbons in it. I wondered why you'd stopped.''

He noticed. What does that mean? Inside, she felt an odd mixture of confusion and hope. Marie forced herself to sound blasé, ''So now you know.''

''I guess so.'' Peter still kept one hand cupped around her neck. He leaned around her, curled his long fingers around the perfume bottle and murmured, ''Here you go.''

Marie reached for it, but he drew it back. Chills ran up and down her spine as he lifted her hair and spritzed her nape. She avoided looking in the mirror. She didn't want to see his expression, but even more, she didn't want him to see how she was responding to his tender ministrations.

''Wrists,'' he ordered.

Marie pulled away from him. She couldn't bear to have him stand that close and touch her. It made her feel things that went far beyond their partnership agreement. Frazzled, she stammered, ''That's enough. Thanks. If, um, I, ah, get that on my stitches it'll burn. Sting. You know?''

His features pulled taut. He nodded once, set down the bottle and strode from her room.

Marie melted onto the edge of her bed. The feel of his touch lingered every bit as strongly as the perfume's fragrance.

Chapter Twenty-Four

Peter headed straight out the door. He had to get away before he made an utter fool of himself—if he hadn't already done a royal job of it. She'd flinched, then recoiled from his touch. *What was I thinking? I'm torturing myself and scaring Marie half out of her wits. She could scarcely stand to have me touch her!* He paced to the side yard and sank onto the bench.

The revelation that Ricky was his son had stunned him in this very place. Ironically, this was the very spot where Darlene had told him she was pregnant and didn't want his child any more than she wanted him. He'd pleaded with her to go to family counseling, but she refused. Finally, he'd agreed to her greedy terms: She'd carry and turn over "the brat" if he'd grant her a divorce and a huge settlement—otherwise, she'd have an abortion.

In the end, she'd already been sucking money out of accounts and running up charge cards. Peter hadn't told anyone that in the Dear John letter she'd left, she'd basically told him he'd have to renegotiate with her for more money if he wanted the baby.

So here he sat, in the early-morning quiet, reliving old hurts and wondering what to do. Last night, he came to the staggering realization that he loved Marie. How could he possibly mess up his life? She'd committed to a partnership—not a true marriage. Companionship and parenting were the bargain—not loving and certainly not love-making. He'd told her he'd never love a woman again. Foolishly, he hadn't counted on the fact that God might have other plans.

Peter hunched forward and rested his forearms on his knees. He'd been down this torturous path before of loving a woman who didn't love him back. This was different, though. Darlene didn't love anyone but herself; Marie loved everyone more than herself. Dedicated to Ricky and Luke, she'd willingly sacrificed her own happiness and freedom for them.

Only he didn't want her sacrifice. He wanted her to come to him freely, of her own will. How was he to break past her fairy-tale memories of a storybook marriage? How could he compete?

He'd had a knee-jerk reaction to Marie's assertion that he was trying to buy her affection and allegiance, but her words haunted him. In fact, they felt uncomfortably true, now that he'd thought about it. He wasn't enough to make Darlene love him, so he'd used such things as money, gifts, vacations… And now, he feared Marie wouldn't love him, so he'd started to do the same thing—only she stopped him and pledged her commitment, loveless as it was. *What is it about me? Why can't a woman love me, Lord?*

"Whoa, that sounded pretty heavy duty."

He lifted his head. "Huh?"

"You groaned." Kate walked up and sat down beside him.

He gave her a questioning look.

"I left for work a little early so I could stop by to see if Marie needed any help. I saw you headed this way." She paused a moment, then quietly invited, "Want to talk about it?"

"There's nothing to say."

She squirmed for a second so she was in a comfortable position, then quietly refuted, "I think there's plenty to be said. You're in love, and after getting burned by Darlene, you're not sure if you want another commitment."

Peter winced. "You knew about her?"

Kate wasn't one for pretenses. "Yes, I did. I wanted to throttle her for being indifferent to you, but it wasn't my place to get involved."

He glanced at her out of the corner of his eye and said softly, "Marie likes you."

"Is that your way of appealing for me to get involved this time?"

Peter rose and paced around the circle of flowers. Raking his fingers through his hair, he said, "I don't know what to do. At first, all that mattered was that the four of us were together. Now, it's much more than that. I don't want a partner or a buddy anymore. I want a wife."

"Have you told Marie that?"

"Are you kidding?" He wheeled around and lifted his hands in a helpless gesture. "It'll send her into a total panic. We made a bargain, and she's sticking to it. If I say anything at all, it's likely to ruin everything we've achieved. The problem is, Marie is still in love with her dead husband!"

Kate nodded. "That's actually a good thing."

"Good!" he exploded.

"Yes. It shows how dedicated she is to those she loves—and that'll open all sorts of opportunities for you."

"I want her to be connected to the boys, but…"

"You want her to want you, too," Kate finished for him. "She will. Peter, Marie may not understand it, but she feels betrayed by her husband—he left her. She feels guilty, and that's what makes her cling so desperately to her memories. Don't try to compete—she'll dig in deeper."

"So what do you suggest?"

Kate looked at him somberly. "Remember that night you told me about, when you finally had a breakthrough at the pool and accepted God's healing from the wounds your marriage left? Marie has to be scared of loving again, Peter—she already got hurt once before."

"I wouldn't ever leave her! I love her!"

"I know that, but does she? You can't guard her from the fact that accidents happen, Peter. You have to make it safe for her to love again. My guess is, you've already done all of that. She just needs to realize it."

"How do we get her to realize it?"

"Pray." Kate waited a moment, then said, "You're too intense, and you'll force the issue before she's ready unless you calm down. Get away. Go on a trip and think things through carefully. When you come back, take things one step at a time. Don't expect Marie to suddenly bow to your wishes just because you've changed. Court her. Most of all, have faith."

Peter's mother came over that day. Marie enjoyed her company, and she appreciated having help with the boys. Each time she moved, her arm burned. As the morning passed, Marie had the strange feeling Lauren had something on her mind. After they put the boys down for a nap, Lauren turned to her.

"Do you need to lie down?"

"Not at all. I'm thirsty, though. How about some lemonade out by the pool?"

They passed through the kitchen, and Mrs. Lithmas clucked and fussed for a minute before insisting she'd bring out a tray. Marie noticed that Lauren stood over by the table and read that morning's verse. *Lord, open her eyes and heart.*

Mrs. Lithmas tilted her head toward the table. "John 3:16 today. It was the first verse I memorized as a child, and it's still my favorite. Do either of you want a sprig of peppermint in your lemonade?"

"You spoil us," Marie said appreciatively.

"Oh, now, who's talking? You're the one who sneaked behind my back and paid the dentist. And who sends an old housekeeper a bouquet just because? Don't think I didn't know who put those new tires on my car, either."

Marie merely laughed off those assertions and drew her mother-in-law outside. A few minutes after they took seats under a poolside umbrella, Mrs. Lithmas brought out a tray and left.

Lauren picked up her glass and took a sip of lemonade. She kept hold of the glass, stared at it and absently played with a water droplet as it wended down the side. "Ever since your arm got hurt, I've been wanting to talk with you."

"Oh?"

"When I wiped up the cookie mess on the kitchen table, I found this." Lauren pulled a verse from the pocket of her neatly tailored aqua slacks and read aloud, "Romans 5:8—'But God commends his own love toward us, in that while we were yet sinners, Christ died for us.'"

She smiled self-consciously. "Luke told me it means even though little boys are naughty sometimes, God still loves them so much, He sent Jesus to die on the cross."

Marie felt a spurt of joy. She sometimes wondered if what she and Peter told the boys got through. She looked Lauren in the eye. "It's the truth."

"I've been thinking about that. About what you did that day, too."

"What I did?"

"You got hurt, rescuing Luke. Then, I realized something. Had I been standing there, I would have reached down to protect him, too. Love makes us act, even though it causes us pain—because we'd rather take the pain, ourselves, than see someone we cherish get hurt."

Every one of her words resounded with truth. Marie hoped this was an open door, an answer to her prayers for her mother-in-law's soul. She whispered an urgent word for the Holy Spirit to grant her the right words. "So when you think that way, what do you think of God's plan for salvation now? Does it make sense to you that He loves us so much, He willingly gave His own Son?"

"I was thinking about that." Lauren then set down the slip she'd taken from the kitchen table. Side by side, the verses started to fit together in a salvation puzzle. "This John 3:16 says so."

"God didn't begrudge us His mercy. He acted out of His compassion and love. He's our Heavenly Father, and He reached down to rescue us."

"Like you reached down to save Luke." A shadow crossed Lauren's face. "If God can do that, why didn't He reach down and protect my Lisa?"

"If evil didn't exist, God wouldn't have ever needed to send Christ. He gives us a choice whether or not to follow Him. Those who don't follow Him can do terrible things.''

''But I'm a good person,'' Lauren said in a plaintive tone. ''I was a good mother. I didn't deserve that, and I don't see why I'm not good enough for Him.''

''Lauren, you were an excellent mother. I look at Peter and his sisters and hope Ricky and Luke turn out half as well. Still, being good isn't what it takes. We're all sinners. God's children admit that and ask for forgiveness. We don't earn our salvation—it is His gift.''

Lauren took another sip of lemonade and stared out across the pool.

Marie thought aloud. ''A while back, you said you were angry at God, that you couldn't accept Him because He gave up His Son. Now you're telling me you understand that sacrifice.''

Lauren sighed. ''I don't even think I'm angry anymore. This may sound silly because I have a husband who loves me, great kids and adorable grandsons, but I sometimes feel so…'' She waved her hand in a helpless gesture.

''Empty?''

''Yes.''

Marie nodded. ''Some of that is grief. Most of it is the fact that we were created with a need to commune with God. When we're not in relationship with Him, there's a void in our lives and souls. He's reaching down to you, Lauren. He wants to fill you up with His love and happiness.''

''I think I'd like that.''

Marie got up and embraced her. They prayed together. Afterward, Marie said, ''The angels are singing in heaven.''

Lauren smiled at her through tear-glossed eyes. ''Someday, I'll make it to heaven to hear them firsthand.''

* * *

Peter knew something was up when Marie met him at the door that night. Her eyes sparkled, and she could barely wait for him to set down his briefcase. "What's up?"

"It's really your mother's news—"

"Mom?"

Marie nodded.

Peter caught his breath. "She's been asking a lot of questions about God. Did she—"

Marie nodded enthusiastically.

He let out a whoop, swept her into a hug and gave her an exuberant kiss.

Marie pulled away and was twelve shades of red. She cleared her throat and wouldn't look at him. "My, um…arm."

"I'm sorry, sweetheart. Is it okay?"

"Yeah. It just got bumped." She rubbed it, looked at his chin and flashed him a smile. "Anyway, I thought maybe you'd like to call Mom before we sat down to dinner."

"Absolutely." He took that as an exit cue and hastened to his study. He desperately wanted to share the good news with his mother…but he also felt a pang. Had he really hurt Marie, or was she simply pushing him away yet again?

Chapter Twenty-Five

*P*ray. *Court her. Have faith.* Kate's advice echoed in his mind. Peter kicked the door shut to his hotel room and tossed the suitcase on the bed. Marie had packed everything for his trip. He hadn't even asked—she simply took it upon herself. She'd ascertained that he needed casual clothes and one suit, then gone to his room and taken care of the task. For the first time, she'd dared to enter his domain. *Was she glad to get rid of me, or did she do it because she wanted to be supportive?*

A whole week away from home. He'd been careful not to do this since Luke was born. If Peter had to travel, he'd always taken the red-eye and allowed only three days' separation. This time, he'd needed extra time to think. This convention was a perfect excuse to get away. The seminars would start the day after tomorrow, but he could meet with a couple of surgical equipment suppliers beforehand to assure his hospital would get priority shipping. Marie would love the boys to pieces, but leaving the three of them felt awful.

Marie insisted upon them all seeing him off. Instead of

going to a major airport, Peter took a charter flight out of a local airfield. They went with him to the check-in desk, then sat with him on a tiny, oak park bench. Each boy sat on one of his thighs, and Marie managed to sit pretty close—but he wondered if it was because the bench was so small. They'd gotten there a bit early so he could stand by the fence with the boys to watch the takeoffs and landings. When his boarding call blared over the loudspeaker, Peter kissed them, hugged them and reminded, ''Be extra good for Mommy.''

When he stood, Marie automatically gathered Luke and Rick to herself. It was an instinctive move—that of a protective mother who would safeguard her children at all costs. Reassurance mingled with disappointment. With a child in front of each of her legs, she wasn't exactly accessible. Peter leaned over and dared to brush a kiss across her cheekbone. ''I'll be home soon.''

She kept her lashes lowered. ''Be careful.''

''I will. You be careful, too. Call Mom or Kate or someone if you need a break.''

''We'll manage.''

''I'll call at seven-thirty, your time, each night.'' He barely resisted gathering her curls in his hand. She was wearing a red satin ribbon in her hair. It looked flirty and feminine. He wanted to fill his palms with her soft hair, cup her head and angle it so their lips would meet…. Instead, he stepped back, lifted his briefcase and strode toward the plane.

Marie's words floated to him. ''God go with you!''

She'd called those words to him five hours ago. It seemed like a lifetime. Peter slipped his wallet out of his back pocket and reached for the phone. He paused for a moment. A picture of Marie and the boys he'd snapped at the park came into view. It had been a happy day—

sunny, filled with laughter. She'd grabbed the boys and seated them ahead of herself on a big rocket ship–shaped slide. He'd snapped the picture as they zoomed toward him. The boys' mouths were wide-open—Luke's with a scream, Ricky's with a laugh. Marie's lips formed a gleeful smile. He treasured that candid snapshot.

The rapid drone of a phone-off-the-hook warning snapped Peter out of his reverie. He dialed a 1-800 number, flipped open the trifold and pulled out a credit card. "Yes. I'd like to send a dozen roses. Red. Long stemmed. I'll charge them…."

Promptly at seven-thirty, Peter dialed home. The phone rang twice, then Marie answered. Her voice had a hollow, echoey quality. "How was your flight?"

"Fine. How are you and the boys?"

"Sticky." Her laughter filtered over the line. "We were just finishing ice-cream cones. I put you on the speakerphone."

"Good idea." He raised his voice slightly. "Hi, boys!"

"Daddy!" Both voices mingled in a heartwarming duet. Even across the miles, their excitement came through loud and clear.

"Were you good for Mommy today?"

"Uh-huh. We gots ice cream," Ricky said.

"Choklit," Luke chimed in.

"That sounds yummy. Tell Mommy she can eat my scoop, too."

"Mommy, you eat ice cream," Luke chirped. "Daddy said."

Ricky tattled, "Mommy doesn't got ice cream."

"No?"

Ricky continued to chatter. "Nope. Mommy says she already sits on enough ice cream." Boyish laughter rippled over the line.

Peter tried to muffle his chuckle. Marie must be blushing again. "Tell Mommy she doesn't need to worry about an ounce."

Luke repeated, "Mommy, Daddy says, 'Don't worry 'bout your bounce.'"

A garbled sound somewhere between a choke and a groan came from Marie.

Peter chortled. Luke's version though mangled, actually fit quite nicely. Peter eased back onto the bed and chatted for a few more minutes. Marie managed to regain some semblance of control. Before they hung up, he promised, "I'll call again tomorrow night."

"Seven-thirty?"

"On the nose."

He had a hard time letting Marie go. Peter talked a while longer and finally hung up. Afterward, he stared at the room service menu and started to chuckle. He grabbed the phone again.

"Hi! How are you all doing?"

"Give me just one more minute," Marie said in a breathless rush. "I didn't want to miss you—" She turned and tossed a towel around Ricky. Luke was racing down the hall in true superhero style, his towel flapping behind his still-wet little body. Marie captured him, flipped the towel around him and barely dried him as he squiggled. "Daddy's on the phone!"

Ricky held the phone and babbled, "Daddy? Daddy? Hello, Daddy."

Marie took the phone from him. "I'm back."

"What in the world is going on?"

"The boys are fine. I just scrubbed at least three inches of grime off of them. The gardener watered that patch he's turned over and mulched. Ricky and Luke got so dirty, it was hard to tell them apart.''

Peter chuckled.

Merriment filled her voice as she confessed, ''I played beat-the-clock to get them out in time to talk to you.''

''By their standards, I'd judge it was a terrific day.''

''You could say that.''

''And how about yours? How's your arm?''

''The stitches came out today. It's ugly, but not sore.''

''Nothing about you could be ugly. You got that by protecting our son. To me, it's a beauty mark. Still, if it bothers you, we'll have a plastic surgeon look at it.''

''That's going too far.'' Her tone lifted in an attempt to change the subject. ''Speaking of going too far, some-one sent a special delivery, chocolate ice-cream cake here today. If there were designated pews at church for the seven deadly sins, I'd be a permanent fixture on the one marked Gluttony.''

Peter's rich laughter warmed her like a towel fresh out of the dryer.

She tried to interject mock sternness into her voice. ''Oh, it's easy for you to chuckle. I'm the one who's going to have to repent to the tune of half a billion sit-ups a day for the rest of my life.''

''When I come home, I'll hold your feet.''

''With friends like you...''

''Happy homes are made,'' he filled in.

His assertion caught her off guard. ''The boys do seem happy.''

''I am, too, Marie. You're a wonderful wife and mother. Thanks for those notes and pictures.''

A flood of warmth filled her. She'd had the boys draw pictures for him and she'd written notes on them. As she packed, she'd layered pictures between Peter's slacks and shirts in the suitcase. She'd also slipped Bible verses into some of his pockets. As soon as he picked up the suitcase and put it in the back of her new van, she'd begun to worry—had that been too corny? Too intimate? Too desperate? No—he liked them. The tension in her shoulders melted away.

After they hung up, Marie read to the boys, helped them say their prayers and tucked them into bed. She sauntered through the house. It felt too quiet. Too empty. By no means was Peter noisy, but he seemed to fill the house with his presence. The whole place felt barren and desolate without him. Marie didn't like the feeling—and she was all too familiar with it. She'd lived with this sensation after Jack died. She'd even asked Sandy to come up and spend the week with her—both because she loved her, and also because she longed for some companionship. This loneliness made her feel so terribly empty inside, but Sandy couldn't come.

Marie wound her arms around her ribs and winced at the pulling pain in her right arm. She tried to ignore the fear and ache in her heart as she looked around the much-too-quiet house and whispered urgently, ''Dear God, bring Peter home safely.''

Peter called each night. Each day, he had something delivered—pizza for lunch, a family of teddy bears, a fruit basket... Marie and the boys anticipated his calls. The last night, they waited in vain for the phone to ring. Marie let the boys stay up a bit later than usual, but she finally decided to call Peter. He'd admitted to being tired the night before. ''Maybe Daddy fell asleep. Let's call him tonight.''

She dialed, and the phone rang only once. ''Hello?''

After a brief pause, a distinctly feminine voice repeated, "Yes? Hello?"

Marie fumbled and hung up. Plastering a smile on her face that she hoped would hide the pain and confusion she felt, she said, "I guess Daddy is too busy. Let's go tuck you in."

Eight-fifteen. Eight-thirty. Nine-thirty. Ten. Marie lay on her side and watched the neon numbers change on her bedside clock. She did the math. Chicago was two hours ahead. That made it ten-fifteen. Ten-thirty. Eleven-thirty. Midnight.

When the phone rang, she stared at it. Did she dare answer? She almost didn't, but what if something happened? What if Peter had gotten hurt? "Hello?"

"Sorry I'm late, Marie. Things got a bit involved."

Man, oh, man—he really had to think long and hard to come up with that line.

"Are you okay?"

"I'm tired," she said flatly.

"Yeah, I'll bet you are. I'll be home tomorrow."

"I know. Peter? Instead of us picking you up, would you mind just coming home in a taxi?" Marie knew she had to put distance between them. A married man—even if it was strictly a marriage of convenience—had no business having some other woman in his hotel room. She was afraid she'd take one look at him and give him a healthy chunk of her mind if she didn't settle down and think through her options quickly.

"Sure. No problem."

"H-have a safe flight."

"I missed talking to the boys. Are they all right?"

I don't want to talk to you. Can't you just let me go? I don't want to think about how you've betrayed me, betrayed the vows we took. I cared about you. I cared for you. At least this happened before I made an utter fool of myself.

"Marie? Are you okay? Is it your arm?"

"My arm is fine." She glanced down at how long and red the new scar was. "The stitches are out." *There. I hope I sound normal. Oh, no. I already told him that days ago.*

"And the boys?"

She owed him information on the boys. Being petty wouldn't do her any good. "Ricky's okay. Luke seemed a bit grumpy when I put him down."

"I hope it's not his ear again. Was he running a fever? Rubbing his ear? Having trouble swallowing?"

"No. It was nothing."

"You really do sound tired, Marie. I won't keep you any longer. Oh, Marie? If Luke gets sick and you need me, I'll be in room…ah, um…821 for tonight."

"'Bye." She hung up before she reacted or questioned him. Why give him an opportunity to lie? He'd had a woman in his room, and now he was going to spend the rest of the night in a different bed. It was almost as if he taunted her, wanted to goad her into asking him painful questions. She refused to play that game—not on the phone, not separated by thousands of miles and several hours. Their time of reckoning would come tomorrow.

As she forced her fingers to uncurl and let go of the receiver, sobs tightened her chest. Marie tried to choke them back, then gave up and buried her face in her pillow. She wept until she had no more tears.

The day's verse echoed in her mind and heart. *Casting all your worries on Him, because He cares for you…* Marie let out a soul-deep sigh of despair. She lay in bed and watched the neon numbers on her clock change for most of the rest of the night. Sleep simply wouldn't come. She knew God cared for her; she wished her husband did, too.

Chapter Twenty-Six

Peter hung up and headed for the sink. He needed to take some aspirin. His head ached. The day started out badly and never improved. The hotel manager woke him at five-fifty with the news that there had been a minor mishap. Peter guessed as much since the bedside light wouldn't turn on and the carpeting squished beneath his bare feet as he'd walked over to answer the knock. "The patrons in the room adjacent to yours left the tap flowing for the Jacuzzi. Since the connecting door can be opened to create a suite of these rooms, we worried the water might have flown freely into here, as well."

Peter frowned at his cold, wet feet. "Rightfully so."

"We turned off the power so you wouldn't electrocute yourself. Please accept my deepest apologies. I'll have someone gather your belongings. We've prepared a lovely suite for you."

"Wait. I need to get—"

"Sir, I can personally guarantee everything will be brought to you."

Peter cinched his robe a bit tighter. "I'll just grab my wallet and laptop."

Once awake, he couldn't get back to sleep. The seminars for that day were poorly presented, and the one he most wanted to attend was canceled. He went back to his room and decided to nap instead of going to supper. Just as he started to coast off to sleep, the phone rang. Some of his acquaintances were going out for the evening and invited him along. The whole time he was out, Peter felt awkward. He knew two of the men had escorts who were not their wives. He'd missed calling Marie and the kids. He slipped away to a pay phone, but the call didn't go through. All in all, the day rated as an unmitigated disaster. Plainly put, he was homesick.

After tossing and turning all night, Peter dozed during the flight home. Though not completely refreshed, he felt better equipped to handle two rambunctious three-year-olds. He'd come to the decision that he'd ease Marie into things gently. First, he'd reassure her that he wanted them to all be one family—forever. He'd adopt Ricky. Then, as time passed, he'd teach her to trust him and love him as much as he cherished her.

A taxi dropped him off at home, and he dumped his suitcase inside the front door. "Where are my boys?"

"Daddy!" Luke and Ricky screamed the duet as they tore through the house and flung themselves into his arms. If only Marie would do the same, he'd truly feel he'd come home.

"I'd like to talk to you about something."

Marie gave Peter a worried look. He rarely sounded this formal. She'd tried to stay in the background and let the boys monopolize Peter's afternoon. It was too hard to be near Peter. Everything inside of her shook, and she fumbled with anything she held. Now that prayers were over and the boys were in bed for the night, Marie had no convenient excuse to avoid him. She gingerly sat on the sofa in his study and stared up at him.

Peter paced the full length of the carpet, turned abruptly and returned. He stared at her, then out the window and finally walked away and back again. Each step seemed to measure more than a stride. It seemed to measure a heavy weight.

Her pulse skipped a beat, then thrummed faster and faster as her anxiety skyrocketed. She couldn't bear waiting for him to build up his nerve anymore. Marie clenched her hands in her lap until her knuckles went stark white and blurted out, "What is it?"

Peter hunkered down in front of her and locked eyes. He took her hands in his, then repeated, "I have to talk to you about something."

There's another woman. He's going to try to ease into a divorce. She gave him her bravest smile, but inside, everything felt like it was falling apart. "Okay. Whatever it is, I'll handle it."

He straightened up and let off a tense laugh. He still kept hold of her hands. After a second, he sat beside her on the cushion and still kept possession of her hands. His fingers were long and warm. The way he hung on to her made Marie's apprehension soar. "What is it?"

"Ricky."

"What about Ricky?" Her mind whirled. *Ricky? What could possibly be wrong with Ricky?* Horror streaked through her. *He wants to keep Ricky for himself. He's found another woman, but he wants to keep both of my boys!*

Peter looked at her with an intensity that made her heart twist. "When we were goofing off in the pool that night,

I realized we hadn't decided what would become of the boys if something were to happen to both of us.''

Marie went completely still. *Is that all? I got paranoid for no reason at all!*

"I'd already made out a will as soon as Luke was born, designating Kate as his guardian.''

She shifted to let go of a bit of her tension and agreed, "I think she's the best choice. As good as your parents are, the boys need someone younger to keep up with them. Jill and Brianna love them to pieces, but they're not settled yet. Sandy would offer, but she has some special needs of her own, and I want her to adjust to them and hopefully have this relationship with Brent without having that possible obligation hanging over her head.''

"Good, then we're agreed.''

"So, see?" She relaxed a bit. "Everything is fine.''

"Fine," Peter echoed. He didn't look very relieved. He then continued, "I can't take care of doing that with the attorney just yet. We have to tend to another matter first.''

The way he paused struck Marie as odd. Her sense of panic crashed back in, only it had doubled. She watched him diligently, her eyes scanning his features carefully to glean a clue as to the gravity of what he'd say next. He said nothing yet, so she waited.

"Marie, I can't do that until I have legal rights to determine what is in Ricky's best interest.''

She scrambled to come up with a reasonable way to dodge this. If he adopted Ricky, she'd never be able to keep custody in a divorce. "That's silly. Anything we've done is subject to legal interpretation and red tape. The courts would have a heyday trying to determine who was the parent of which child." She paused a moment, then proposed what she hoped would sound like a compromise. "Wouldn't it be simpler if we just asked an attorney to draft a joint will or a…what do they call it? A living trust.''

''Yeah, we could do that.'' Peter still didn't look finished. Marie smiled at him. ''Peter, don't be so upset. I seriously doubt the boys will ever have to face this. The odds of anything happening to both of us are incredibly slim. I'm sure anyone would agree, we've already suffered more than our fair quota of disasters.''

''I know, but there's just one more issue.''

''Another one?'' her voice shook. *Is this ever going to come to an end?*

''It's about Ricky.'' Peter's fingers held hers more securely as he softly said, ''His name.''

Marie frowned. ''His name? What's wrong with his name? Do you want to call him Richard? Dickie?''

''No, Marie. I want to legally change his last name.''

It took a moment for the words to sink in. Marie jolted. He was using this as a back door into adoption. He'd thought it through and approached it far more shrewdly than she'd ever imagined. He'd always been honorable with her—and this maneuver almost blindsided her.

Peter's hold on her tightened. ''You took my last name. Ricky's the odd man out. I think it would be best.'' He paused momentarily, then hastily added, ''And he truly is my biological son.''

Her fingers went ice-cold. All of her went cold—ice-cold. She shivered, then stiffly pulled from Peter's contact. He could have held on, but he relinquished his hold as soon as she started to draw back. Marie stared at him and rasped, ''Then what about Luke?''

''What about him?''

''Do we change his last name to Cadant?'' Her chin went up a notch, as did the volume of her shaky voice. ''He's Jack's biological son.''

Peter's dark eyes narrowed, and his face went taut. For a moment, he stayed silent and the muscle in his cheek twitched. Clearly, this matter was just as emotionally charged for him as it was for her. She'd countered with a move he hadn't anticipated. Finally he shook his head. "I want us to all have the same last name."

Marie felt as if he'd punched his fist into her chest and pulled out her heart. She stood on very stiff legs and woodenly shook her head. "No. No. You can't do this."

"Why not?"

You're the one who told me the marriage was inviolate. You're the one who promised you'd never fall in love with another woman. You said we'd be together and make a home for our sons. How can you do this?

Peter stood, too. He folded his arms across his chest in a move of pure stubbornness. "Why can't I? If this is about Jack—"

"Oh, you want to talk about Jack?" she cried. "You want to make this all about Jack? Okay. We'll do that. You've tried to wipe out every bit of Jack in my heart and life and want to pretend he never existed, but you can't do that. He was my husband and he fathered our son. That son is all I have left of Jack."

"But, Marie—"

"How can you be so cruel that you'd rob Jack's son of his birthright?"

"Luke never knew Jack, Marie. I'm not being cruel at all. The only name he's ever known is mine."

She stared at him through a sheen of tears. She'd trusted him. *I've been a complete fool. I knew you loved the boys, but I never imagined you'd go to these lengths to have them all for yourself.*

"It's important for the boys to both be mine."

"Yours!" Angry beyond anything she'd ever felt, Marie choked on that one word.

"You know what I mean."

He looked like he expected an immediate capitulation, but Marie knew he'd never accept it if she flatly refused, so she whispered thickly, "I'll think about it."

"Marie—"

"I'm tired. Really tired. Good night." She half dashed out of his office, down the hall and into her room. She shut the door and sat on her bed. Even here, she found no refuge. This wasn't their house—it was his. Marie hugged a pillow to her chest, bowed her head and tried to gulp back tears.

He didn't want her; he wanted her son. From the time she'd admitted to herself that she felt a spark of attraction for Peter, she'd wondered if he could feel the same for her. Now she knew: He didn't want her for herself. He only included her because it meant he'd have Ricky. She was merely a means to an end. Once he adopted Ricky, she'd be expendable.

God, please don't let this be.

How long she sat there with tears streaming down her face, she couldn't say. Steeped in misery, she'd lost track of time. The sound of Luke's crying broke through to her. Marie set aside the pillow, hastily wiped her face and headed into the boys' room.

Peter got there before she did. He picked up Luke and cradled him to his chest. His voice was low and comforting as he crooned nonsensical sounds. He glanced up at Marie and said, "He's hot."

She closed the small distance between them and instinctively reached for her son. "How hot?"

Peter pulled away and held Luke tighter. "You can't have him."

Marie started to shake, and tears welled up again.

"Marie, your arm is too sore to hold him. Go get the thermometer. I'll meet you in the playroom." Peter brushed past her.

Marie quickly checked on Ricky, then did as Peter bade. Her heart was breaking, and every step was an effort. Peter sat on her old couch in the playroom. Luke huddled close and looked pitiful. "It's probably his ear again," Peter said. He took the thermometer from her nerveless fingers. "Let's get his temperature, then I'll call the doctor." He frowned. "Are you okay? You're flushed, too."

"I'm fine." *As fine as I can be, considering you're stomping on my heart.*

"Sit down." He shook down the thermometer, then tucked it under Luke's arm. He was running a bit of a fever and complained about his ear. Peter directed Marie where to find some numbing eardrops and the liquid fever reducer the pediatrician prescribed. Once they took care of things and Luke fell back to sleep, Peter carefully tucked him back into bed. They tiptoed out to the hallway. Peter halted her by lightly cupping her shoulder. "Are you sure you're okay? Is it your arm?"

Marie self-consciously wrapped her arms around her ribs, careful to slip the left one over the right to cover the unsightly red scar. "You don't need to worry about me."

"Of course I worry about you. You're my wife!"

"For how much longer? Until you can secure your rights to Ricky with an adoption?"

"Marie!"

She jerked away from him and whispered harshly, "I'm not stupid."

"Then I must be. What in the world are you talking about?"

"Oh, come on, Peter! Don't act like I'm a total fool. You pushed me to let you adopt Ricky right after you went away and stayed out 'til all hours of the night. A woman answered your hotel room phone. I—"

"What?"

"They're my sons, too. I'm not—"

"I know they're your sons, too!"

"Then why are you doing this to me?" She couldn't hide her pain and fear anymore. Marie started to sob.

Thunderstruck, Peter stared at her for a split second. When she tried to turn and bolt away, he lunged and swept her into his arms. He carried her over to the corner of the living room and sat in the center of the oversize love seat. Marie tried to squirm away, but he held her tight.

"Let go of me!"

"No. Not now. Not ever."

His words only made her weep harder. She shuddered and soaked his shirt with her tears. Peter held her close. She finally went limp across his lap. He tenderly stroked her back and tucked her hair behind her ear so he could look down and gauge her expression. She'd taken him by complete surprise with her accusations and this emotional storm. He'd been so wound up in his own doubts and concerns, he hadn't thought to look at things from her vantage point.

Her shoulders still jerked as she gulped in choppy breaths. Anguish painted her features. She stared blankly ahead, as if she were alone. His heart skipped a beat. Alone. She truly did feel alone. He'd denied her the comfort of a mate. He'd let her shoulder the responsibilities of caring for the boys, readjust to a new home, and instead of connecting with her and holding her hand through those changes, he'd never looked past her facade of control.

"Marie," he said softly as he traced the shell of her

ear. "Sweetheart, please listen to me. I'm not trying to take Ricky away from you. I only wanted to share him. I hoped if we took that step, you'd feel like our marriage was stronger and safer. I told you this was forever, and I meant it. There isn't another woman. There's only room in my heart for you."

Her lids fluttered downward, and she looked like she'd lost all hope. Peter curled around her more closely as he saw her lips moving. Her words stunned him, humbled him. They also gave him hope. Marie was praying.

He brushed his lips across her forehead, then prayed aloud, himself. He gave thanks for the boys and asked for Luke's ear to feel better. "Most of all, Lord, I ask you to heal our hearts so we can love each other as a real man and wife—not as partners, but in the fullness of a loving marriage so our hearts and minds will be one in Your sight."

After he prayed, he continued to hold her. "My hotel room flooded, Marie. They moved me. I haven't even looked at another woman since I met you. There isn't any other woman in the world who could interest me. My heart is already taken. I know you're adjusting to so many changes, and things are hard for you. It's not fair of me to change our arrangement, but I want to—I want you to be my wife. Not my partner—my *wife.* Our marriage started out as a business arrangement, but I soon found I couldn't take my eyes off you."

She whispered sadly, "It's hard not to like someone when they love your kid."

"Honey, it goes far beyond that."

"I made an utter fool of myself, and you're being noble."

"Then I suppose you'll tell me the rings I have in my suitcase are a noble gesture, though I had no notion we were going to have this discussion when I bought them. Marie, I bought a whole trio of rings for us—an engagement and wedding ring for you, and a matching band for me.''

''You already gave me a ring.''

''That is a partnership ring. I want us to truly be married. In the church. I want us to be free to love each other openly, to share our hearts and lives and bodies. When I was away, I decided I'd come home and court you slowly.''

''But I got hysterical and ruined your plans.''

''You were hurting too much, Marie. I couldn't stay quiet when all I wanted to do was reassure you that I'm head over heels in love with you.''

''Really?'' She searched his face carefully.

Peter gave her a moment, then tightened his hold around her and stood up. He chuckled at her gasp and carried her into his bedroom. Once there, he laid her on his bed and unlatched his suitcase. There, from the suitcase, he drew out a small jewelry box.

Marie's breath caught.

He knelt by the bed and opened the box. Three golden rings glimmered on the white satin lining. ''Marie, I believe God brought us together. Circumstances were strained, but He can work miracles. The boys were blessings, but they were mixed up. God created something wonderful out of that mixed blessing. Our love is a miracle. Please, sweetheart, marry me. For real. Be my wife.''

''Oh, Peter!''

''Was that a yes?''

''You love me?''

''I love you in a way I never knew possible. I've been crazy, trying to be subtle and supportive when all I wanted to do was grab you and kiss some sense into you.''

Marie let out a small laugh.

"Oh, so that's your reaction to my declaration of love?" He gave her a look of mock dismay.

"Let me make it up to you." She leaned closer and cupped his cheek. "Far be it from me to hurt anyone— especially the man I love." She brushed her lips against his.

Peter reached to the side and fumbled to set the rings down, then wrapped her in an unyielding embrace as he deepened the kiss. When he finally eased away a few inches, he then tipped his head forward and rubbed noses with her and murmured huskily, "So tell me you'll marry me—for real."

"Yes," she whispered. Joyous tears filled her eyes as he traded the eternity band to her right hand and slipped the swirling gold-and-diamond engagement ring onto her left hand.

Two days later, Peter slipped the matching wedding ring onto her hand. Their family surrounded them once again, but this time, they stood in the church's small, stained-glass prayer chapel. The vows spoken this time carried true meaning and heartfelt love.

After a very satisfying kiss, Peter dipped his fingers into his pocket and produced a tiny box. "Pastor Fuller and I planned a little something extra."

Marie watched as the pastor knelt and drew both boys in front of himself. He spoke a few simple words and declared the boys brothers. She looked up at Peter, and he snuggled her a bit more securely, as if to tell her, "This is the way it's supposed to be. This is right." Pastor Fuller opened the box Peter handed to him and latched identification bracelets on the boys' wrists. They were volubly pleased.

When they left the church, Peter's parents took the boys back to the house. Peter tucked Marie into a limousine and whisked her off to a nearby honeymoon suite where he kissed her breathless.

Finally, she whispered, "You're eager to start this honeymoon."

He chuckled, then said under his breath, "I've waited long enough to love you, but believe me, you were worth the wait!"

"Why, thank you, Mr. Hallock."

His eyes twinkled as he tenderly settled her in the center of the bed. "You're more than welcome, Mrs. Hallock."

Though only three days long, their honeymoon was the stuff of fairy tales and fantasies. Even when they returned home and the boys misbehaved, life was sweeter than either of them ever dreamed it could be.

On their seven-month anniversary, Marie left the boys in Mrs. Lithmas's care for the afternoon and unexpectedly dropped in on Peter at work.

Peter looked up from his desk when she slipped into his office. "Marie! What are you doing here?"

She shrugged.

"Why don't I take you to lunch? We can drop by and see how things are going at Issac's House. They were supposed to install all of the computer equipment today."

"That'd be nice." She got close enough to give him a hug, and he enveloped her in his warmth. When he dipped to kiss her, she turned her head. "Peter?"

"Yeah?"

She gave him a dazzling smile. "I—I have your son."

He chuckled. "You've got both of them, and if Luke dares to—"

She shook her head. "No, Peter."

"So it's Ricky this time? What did that little rascal do?"

She looked down for a moment, then back at him. Tears of joy glistened in her eyes. "Peter, it's not Luke or Ricky. I'm carrying your son...or daughter."

His arms tightened, and he let out a joyous whoop then they kissed with all of the love in their hearts.

*   *   *   *   *

Dear Reader,

In my other life, I'm a Lamaze teacher. (Yes, it's an absolutely delightful profession.) One night, after class, a father-to-be asked, "What if the worst happened? What if our baby got swapped?" He was thrilled to learn our hospital allows daddies to stay with mother and child the whole time. That lucky baby girl has a father who loves her, wants her and is protective.

If an earthly father wants good for his daughter, how much more does the Heavenly Father want for His daughters? Luke 11:13 says, "If you then, being evil, know how to give good gifts to your children, how much more will your heavenly Father give the Holy Spirit to those who ask Him?"

Even then, we all have problems. Burdens. Tragedies. Marie and Peter experienced one of the worst imaginable. Their hearts were torn, their faith tested. In the end, the Lord helped them see the potential, the blessings and the triumph He sees when asked to be with us as we walk the path set before us.

My prayer for you is that you will hold tight to the Heavenly Father's hand on the days you skip with joy, and that in the dark of night when all you have are tears, you'll know the comfort of His drying them. All we have to do is ask.

I'd love to hear from you. You can write to me through my Web site http://members.aol.com/cathymariehake or through Steeple Hill at the following address: Cathy Marie Hake c/o Steeple Hill Books, 223 Broadway, Ste. 1001, New York, NY 10279.

Cathy Marie Hake

TESTED BY FIRE

BY

KATHRYN SPRINGER

Ex-cop John Gabriel was roped into a favor
by his former boss—keeping an eye on rookie
officer Fiona Kelly, the chief's granddaughter.
The fiery redhead wasn't getting department
support as she investigated a serial arsonist.
But could Fiona's strong faith rub off on the
scarred cynic and make him believe in the
healing power of love and the Lord?

Don't miss

TESTED BY FIRE

On sale August 2004

Available at your favorite retail outlet.

www.SteepleHill.com

LITBF

Take 2 inspirational love stories FREE!

PLUS get a FREE surprise gift!

Mail to Steeple Hill Reader Service™

In U.S.	In Canada
3010 Walden Ave.	P.O. Box 609
P.O. Box 1867	Fort Erie, Ontario
Buffalo, NY 14240-1867	L2A 5X3

YES! Please send me 2 free Love Inspired® novels and my free surprise gift. After receiving them, if I don't wish to receive anymore, I can return the shipping statement marked cancel. If I don't cancel, I will receive 4 brand-new novels every month, before they're available in stores! Bill me at the low price of $4.24 each in the U.S. and $4.74 each in Canada, plus 25¢ shipping and handling and applicable sales tax, if any*. That's the complete price and a savings of over 10% off the cover prices—quite a bargain! I understand that accepting the books and gift places me under no obligation ever to buy any books. I can always return a shipment and cancel at any time. Even if I never buy another book from Steeple Hill, the 2 free books and the surprise gift are mine to keep forever.

113 IDN DZ9M
313 IDN DZ9N

Name	(PLEASE PRINT)	
Address	Apt. No.	
City	State/Prov.	Zip/Postal Code

Love Inspired

FINDING AMY

BY

CAROL STEWARD

It was a mother's worst nightmare—while
Jessica Mathers was undergoing surgery, her
daughter and the sitter disappeared. Detective
Samuel Vance reluctantly agreed to assist in the
case, but his first impression of Jessica was not
favorable. Yet Sam quickly learned that Jessica was
a warm, caring mother. Could their faith help them
find Amy…and forge a relationship?

Don't miss

FINDING AMY
On sale August 2004

Available at your favorite retail outlet.